BORN UNDER THE BLAZING COMET

Other books by Katharine Johnson

Belzi's Blizzard
Born of an Eclipse
Sylvie's Silence
Born in a Red Canoe
The Wind and the Drum
Mukluk Ball

BORN *Under the* BLAZING COMET

Katharine Johnson

SILVER FOX BOOKS

SILVER
FOX
BOOKS

PROLOGUE

I am Luna.

I was born in a red canoe at the moment a blazing comet flew overhead. My father believed the comet bestowed a mystical gift on me. He hoped I would become a great fortune teller, a clairvoyant, communicator with the spirits, or even a magical shape shifter—anything that could make us rich.

That was not to be. My gift was that portals of the dead opened up to me.

There was nothing at all advantageous or enriching about my gift.

Disappointed, father sold me to a farmer. I escaped in the red canoe which seemed to possess its own magic. First, it brought me to Ossi; then it whirled the both of us during a great snow storm to the steps of Huldor's inn. It was there I spent the winter and summer healing and helping with the duties of the inn and the whims of the guests.

Ossi and Huldor were like the family I'd never had. I was safe and happy with them.

I hoped my dark and dangerous days were behind me.

CHAPTER I

The last of the inn's overnight guests left early in the morning. Huldor and I hurried to sweep the floors and bring the used sheets to the bath house where we washed and then hung them to dry in October's warm sun. Working next to Huldor was one of my favorite things. She hummed sweet melodies and smelled of roasted carrots and freshly baked bread. I hummed along with her.

When we finished and were sharing the last of a blueberry tart, Ossi came in from feeding the goats and declared, "Today, we celebrate!" He and Huldor grabbed my hands and spun me in a circle. "Today we become a true family, not only in our eyes, but in the eyes of our neighbors."

Dizzy with happiness, I sang to myself. "Family. I'll have family. At last." It would be a perfect day. A day I had never even dared hope for.

The blacksmith, his wife, and children came with the goat herder and voyageur from a nearby village. The farrier, cooper, logger, trapper, and a dairyman all came with their families. Last to arrive were some nomadic tradesmen. When all were gathered, Ossi said, "Today Huldor and I unite ourselves to each other with you all as witnesses. And we take Luna to be our legally adopted daughter."

All summer, I'd bubbled with joy and warmth as I watched Ossi and Huldor grow close and enjoy each moment they were together. I'd seen the looks that passed between them. The pats on the hand. The smiles. The twinkles of their eyes. They'd known each other as youngsters. Long ago, Ossi had hoped to take her as his bride when he returned from his separation journey, but while he was away, marauders attacked and burned their whole village. Huldor, who'd been known as Oriina back then, had been abducted and sold to a horrible man who abused her every day until he died. She and Ossi had been apart for twenty years. And now, they were finally going to say the words that bound them together and make me part of their family.

The sun shone brilliantly. Squirrels chased and chattered as they collected acorns, hazelnuts, pinecones and ran along tree branches. In spite of the joy I felt, something bothered me. I felt a sudden and uninvited foreboding deep within myself. At moments, I saw, or rather I felt dark clouds that made me uneasy even though no one else seemed to notice them. Worse yet, my hands itched. I'd come to know the itching as a warning. I plunged one hand into my pocket and held my moonstone, hoping for reassurance that all would be well. The stone was as cold as could be and gave me no comfort. I rubbed my hands together hoping to get rid of the itch. I rubbed my moonstone hoping to warm it and for its colors to swirl soothing me. Nothing worked.

As our neighbors gathered beneath the branches of a great oak tree, I did my best to shake the gloom away. Ossi held Huldor in his arms saying, "Huldor, I have looked forward to this moment for many years. Now it is finally here. I vow to be a good husband for you. I'll respect you as I would my own mother and grandmother, and share all I have with you." Then he turned to me, "Luna, I vow to be a good father to you. I'll treat you kindly and share all I have with you, too."

He took my hand and one of Huldor's and held them to his heart as he continued. "I'll never take a stick to either of you. These things I promise until the day I am old and have no more steps to take on this earth, and I leave my earthly body behind to join with my mother, father, and grandparents in the star sky."

My knees trembled. I tried to smile. I grasped Ossi's hand tightly, but at that instant, the cloud hanging over the inn darkened. I tried to smile again, but none reached my lips.

Huldor beamed as she held my and Ossi's hands to her heart. "Ossi, thank ye for all yer wonderful promises an' for comin' back to me 'alf dead on that stormy winter night jist a few moons ago. I promise to be a good wife to ye. I never be scoldin' or naggin'. I take no more than me share of what ye bring me. I be comfortin' ye when ye be needin' comfort. I be joyous with ye when ye be joyous. And Luna, I be takin' care of ye as good as I know how to take care of a daughter. These things I promise 'til the day I be too old to take any more steps on this earth and be flyin' off to the star sky."

Even though I should have been feeling gladness, a lump formed in my throat. My heart skipped a beat. I choked back my tears as Ossi and Huldor held my hands and everyone clapped. One of the neighbors said, "Speech! Luna, your turn!"

I didn't know what to say. The cloudy haze swirled and enveloped the inn. I tried not to look at it. My hands still itched. I dared not touch my moonstone knowing it would be cold. I shook my head and blinked my eyes trying to clear the haze. I held tightly to Huldor's and Ossi's hands wanting to feel their strength and hoping to chase my fears away. After trying to clear my throat, I somehow found the words that were in my heart. "Ossi and Huldor, you are already my family—the family I always needed and yearned for—but I am honored you say this in front of everyone. Ossi, you saved my life and always treat me with kindness. You taught me about our people—the Ice People—and the prophecies of the comet under which I was born. You are a true father."

I paused. My throat tightened. Tears threatened, but I continued, "Huldor, you, too, saved me, fed, and taught me. I never knew my own mother, but I hope she would have been as good as you. I am happy to be your daughter."

I meant every word I said, and I looked forward to many years living with them at the inn. I dared not look up to see if the dark cloud still hung above.

After feasting on roasted root vegetables, venison, and pumpkin cake, the guests wished us well as a family. I should have been joyously happy, but the haze was still there. With so many smiles around me, I tried to convince myself that the haze boded nothing bad.

After the last guest left, I stacked plates and bowls and carried them into the kitchen. I was heating water for washing when Huldor shooed me away saying, "We be cleanin' the dishes an' such on the morrow. No more fussin' tonight."

I gladly left my chores for the next day and told myself that my edginess was just because I was so excited. To rid myself of the feeling, I romped through the fields with Shadow. Then I snaked my way through the trees leading to the bank of the river that flowed past the inn. I lay on a thick bed of moss and fallen leaves. I listened to the ripple of the waters. I smelled the spiciness of mosses. I watched bees flit from flower to flower. I plucked a red wintergreen berry and crushed its sweet juices with my tongue. Above me the sun filtered through the colored leaves. I stretched my arms high and felt the warming rays. I dared not look toward the inn. Shadow snuggled next to me.

Late afternoons had always been my favorite. My chores were done, and the sun hadn't lowered behind the trees. It was then, like now, that I could be alone and away from the busyness of the inn. I could paddle my canoe down the river, or I could just stretch out on a bed of moss.

When the sun lowered and I felt the evening's chill, I reluctantly got up, and headed toward the inn. I kept my head down not wanting to see if a cloud still hovered. I carried my birch bark pack into the goat shed so I could sleep in the straw leaving Huldor and Ossi alone to enjoy their time as a married couple. I'd slept in the shed most of summer, leaving my bed to be used by guests who came, so I hung my pack full of all my belongings onto a wooden peg. Despite my earlier uneasiness, I smiled to myself and thought of Ossi and Huldor now sharing a bed as well as their lives with each other.

Shadow and all the cats and kittens burrowed next to me for the night. Their licks and purrs wiped away all thoughts of the lingering cloud. Bone-deep tired from the busy day, I fell asleep in an instant.

CHAPTER 2

I jolted awake to Shadow barking, tugging at my sleeve, and running in a circle. The goats baaed loudly, jumped, and ran every which way. That was when I saw a great flame lighting the night sky and smelled the acrid smoke. No! It couldn't be. The inn was ablaze! Without thinking of my own safety, I ran toward the scorching inferno screaming, "Fire! Fire! Ossi! Huldor! Fire! Fire!"

My face and feet burned as though branded. My hair singed. Choking on smoke, I yelled until my throat stung raw.

"Ossi! Huldor!" I ran, circling the burning inn hoping to find them.

"Ossi! Huldor!" I yelled again, panic rising. "No! No! No!" I howled.

"Ossi! Huldor!" They were nowhere to be seen. There was no answer—just the roaring of the fire. I sobbed. I must be dreaming. This couldn't be real.

"Ossi! Huldor!"

There was no answer—just the roaring of the fire.

I tried to run past the flames. I had to find Ossi and Huldor. My face and feet burned. My hair singed. The fire was too hot. The blaze too fierce.

I backed away brushing a spark from my dress. I tried to close my nose to the cruel and smothering smoke. I tried to close my ears to the crackling, sizzling bursts of the flames and the crashing of timbers as the fire burned Huldor's inn to the ground.

My burns tortured me to near madness. The fire raged ceaselessly. I called for Ossi and Huldor. No answer. This couldn't be happening. They had to be alive. Huddled somewhere. Safe.

I endlessly circled the inferno. Looking. Calling. Hoping. Ignoring my own festering burns. When the great roof timbers fell shooting sparks to the sky, my tears ran freely. Numb to the very core of my being and feeling the scorch of my burns, I finally ran to the river and jumped into its cooling waters.

I dug my fingers into river mud. I gnashed my teeth as I smeared sludge over my burns. Shaking and shivering, I headed toward the dying flames again. The blaze now glowed and smoldered. Sparks and flickers still burned in the dark. Desperate, I ran to the chicken coop. Maybe Ossi and Huldor found shelter there. No! I ran to the goat shed. They weren't there either.

As the moon traveled across the sky, streaks of dawning light foretold a new day.

Embers glowed. Ashes swirled in the early breezes lit by the light of a gibbous moon.

The stone fireplace chimney stood tall, hauntingly majestic amongst the ashes. I wandered. Looking. Praying for Ossi and Huldor to somehow, miraculously, emerge from the ashes, covered in soot, but alive and holding hands.

It wasn't to be. I shivered from the bleak reality that Ossi and Hulder were gone. I alone stood amongst the ashes and ruin. A paralysis of grief swept over me as I listened to the creaking of failing timbers as they tumbled. The inn where I'd found a home and family was ashes.

I smelled the choking smoke. I felt the heat of the destruction. I closed my eyes so I could no longer see the rubble as the bones of the once beautiful inn trembled and collapsed. I felt my legs tremble as I, too, collapsed.

For a long time, I lay face down trying to suppress images of the cruel blazes. I didn't want to stir. I didn't want to move. I didn't want to live. Remembering the fire and all I'd lost, I just wanted to die and become one with the ashes surrounding me.

Smoke still hung in the morning air. Acrid. Throat burning. Ashes and mud covered me. I hurt inside and out.

In my sorrow and hurt, I wondered what to do next. I cried out, "Ossi and Huldor!" I hoped they'd magically appear before me—alive and well. It was all my fault they'd died. I'd seen the shadow hanging over the inn, but I hadn't told them or anyone else. Now, I just wanted to be alone covered with my guilt. Shadow nudged me with his nose. I was sure he wanted me to go into the barns to feed the animals. To feed him.

I looked at the burned and charred remains of the inn. The sheds where the rabbits, chickens, cats, and goats waited to be fed had escaped the fire. I slowly got up and made my way to the coop where I collected eggs from the chickens. They cloo-coo-ed at me as though asking what had happened. Then I pumped water for the animals. Burns blistered my face and hands. I hurt all over, but worst of all, I felt my stomach heave when I thought of Ossi and Huldor.

In the bath house I carefully washed myself from head to toe. I even dunked my whole head into a bucket of cold water to wash my hair. Then I scrubbed mud, soot, and ashes from the dress I'd been wearing.

While dabbing my burns with resin from a nearby spruce tree, I felt a surge of grief swarm and surround me. "Ossi. Huldor." I said their names over and over as though it would bring them back. They'd taken me in and made me their daughter, but now I was alone again. What could I do? Where should I go? How could I go on? How could I find the Ice People?

CHAPTER 3

For the next three days, I lived in the goat shed. I felt anxious and edgy. Without Huldor and Ossi, my world was empty. I didn't belong there any longer. Even the goats looked at me as though to ask *What are you doing here?* I felt a tug. I needed to be somewhere else. Not here among ashes and memories. But where? The inn had burned. Ossi and Huldor were gone. I could go back to the hut I'd lived in with Father, but it held too many bad memories. I could find the land of the bubbling mud pots where Lamb-i-kins had lived, but what if she was still there and tied me up again? There was no going back. I felt a deep loss. A deep void.

Each day, I fed the dog, chickens, rabbits, goats, and cats. I did all the chores as if in a trance. I felt no comfort in its normalness, not even when I lay in the hay cuddling and stroking the soft fur and listening to the gentle purr of the kittens.

I wandered the lands surrounding the burned inn wringing my hands and blaming myself. What had happened? How did the fire start? A candle not blown out? An ember from the fireplace? I should have stayed in the inn that night, then I would have smelled the smoke, and could have warned Ossi and Huldor. Whatever it was, it was my fault. I could have smelled the smoke earlier. Seen the blaze. I should have done something.

I couldn't shake the sadness and guilt that plagued me. Being born under the blazing comet was supposed to bring me a gift. All it had brought so far was sorrow. My mother had died giving birth to me—or so my father had told me. He had been filled with grief thinking I'd taken my mother's breath and heart beat so I could live. And now Ossi and Huldor. They'd been good to me, but they were dead because of me. I should have told someone about the cloud I'd seen and felt, but would anyone have believed me? What could anyone have done?

No matter how silly the goats were as they romped, chased, and butted one another; no matter how playful the kittens were, I felt no joy in watching them. I felt weak kneed. With only Shadow to keep me company, I escaped to the river bank and sat in my canoe and sobbed. Each tear ripped painfully inside me. The sounds of crackling flames and charred timbers crashing to the ground haunted me. Ossi and Huldor's deaths were more than I could bear. When I thought of them, my chest felt so crushed I could hardly breathe.

In my sorrow, I squeezed my eyes shut and focused. I wished I could enter a portal of the dead to find Ossie and Huldor. I wished I could find them and bring them back. Even as I wished it. Even as I imagined it. Even as I wanted it so much that I ached, I knew it wasn't possible. Needing to touch reality, I ran my hands over my patched canoe. A new wish. A new desire overcame me. The canoe. The canoe had helped me escape the farmer. It had brought me to Ossi and then to Huldor. Now, maybe, it would help me flee from my guilt and memories. Maybe it would bring me to my mother's people—to a new family.

The waters of the river rippled. Inviting me to follow. Trees swayed in the breeze. I listened to the trembling leaves. They spoke of new places. A raven fluttered to a branch above me. *Gronk! Follow me.* The canoe beckoned. Ready. I listened to my heart. It knew. It was time for me to go. Go where? I wasn't sure, but I thought of finding my mother's village. Ossi and Huldor had lived there, too, before the marauders destroyed it. It was late in the season with the leaves already turning colors. I didn't want to be on my own in the middle of nowhere when the snows came, so I would have to leave soon.

For one last time, I walked through the ashes of the inn, looking for anything that had survived the flames. Where the scullery had been, I found kettles, knives, grinders, and the blackened remains of everything Huldor had been so proud of. In the area where the larder had been, the shelves had burned tumbling the crockery pots to shards. The large crock in which Huldor soured pickles and cabbage stood unbroken on the floor. I cleared the area around the crock and slid it to the side. Beneath it was the loose board that had been protected from flames by the crock. I pulled up the board, and found the old metal pot half-filled with coins Huldor saved during the busy summer season. There were a few coppers, a lot of silvers, and even a few golds. It was money guests paid for their bed and meals. Whenever Huldor went to the village, she always slid the large crock aside and lifted the board to take out the coins she needed to buy provisions. At least I wouldn't be penniless on my journey.

I wrapped the coins in a rag I found in the bath house. My mouth soured as I touched the bundle of coins Huldor worked so hard to earn. They reminded me of the coins Father got when he sold me to the farmer so he could be free of me. Free of me—so he could catapult himself to the star sky looking for my dead mother among the stars in the Pleiades.

Next, I looked in Ossi's workshop. An axe, a saw, and a hammer. They might be useful.

In the garden, I found three fat ripe squashes, a rutabaga and a handful of carrots. Last of all, I climbed to pick the few apples still hanging on high branches of a twisted apple tree.

As I packed, I looked to the sky. Last night, the moon had almost passed from the waning gibbous to half-moon. In three weeks, the full moon would signal the Harvest Moon Festival taking place again. Going there was the only time Father and I had ever left our dreary log and moss-covered hovel. At the festival, Father used to put on his professor's robe after hanging a sign proclaiming that he was the All-Seeing Eye. He lured customers by promising to tell their fortunes. They eagerly laid coins in his hand. Those coins had bought our winter supplies and Father's elixirs.

After feeding the chickens, goats, rabbits, and cats for the last time, I opened their gates and doors as I shooed them to freedom. My throat strangled as I said, "Find new homes." At the very end, I caged two of the hens and one rabbit. *Eggs and food.*

Trembling with sadness, I filled my canoe with a soot-blackened kettle, a knife, Ossi's saw, axe, and hammer, rutabaga, carrots, the hens and rabbit. There was just one more thing to do—get my birch bark pack from where it hung in the goat shed. Before I left, I packed the spark stones from Ossi on top of everything.

Almost ready, I tied the rag pouch of coins around my waist and made sure my moonstone was safe deep in a pocket. I patted each of the goats, telling them and the chickens to be good and to find new owners. Tears fell as I kissed each of the kittens and rabbits on the head.

Shadow followed me as I made my last walk around the burned inn. Each step was a memory. Each step was a goodbye to all I'd loved. Each step brought me closer to my unknown journey. A raven watched from high on a branch.

"Come," I told the dog. "It's just you, me, rabbit, and two hens, now."

He wagged his tail and scampered ahead of me.

CHAPTER 4

A gentle breeze followed as the river's current guided us down the river. Once in a while I used the paddle to direct the canoe around rocks or dead tree branches. In the dimming light of evening, I found a sandy shore, pulled the canoe onto it, and found a willow with drooping branches to rest under. Shadow set out finding his own supper. He scrambled through fallen leaves chasing something.

A sharp spasm gripped my chest, and I felt a heavy pall surround me. I was afraid. I was far from the hut I'd shared with Father on Lake Kawishami. I was far from the inn where I had found kindness and caring. I was far down a river and heading into a strange land. I missed Huldor and Ossi. Their warmth. Their laughter. Their everything. I choked back tears and sat on a rock. A tiny spider tickled my wrist as it crept onto me. I watched it lift each leg as it explored by hand. I felt a sudden urge to smash it, but instead, brushed it to the soft ground. The spider had done nothing to hurt me. I was the one filled with guilt and looking for a reason to live.

I tried to shake the grief and sadness that gripped me, but it didn't work. I was exhausted and as lifeless as a branch that had fallen from a tree and floated down the river. A broken branch soon dies without the tree. Is that what I was now? A broken branch? Without family? Would I forever float, carried by the current, every which way? Or would I die alone in the wilderness? Alone, but searching for my mother's people?

The clucking of the hens and Shadow nudging me with his nose brought me back to the hard rock I sat on. I opened the cage and sprinkled dried corn. The hens cloo-cooed as they pecked at the corn. They probably were asking why I'd put them in the cage and when would I bring them back to their coop. Then they strutted around scratching the earth to find bugs. I set the rabbit in the grass to hunt for her own meal, too. Soon she was scratching her ear and munching on clover.

For myself, I ate a carrot and an apple. I hoped the hens would calm down and lay eggs. If not, I would roast them over a campfire. I laughed at the thought of myself roasting a chicken. Would I be as good at it as Lamb-i-kins had been? At least I'd learned something from finding her in the Land of Lucifer's bubbling cauldrons. I wondered where she was now and why she had left me tied to a tree and never returned. Luckily, Ossi had found me there.

The canoe was my bed for the night. With only one thin blanket for cover, I shivered and wished for the warm furs Ossi had given me, but they'd burned in the fire. Shadow snuggled close gently snoring; his tail wrapped over his nose.

A night owl hooted. A rustling of leaves—maybe a fox sneaking close to snatch the chickens or bunny, but I'd caged them again. The snapping of branches. A deer? The rippling of the river. Fish jumping? All the night sounds kept me awake and alert.

I felt a deep aloneness. Ossi had told me of the many times a lone wolf had watched him as he puttered around his camp on the high rocky ridge. "A lone wolf," he told me, "travels and hunts for food by itself." Ossi often saw it hiding in the trees on the edge of his camp and he wondered if the wolf was looking for companionship or a new pack. I smiled to myself as I thought how Ossi and I had both been lone wolves until we met and joined Huldor to become a family. But they were gone now. I ached in my solitude. Once again, I was a lone wolf yearning for a pack.

The river burbled. The moon shone on the waters making a path to the deeper unknown I'd have to travel. Where was I going? Would I ever find the Ice People and another family? A gentle breeze touched my neck. I reached for my moon-stone. The colors swirled gently.

CHAPTER 5

The tamaracks on the river bank glowed golden in the morning sunshine. Their color was another reminder that I needed to find shelter before the oncoming cold. Soon there would be frost on the ferns and grasses in the morning. A raven perched on a branch preening its feathers. A flock of geese flew overhead. Honking.

After letting the hens and rabbit loose to find their own food, I followed Shadow into the woods to search for withered mushrooms or any berries the birds had left on bushes. I found nothing, so bit into an apple as I sat on the river bank, I wished the ground beneath me would tremble. I wanted to feel queasy and have mists blur my vision. I wanted the world around me to twist. I wanted to enter a portal of the dead so I could find Ossi and Huldor. Or maybe even my father. But none of that happened. As much as I wanted, no portal opened.

Shadow shook me out of my reverie when he ran up to me with a squirrel in his mouth. Catching the hens and rabbit wasn't easy, but I finally got them into the canoe. Then I launched my canoe for another day of paddling and looking for a town. I passed a few farms, but remembering the farmer Father had sold me to, I paddled faster. Father was often on my mind. Had he been able to catapult himself to the Pleiades? Had he found my mother there? Was he dead? Alive? Would I someday be able to find him in a portal of the dead? And then I wondered, what would I do if I entered a portal and saw father leaning against a tree, or donning his robe to become The All-Seeing Eye at a festival? I didn't know what had happened to him after he abandoned me. I sobbed as I blamed myself for his sorrows and that I couldn't be the person he'd loved the most.

I paddled for five perfect autumn days that belied the coming cold season. Once, when I stopped to rest, the hens flew high into a tree. When it was time to leave, I coaxed them to come down. Nothing worked. I tried to climb the tree, but it was too slender to hold me. I found dry berries and offered them to the hens. They still didn't come down. Finally, I left them behind knowing a fox would probably enjoy a chicken dinner or two. My own food stores were dangerously low. And now I had no chickens. I needed to ration carefully. I didn't know if I'd ever find a village of my mother's people or even a village where I could find a place to stay for the winter.

One day, the sun was barely past its height when I heard the ringing of bells off to the right bank. I stowed the canoe in a small inlet and prepared to investigate if I'd found a village or larger town. I was about to sling my pack to my back when a chill rippled my spine. My thumbs pricked and tingled. I patted my moonstone. It was cold. I knew the signs well. Beware.

Despite the warnings, I took the pouch of coins from around my waist. I needed to get more food, a pair of boots, and a warm cloak for winter. I counted out a few coins and then buried the pouch next to a nearby rock and covered it with fallen leaves.

I crept in the direction I'd heard the ringing of bells. Peering through branches, I saw a narrow and rutted path leading to a gate. Stone pillars stood tall on either side of the gate that was made of hammered iron unlike anything I'd ever seen. A man stood silently just inside the gate. An old cracked wooden sign hung at a tilt and spanned the two pillars. The faded words read: *Sanctuary for the Exotic Born.* A newer sign hung below the first. It read: *Sanctuary for the Comet Born.*

What did those signs mean? Sanctuary? Exotic? Comet Born? Intrigued, I ignored the tingling in my thumbs. The sign captivated me. I was a child born when the blazing comet was overhead. A sanctuary was a place to be safe. Would I find safety there? If so, why were my thumbs pricking? And who were the *Exotic Born*? Were they the same as the *Comet Born*? Maybe. Maybe not.

I was curious. There were people here. Perhaps I could find a place to spend the winter, or at least buy food and a warm cloak.

Even though my palms grew clammy, I thought maybe the sanctuary was where others like me could learn about the gift they'd been given. Father hadn't known I could enter portals of the dead. If he knew, he'd have been disappointed because I didn't have a gift for fortune telling or any other mystical ability that would make him rich. If I entered, and told the people there I had been born of the comet, would someone help me understand my gift and forebodings? Forebodings—like the one I felt now?

Filled with curiosity and wanting to know more, I prepared to show myself at the gate. I'd pretend, well, I didn't even have to pretend that I was a traveler on my way to find family at an Ice People's village. Maybe someone would even be able to tell me the direction to travel.

The watchman waved his hands for me to stop when he saw me emerging from the woods. "Who comes to my gate? Tell your name. Your business. Or go!"

He shook his arms wildly and lurched closer to the gate. That's when I noticed his knees didn't bend forward like mine and everyone else's. His legs twisted. His knees bent outward making him walk in a strange way. I wondered if he was one of the "exotic born."

He yelled at me again, "Go! You have no business here!"

Stunned at the rude reception, I stepped back from the gate and was about to say my name, but my thumbs pricked. I would not tell the ill-mannered man that my name was Luna.

"P-Purslane," I stammered giving the name I'd hated so much, but Father had chosen for me. I repeated, "My n-name is Purslane." There was nothing exotic about the name of a weed. "I'm here because I need food, boots, and a warm cloak. I was hoping I could get them here." I touched my coins, but cautiously added, "I could work for them."

"No boots here. No cloaks. No food for strangers. Go away!"

I was about to turn when a wide-hipped woman rushed to the gate. "What's going on here?" she asked. She wore a bright rose-colored shawl that hung below her knees. Her dress swirled with every hue of rose. Most notably, the skin on her left cheek was splotched as rosy red as the dress and shawl she wore. I tried not to stare as she looked me up and down. Was she one of the exotic-born who sought shelter in the sanctuary, too?

"Girl here says she be begging for food and needing new boots and cloak. I told girl here to scram." The gatekeeper no longer shouted. His shoulders slumped. His head sagged to his chest, and his fingers twitched as he talked to the woman in a voice barely above a whisper.

"Well, spin around there, missy, so I can look you over."

I did.

"How old are you? And what's your name?"

A foreboding deep inside held me back from saying *Luna, my name is Luna*. I had already told the gatekeeper my old name, so I said, "Purslane, ma'am." My heart pounded. A trickle of cold sweat ran from under my arms.

"Purslane? What an atrocious name! We could always change it, but never mind your name. What I really need to know is how old are you?"

I glanced up at the sign for comet-borns. I was quite sure I'd been fourteen at the last Harvest Moon Festival Father and I had gone to a year ago. I must be fifteen. That's how old all those born under the comet would be now. Was it safe to say I was fifteen? Would she let me in if I did? What would happen to me? Beyond the gate, I saw buildings, but no people. My thumbs pricked. My moonstone was cold. I hesitated, then said, "T-thirteen, ma-am."

The woman raised an eyebrow. I didn't think she believed me so I twisted my fingers and added, "I'll be f-fourteen s-soon."

She looked at me closely. "Thirteen. Nearly fourteen. Too young to be comet-born if you're telling the truth." She scratched the red splotch on her cheek. I noticed her hand was covered with a bright red blemish, too. "Hmmm. Purslane who's not quite fourteen. You faltered. You want me to believe what you say, but something tells me it's not the truth."

"Let her in," she said to the gatekeeper. "We'll make her feel at home. A bite to eat. A scrubbing behind the ears, and a pillow for this lone traveler won't hurt. Perhaps then we'll find the truth. Even if she's not a comet-born, she might still be of value to us."

CHAPTER 6

I hugged myself close as I followed the woman along the cobbled walk into the village. No matter how I tried to calm myself, something didn't seem right. A chill pierced the depth of my bones.

When we were well past the tall gated area, a group of young boys wearing strange silver discs over their faces suddenly filled the cobbled street to gawk. *Why were they wearing masks and what did the masks cover?* Born exotic came to my mind. The boys didn't say anything as I passed, but they did point at me.

One mumbled, "She's one of 'em."

"No, she's not."

"How do you know?"

"Just look at her, for sure, she's one."

"Ah, you can't know just by looking at her."

"I wonder what she can do? Maybe even heal with a touch? Maybe go invisible?"

"Nah. Something better. Like turn you into a skunk. But then that'd be much too easy 'cuz you're halfway there already." All the boys laughed.

"You!" The wide-hipped woman said pointing at one of two identical girls who'd appeared from around a corner. They wore matching frilly white blouses under thick grey woolen sweaters and long black skirts, but no silver masks. "Bring this filthy wraith to the bathhouse. Heat it plenty warm. Don't skimp on the water or soap. Scrub her elbows, feet and knees. Make sure you get between her toes and behind her ears. Look for any marks or deformities that tell the story of who she is. Look especially hard for any sign of the comet."

"And you!" She pointed at the other one. The girl stepped forward as if on command. "Find her clean clothes. Burn what she has on!"

"No," I shouted louder than I intended. My voice strangled in my throat. Stuffing my hand into the pocket, I grasped the coins and my moonstone. I repeated, "No! They're mine!"

The wide-hipped woman looked me up and down. I looked, too. My dress that had once been a beautiful green was now stained and worn. The hem dragged on one side. It had a rip in one sleeve. I reached to touch my tangled hair. I looked at my chewed and broken nails. I winced. I did look like a dirty ragged waif.

The sky clouded. The wind swirled leaves on the walkway. The woman frowned. "Let her keep the wretched dress. Just get her to the bath, and don't let her leave!" She started to walk away, but turned back. Her voice took on an ominous tone as she said, "We *will* find out who you really are. The truth will come out. One way or another."

What the woman said echoed in my ears. *The truth will come out.* What truth? My name? My age? I wanted to get away from there. Everything happened so fast I had no chance to ask if they knew where the Ice People villages were. I didn't even know what direction to go when I left.

I tried to pull away, to leave, but the two girls held my hands tightly as they led me into a bathhouse. Buckets of water heated on a stone fireplace in the middle of the warm and steamy room. Branches of cedar hung from the ceiling giving off a heady aroma. Several large copper basins surrounded the fire. One of the identical girls took my clothes, then she filled a basin with water and pointed to it. I got in. My feet hung over the edge. I tried to relax in the warmth as the other girl inspected my burn scars that were almost healed.

"The ma-am is going to want to see these," she said as she mopped dirt from me with a large cloth.

I hadn't seen anything exotic or different about these two girls, so I asked, "Are you comet-born?"

"Us? No! Thank goodness, but. . . ."

Her sister shushed her. "Don't be saying anything. Harmonia will make you swab the waste buckets for who knows how long if she finds out."

The girls looked to the door with fear in their eyes. Then they began to sing as though nothing had happened. They sang as they scrubbed me from head to toe, treating me as if I was just a child.

Toe-sies. Toe-sies.
Scrub them clean.
Toe-sies. Toe-sies.
Ten of 'em.
Scrub 'em.
Wash 'em.
Make 'em shine.

In spite of my feelings of foreboding, I smiled. Maybe if I made friends with them, they'd tell me more about the signs at the gate. More about the comet-borns and more about the boys with the silver discs. I helped rinse my own hair as one twin dowsed me with buckets of clean water. My chest tightened when I remembered Ossie and the bathhouse he'd made. I ached as I remembered him and Huldor and wished they hadn't died. I held back a sob so the girls wouldn't see me cry.

The girl who'd been scrubbing my back started combing her fingers through my hair to untangle it. When she finished getting the big snarls out, she poured another whole bucket of warm water over me then gave me a huge linen towel to wrap in. She pointed to a wooden bench away from the fire. "Sit there. I'll smooth your hair some more while it dries. By the way, my name is Neoma. My sister is Ayla. What's your name?"

I said my Purslane name just in case they'd heard what I'd told the woman.

Neoma whispered, "Are *you* comet-born?"

Remembering how the girls had acted earlier when I'd asked them the same question, I shook my head and murmured, "No."

Ayla looked at the door, then said, "Wait until you see our brother. He's Elio. Our mother carried us all in her womb at the same time. Can you imagine how big her belly must have been? Of course, we were much smaller then. We're triplets, but you wouldn't think so because Elio doesn't look like us. His ears are big and stick out, and he's always sneezing."

I wanted to ask them why they seemed frightened of the woman they called Harmonia. I especially wanted to ask if there any comet-borns in the sanctuary, but just then the wide-hipped woman came back with an armload of clothes. She stopped short and looked at me intensely. I worried when she looked at me so closely. Even as she laid the clothes on a bench, she kept an eye on me.

Hands on her hips, she said, "Well, Purslane or whatever your name really is, you're looking much cleaner and more presentable. Ayla, did you see anything odd about her?'

"No, nothing at all. Just some burns that are almost healed."

The woman sorted the clothes into piles while she spoke. "My name is Harmonia Anikula. Harmonia is the goddess of harmony and cosmic balance. I come from a royal family that has lived and ruled on a shining star of the Pleiades for millennia. Thus, I bear the blood marks—proof of my royalty. If you or anyone needs further confirmation of my royal blood line, look." With that she dropped her shawl. Large blood-red blotches marked her arms as well as her face and hands.

"I'd show you more, but it would be inappropriate for me to lift my skirt. When one sees the extent of my royal markings, one knows for sure what I say is true, and must follow my royal commands. As my name suggests, I do not like discord, so don't go thinking you can mix everything up here. This is a place of harmony and conformity—conformity of thought and action, not of physical character-istics." While she spoke, she gently ran her fingers over my burn scars. "Hmm. Hmm. Fire you say? What happened?"

I told her about running through smoke and flames looking for and trying to save Ossi and Huldor, but I'd been too late. She stood me up, pulled an under-garment over my head followed by a woven shift and then a knitted woolen shawl. "It'll be getting icy cold because Winter Maker will be here any day now," she explained as she handed me a pair of long stockings and leggings made of a soft pelt. "We don't want you getting cold. Snow Maker will come, too." She examined the birch bark boots Ossi and I had made together. "They'll have to do for now," she said. "Tumla is our shoemaker. It'll take him a day or two or even three or more to get shoes ready for you. It all depends on how much his back is paining him."

When Harmonia led me out of the bathhouse and into the chilly day, several of the boys with silver masks on their faces stood outside waiting. They pointed at me like I was something very strange.

"She got deformities?" asked a red-haired little boy.

"No," Harmonia said. "And remember. No making fun. No teasing. No laugh-ing at anyone who was born different than you. Be kind, and remember that being different is a wonderful gift."

I wanted to ask why they wore silver discs over their faces, but remembered what Harmonia had just said. Just then the boys began tossing my birch bark pack back and forth. I hurried to rescue it before they dumped everything to the ground.

"Mine," I said hugging the pack to my chest. I thought of all my earthly belongings that were inside. I quickly stuffed the dirty dress I'd been wearing inside it, too.

Harmonia shooed the children away saying, "Find something else to play with. Go now!" Then she waved Neoma over. "Show her the village. Don't go beyond the towers that stand at each outermost corner of the village. Remind her that I demand harmony and compliance here. Follow the rules." She paused to tuck a stray hair behind her ear. "Neoma, don't let her out of your sight. You'll be watched the whole time. Later, we'll find out who she really is."

CHAPTER 7

As soon as Harmonia left, I felt relieved. She scared me, and I was troubled by what she meant when she said she'd find out who I really was. I decided it was best to leave right away. I told Neoma, "You don't have to show me the village. I'll go now."

My fingers tingled and pricked making me nervous. I turned to leave even though I was curious if there were comet-borns like me in the sanctuary, and I had many more questions to ask of Neoma.

"No! Please don't go! I have to do what Harmonia says, or I'll get into trouble. You heard what she said about *harmony*. Just come with me now, then you can leave."

Neoma grasped my hands so tightly and looked so frightened that I agreed. Staying there a little while longer wouldn't hurt. Even though I was nervous, it felt good to be clean and wrapped in warm clothes. Together we walked along the rough paths cobbled with rounded stones. The raven I'd seen earlier followed us. When we came to the base of the first tower Harmonia had pointed out, I asked Neoma, "What are these for?"

Neoma looked around as though she'd been caught doing something wrong. She whispered, "Harmonia says they remind her of the realm she's from. Maybe they're important in the stars of the Pleiades." Still whispering, she said, "Sometimes she locks someone in who doesn't do what she wants."

"They look formidable. Have you ever been locked in?"

Neoma shook her head vigorously and whispered, "And I don't intend to make her angry enough to lock me up. Come now. Let's go."

I shuddered a bit as I studied the towers. Each base was eight-sided with a door and a tiny window near the top. The towers themselves had white stone caps with a peaked roof that glowed in the sunlight.

After we'd walked the whole perimeter from stone tower to tower, Neoma pointed in the direction of the village itself. It was laid along two long intersecting lanes. On our walk, I hadn't seen any people, so I ventured to ask, "Where is everyone? The comet-borns? The exotics? Are they the same?"

Neoma held a finger to her lips and hushed me, then whispered. "No, they're different. The exotic ones, like my parents, don't come out unless it's time to go to the dining hall, work, or some other reason Harmonia says they need to be out for."

I didn't know if it was polite or not, so I asked as nicely as I could. "What does it mean to be exotic like your parents?"

"Well, my mom was born with extraordinary hands. Her three middle fingers on each hand are fused together." Neoma held up her hands and pressed her middle fingers together. "Like this. Her fingers each have a nail, but they look more like talons. Like on a bird." She put her hand to her mouth. Looked around, and said, "Don't tell anyone I said that. Even though my mom's hands are rare and wonderful, when she was growing up, other kids laughed and called her *turkey hands* and other cruel names."

I felt sorry for her mom having to endure name calling. Neoma continued, "She couldn't get a job. Nobody would give her work. They just laughed at her. So, to earn a living, she joined a traveling band of others who had been born with rare differences. They rode from village to village in a wagon that had signs painted in red on the side. *See the World's Greatest Exotics! See the Two Headed Man! Touch the Alligator Woman!* People paid to go inside to see and laugh at them. My parents hated riding around in that wagon and being made a spectacle of."

"How awful! People can be so mean! No wonder Harmonia was so stern with the boys who wanted to know if I was exotic in some way."

Neoma looked around again to see if anyone was listening. "Harmonia is stern and demanding most of the time, but my parents and others are thankful for her kindness. When she first saw the covered wagon filled with people who were born different, she felt sorry for them, so she bought them—wagon and all—and brought them here where they built this village together. She's kind to them. They no longer have to put up with prying eyes from people who point, laugh, and make fun of them. Here they have good lives and live in harmony."

"I noticed she could be gentle at times, but at other times she scares me. Thanks for showing me around, but I don't want to stay. I need to leave as soon as possible."

Neoma stopped me by grabbing my arm. She looked around again and said, "Shhhh.

Was she afraid of whomever it was Harmonia had said would be watching us? I didn't care. I hadn't seen anyone, but I was still a little curious about the people who lived in the village. I wanted to see the comet-borns, too, so I walked close to Neoma as I peeked in the windows of the many shops. One sign read: *Hirsute Master. Enter for a Clip and a Snip*. Another: *Tick Tock—Chimes Made to Your Order*. The next shop must have belonged to Tumla the boot maker Harmonia had mentioned because the sign read: *Soles for Your Feet. Complete with Tongues, Heels, and Toes*. Shops and signs, but no people.

I counted as we passed each shop. There were twenty including a bakery, a wiggery, a stitchery, butchery, coffin maker, cooper's shop, a cravat and hat maker, a fiddle shop, one that advertised Teas and Herbal Draughts, a bone cracker, a bone setter, a blood-letter—the sign showed leeches—and a witchery that promised Fortunes, Foretellings, and Fates just by looking at your hands. Skeins of wool hung in the window with a sign Knittery. I thought of Father as I looked in the window of a shop proclaiming Tonics and Elixirs. He would have liked that one. The last two shops were the Grain Grindery and Wood Carpentry.

Neoma held her head down and was quiet as I studied each shop. There seemed to be everything the villagers needed. Keeping my voice low, I asked, "What are some of the other rarities the people here have? Like what makes your father different?"

Neoma frowned, but whispered, "My dad does have an extraordinary gift. Harmonia says only special people are given gifts—like the comet-borns, too. My dad was born with short arms. His hands only hang to his waist. Because there are lots of jobs he can't do, he cares for the sheep. He leads the herd to their grazing spot each morning and back to their shelter at night. He loves the sheep, and they love him. They nuzzle close to him. It's almost like they take care of him while he cares for them. While he watches them during the day, he uses special combs made to fit his arms and hands to card wool so the women who do the weaving and knitting don't have to pull burrs from the wool. It's amazing to watch my dad do that with his short arms. I'm so proud of him."

I noticed Neoma stood taller as she talked about her father. She was proud of what he could do. He had a job he liked and wasn't letting what some people would have thought of as a challenge stop him from doing his job. "What about the weavers and knitters? Surely, they don't have arms and hands like your mother and father?"

"Right. One has a rare formation to her foot. Another has a facial twist, but you should see how their hands fly as they work their looms and knitting needles. They are gifted and make the most beautiful sweaters and blankets."

I was beginning to understand how the exotic people didn't let anything stop them from finding something they could do that was important.

At that point, Neoma and I entered a street where small houses with steep thatched roofs of straw stood in rows. They were exactly alike except for color. A curved path of gravel led to the front doors. I counted—exactly seven little bushes lined each path to each door. A small hexagonal window glinted at the top of each door. The houses were painted in a full rainbow of colors: greens of every hue, blues, violets, yellows, oranges, and reds. I thought of the rough log hut Father and I had lived in with its rocky path and the tin roof that leaked when it rained. Here in the midst of so many houses, I felt lost and alone. I felt a strange emptiness. Houses, but no people. No children. Just me and Neoma, and she was silent. I wanted to be far away from this place. I felt a tiny bit of comfort when I saw a raven perched on the thatched roof of a sky-blue house.

"Why are all the houses so much alike?" I asked.

"Harmonia says uniformity preserves order and harmony. I suppose because the people are all so different that she tries to make other things the same. Whatever you do, don't ask her. She doesn't like questions like that."

The colorful houses with their perfect little yards and carefully planted bushes looked as though no one lived in them. No children played in the yards. No smells of roasting squirrel. No bubbling stew pots over open fires. Here, silence met me wherever I went. It was as if the whole of the village had been abandoned just a short time ago. Where were the children born of the comet? Even Neoma hardly said a word except in a whisper.

Not a single person crossed our path as we had walked the village. Not a single voice rang out from the small shops. A wispy cloud passed over the sun. At the end of the street with all the houses, I looked out at the fields beyond the village. A high fence encircled a large area. The fence was so high I couldn't see what was within it. Tingles ran up and down my spine. As though I was afraid to know the answer, my voice trembled as I pointed and asked, "What's over there?"

Neoma scowled and held her finger to her lips again.

I'd received so much attention when I arrived. Everything had seemed like a normal village. I'd been scrubbed in warm soapy water, given clean clothes, but I still felt a gloom and wariness increasing as I thought of how unnatural every-thing was. Harmonia, who seemed nice at times, had frightened me with the way she appeared to be looking into me deeply, looking, searching for something, as if I were hiding something. I shivered when I remembered she'd said *Then we can find out who you really are.*

I whispered to Neoma, "Do the Children of the Comet live in these little houses, too, or are they in that fenced in area?"

Neoma didn't answer.

CHAPTER 8

The sun sank below the horizon. Darkness crept into the sky. The air chilled as Neoma and I finished our third walk around the pillars and through the cobbled lanes. Even though Harmonia had warned we'd be watched, I hadn't seen a single other person, dog, or cat.

"I have to leave now. Thanks for showing me the village," I said to Neoma.

Neoma looked around as if looking for Harmonia. "You don't have to thank me. I probably would have had to sweep the outhouses if you weren't here."

"Thanks anyway," I said, then turned toward the watchman's gate to leave. I wanted to get into my canoe and paddle until I found a good place to settle for the night.

I hadn't gotten very far when a bell tolled. Neoma caught up to me, grabbed my arm and implored, "No! Don't go. Harmonia told me to keep an eye on you."

At the same time, the street behind me that had been empty, filled with people streaming from all directions. They walked arm in arm, laughing and talking. I was worried about Shadow so I shook off Neoma's hand. "Sorry," I said to her and hurried toward the gate once again.

"Purslane! Oh, Purslane, I'm so glad to see you!" It was Ayla rushing toward me. "Where have you and Neoma been all day?"

"Neoma and I walked around the village. Where has everyone else been?" I asked just as Harmonia stepped out of the crowd and took me by the hand.

"Come have your evening meal with me." Her voice was like a song, and she smiled sweetly. "Then I'll introduce you to our shoemaker so he can get working on your shoes."

My stomach groaned with hunger. It had been a long time since I'd eaten. One squash, some wrinkled apples, and the rabbit were all I had left of my food, so I was grateful for a chance to fill my stomach. I decided I would eat, then hurry to the canoe, let the rabbit out into the grass for a while as I readied the canoe for paddling away. Poor Shadow. He was guarding the canoe and the rabbit and probably wondering if I'd be back with something for him to eat.

My empty stomach rumbled again as I followed Harmonia to dining hall. All the people stood outside waiting for Harmonia to go in first. Inside, the hall was large with windows reaching from floor to ceiling on one side. The opposite wall was covered with a magnificent painting of a dark sky and numerous pin dots of white. I made out the stars of Orion's belt that pointed to Aldebaran and to the Pleiades. Father had said my mother came from the Pleiades to be his bride— the same constellation Harmonia said she was from. I'd never believed Father's story, but maybe it was possible for people to travel through the galaxy. Painted in the center of the wall was a huge swoop of white and a great ball of yellows, oranges, and red—the comet. The comet under which I'd been born.

As I took in the whole room, the villagers entered and found their assigned tables. The room buzzed with conversation. I tried not to stare at anyone. I'd never seen anything like it. All of the older people had a rarity. Some were more obvious than others. Despite their exotic looks, the people laughed, and talked, and scraped stools while settling at their tables. The several youngsters who came in with Neoma and Ayla weren't exotic in any way. They, like Neoma and Ayla must be the children of the people who'd been born exotic. The youngsters sat together in a corner and began singing a rowdy song with a chorus that they sang loudest of all.

Comet, comet.
Many years a coming'
A comin' and a bringin'
A coming' and a bringin'
Bringin'

Harmonia stood next to a stool and signaled me to sit next to her. Two men and two women joined us at the table. One of the men had skin on his cheeks that looked like it was covered with fish scales. The other man set his crutches aside as he nodded to me. The woman sitting closest to me had a large lump on the side of her neck. It looked like a tiny head. There were indentations where the eyes should be, a bump where a partially formed nose jutted out a little, and lots of hair. The other woman had no hair. No eyebrows or lashes even. She smiled at me and said, "You have beautiful hair!"

I became tongue-tied. Not knowing what to say, I just looked down at my hands and mumbled, "Thank you." I found it hard to look at the people sitting near me, so I looked at those at other tables. I didn't want to stare, but their oddities were such like I'd never seen. One person had a small head that grew to a point at the top. Another had a very large head. Others had facial distortions of every kind. I felt bad they had been stared at and made fun of all their lives before Harmonia brought them to this village. She'd made them feel as though their differences were gifts. Even though I was still a little bit frightened of Harmonia, as were Neoma and Ayla, I pushed those thoughts aside and tried to think of her kindness for bringing these people to a place where they could have good lives. It must have been terrible to earn a living by being stared at and made fun of while being carted around in a wagon. As much as I wanted to keep looking at each one of them, I looked down at my hands. I didn't want to be rude.

I was relieved when Harmonia clapped her hands and addressed the villagers, "Look here, we have a visitor from outside. She says her name is Purslane and that she is almost fourteen. I will test her later to determine if she speaks the truth or not. In the meantime, make her feel welcome. Now, let's not waste any more time."

Instantly, I heard a low hum. The hum started no louder than a buzzing bee I had once watched on the flowers of a wild plum tree. Little by little, the hum grew louder. I looked at my tablemates. They tilted their heads back as they hummed. Across the table from me I watched the hairless woman's throat as it vibrated with the hum. Next to her, the lame man's bristly chin wobbled. Their eyes were closed. Harmonia's eye lashes quivered as she hummed, and her brow creased.

I watched as the chests of the five at my table rose and fell at the same time. Harmonious and perfectly synchronized! They breathed in exactly at the same time. To my amazement, the humming in the room began to swell and recede. It reminded me of the waves on Lake Kawishami where I'd lived with Father and spent long summer evenings watching and listening to the waters. The undulating humming lasted a long time. Even though I found the humming and everyone breathing at the same time a bit unusual, I felt myself relax and sink into its soothing rhythm.

How much time passed, I do not know, but it was full dark outside when I surfaced from a deep trance and found a bowl of steaming stew already in front of me with a slab of thickly buttered bread and an apple. My tablemates slurped broth and chewed chunks of vegetables. The man across from me smiled broadly and said, "Welcome, Purslane."

Everyone at the table turned to me and said together, "Welcome, Purslane."

I smiled back, but they'd already bent their heads to their suppers. I took my first taste of the thick stew, too. It was rich with a zesty spice and thick with vegetables. Around me, people ate, talked to one another, laughed, and burped.

Between spoons of the stew, I listened to the talk at my table. The men talked about the weather and the coming of Winter Maker. The women wished the cold season wouldn't be too long and harsh. One said, "I hope there'll be enough tallow for candles and fats for the lanterns."

The man with the cane said, "Good thing the rutabagas are plentiful. The apples from the orchard are smaller than usual so we spent a lot of time hunting wild apples. There are plenty of those, but most are small and wormy."

The woman without hair said, "At least they'll be good for cider, but not much else."

Then they all discussed lambs and hoped many would be born in the spring. Finally, the conversation turned to ways of keeping the grains dry and out of reach of rodents.

I bent forward and ate until my spoon clanked in my almost empty bowl. The woman nearest me asked, "Are you staying to celebrate the Festival of the Coming of the Night Sky Dancers?"

A festival! I became excited and curious because I had never heard of that one before. Would my twin sister Selene and Lady Magda be there telling fortunes? I had planned to leave before Harmonia could carry out her plan to learn more about me, but now I wanted to stay. Maybe I'd see my sister again. Now that Ossi and Huldor were gone, I could travel with her and Lady Magda. My sister and I could be a real family for the first time. Suddenly full of hope and eager to see my twin, I asked, "When will the festival be?"

"Tomorrow night. It's such a grand festival, you'll want to be there."

CHAPTER 9

Getting away alone to check on my canoe and animals was impossible. After the meal, Harmonia grasped my arm and led me to Tumla's Bootery. In some ways, I was glad to be getting new boots for winter, but I was still worried about Shadow and the rabbit.

"Keep her here until I come get her," Harmonia demanded of Tumla who wore a silver disc over his face. Then she whispered to him, "Just a pair of flat shoes, forget about sturdy boots."

After Harmonia left, Tumla welcomed me to his shop and asked, "Do you mind if I remove this cursed mask?"

"Of course not," I answered as I looked around taking in all the hides of deer, goats, and sheep hanging on every wall.

"I warn you, my face is a scary thing to look at. But I find it so much easier to work without it."

I thought he was joking, but when he removed the mask, I saw what he meant. His face was a mass of lumps, bumps, and scars. Instinctively, I asked, "What happened?" As soon as I said the words, I was sorry I'd asked. I didn't want to be rude and thoughtless.

"Not one thing," he answered. "Many things. As a child, I got into many scrapes and fights, but always came out the worse for wear. A bump here. A scar there. Some of the worst ones are from fighting a bobcat when I was only about ten. I learned my lesson the hard way. Never try to take a bobcat kitten from its mother. My mother was at her wits end keeping me out of trouble, or trying to. My uncle finally took me in and taught me boot-making to keep me busy and out of scrapes." While Tumla talked, he gathered some interesting looking tools.

"I loved the smell of tanning skins and working in his shop so stayed even when I got old enough to be on my own. I wasn't nearly this ugly when a traveler came in for new boots and told us stories about great herds of animals that roamed the plains of the West. Uncle was fascinated. I was, too. We decided to go on an adventure hunting them for their skins."

Tumla chuckled as he told his story and ran his hands over a large fur. "Bison," he continued, "Not found in these parts. Uncle and I bought a rickety, creaky cart and a pair of oxen so we could join a wagon train of bison hunters going out West to gather skins for coats and blankets. We started out just as the snows fell to get there in time for when the beasts had the best coats of fur. It took us weeks to get to the wild plains. Woof, you can't imagine the cold! The hardships! This little shop isn't much, but it's a luxury palace compared to what we went through. A blizzard almost did us all in. Eating beans and salted hog fat for days on end was almost worse than the blizzard."

Tumla cleared a stack of leather strips from a wooden bench. With a bow and sweep of his hand, he said, "A golden jeweled throne for m'lady to sit."

I laughed along with him. As eerie as I'd felt walking the village streets, in the dining hall, and meeting other people, I relaxed with Tumla and liked his cozy shop. His scarred and bumpy face was better to look at than Harmonia's smooth one with splotches of red.

"The bad food and constant jiggling and rocking on the rutted trail we took to get to the bison plains was nothing compared to what was coming. My first sight of the massive herds almost sent me running in the other direction. It seemed there were more bison than stars I could count in the sky. The hunt! The thundering of their hooves! The shaking of the ground! All that and Uncle and I didn't know the first thing about hunting the great beasts."

Tumla stopped to look for more tools. "You'd think my uncle and I would have been smart enough to turn around and go home once we saw the massive beasts all in a herd, but we weren't."

He wiped his nose on his sleeve, then continued, "I'll never forget how foolish we were. Every time I walk by a reflecting glass, I remember. Dummy that I was, I was lucky to end with my head still attached and not just a hoof print or two on my face. Just a word of caution for you, if you ever meet a mama bison who is trying to protect her little one, run! Run for your life, or she just might do the Mama Bison Polka on your face."

I laughed as I imagined a bison dancing the polka. Tumla knelt on the floor in front of me and pulled off the boots Ossi had made. In some ways, he reminded me of Ossi. Kind, caring, and making the best of what had happened to him.

"I'll never make anything with that pelt," he said pointing to the wall where the bison skin hung. "I just keep it for show. You're the first in this whole village, I've told the story to."

"Why is that?" I asked. "It's a good story."

"Well, everyone else here was born the way they are. I was born ordinary, but was foolish and got my scars as a result. Harmonia was kind enough to take me in when no one else would give me a place to live and a job to do. Most of the people dwell here because it's a safe place. A sanctuary. They have jobs and aren't poked fun at. But others stay here because they are devoted to Harmonia. They'd do anything for her. I am thankful for her kindness when she is showing it, but I don't know who to trust. In their loyalty to Harmonia, they. . . ." He looked at the door. "Enough said. I've probably blathered too much already."

He stopped and began measuring my feet, so I said, "Some boys were wearing masks like yours. Do they have scars, too?"

Tumla laughed so hard he had to wipe his eyes and hold his belly as it shook. "No scars on those young ones. They used to make fun of me even though Harmonia forbids that behavior, so I made them masks and invited them to join the Tumla Club. They come to help me every day after their lessons. They sweep the shop. Dust. Keep things orderly. And sometimes even help make a boot. They still like to run around wearing the masks, but now it's in fun. They think it's a badge of honor—something to be proud of."

"You're not really that scary to look at," I said. "In fact, when you laugh and smile, your eyes twinkle, and you make me smile, too. People would get used to your scars, and you have a good story how you got them. You don't need the mask."

"I've considered that, but Harmonia insists I never go out and about without it. What she says is law here. She calls this utopia—a perfect village—and wants everything harmonious. No disagreements allowed. If I didn't make such good boots and shoes, I'm sure she'd send me packing with barely the shirt on my back." He lowered his voice as he looked at the door. "Hah! No utopia here even though there is good to be found in Harmonia. But this is more like a Dis-harmonia-topia. Be wary of her. My advice is to get away as soon as possible."

I thought about what he said. Tumla was a smart man. He'd changed a bad situation into something good with the boys who'd made fun of him. Maybe he'd help me, too.

"I plan to leave after the Festival of the Night Sky Dancers. I'm trying to find a village where the Ice People live. Do you know where there is one?" I asked.

"Never heard of them. Why do you ask?"

"That's where I'm going. They're my mother's people. I want to be with them, but I have no idea what direction to travel."

He looked up from his work, then at the door. He asked softly, "Are you one of the children born of the comet Harmonia and the others keep in the stockade?"

My heart thudded. Comet-born children kept in a stockade? No wonder Neoma wouldn't say anything. And now, there was something about how Tumla had been so cautious asking the question that made me wonder. Made me wonder why Harmonia wanted to find out who I really was. Tumla—kind Tumla— who was making me boots like Ossi had. Could he be trusted?

"I just got here today," I answered, not really answering. "I know nothing about children being kept in a sanctuary except for what the sign at the entry said. I didn't see any at supper."

Tumla bent to his work again and began to speak so softly I could barely make out his words. "The boots and shoes I make are strong and sturdy, but Harmonia orders other kinds of shoes for the sanctuary children. Flimsy, floppy ones. Not even real shoes, just a sole and one or two narrow straps. Shoes no good for running away." He looked at the door as if he expected Harmonia to come bursting in and scolding because he'd told me too much. "She wants me to make flimsy shoes for you, but I'll make good ones. You'll need good boots for your travels."

In a whisper he continued. "I don't like how she keeps those youngsters confined in the stockade way out there on the windy hillside. I don't even like that we'll be going there for the Festival of the Night Sky Dancers. It's supposed to be a fun time before the cold and bluster set in, but in the end, Harmonia is going to select some who have been showing great promise."

Tumla shook his head as though shaking terrible memories away. "The whisperings are that every once in a while, she sells one or two of the comet-borns with supernatural powers. Or if she thinks one doesn't have powers, she teaches them to pretend they do. Word is, she puts them on an auction block and sells them to the highest bidder. She tells the buyers they'll get rich owning one because of their magic."

I shook my head, too, as I thought about what he'd told me. It spelled danger to me. I was a child born of the comet. If Harmonia knew, she'd put me in the stockade with the others. No wonder she asked how old I was. A chill ran up my back. I didn't think she believed me when I'd said *almost fourteen*. Maybe she didn't even care if I was comet-born or not. I looked the right age, so maybe she'd put me in the stockade and sell me anyway.

I wanted Tumla to keep talking. I needed to know more. "Harmonia asked how old I was as soon as I came here. She said she wants to find out who I really am. I've already told her, but I don't think she believes me. I'm afraid of her."

"You, me, and a few of the village folks, too. Most of the others have bought into Harmonia's promises and are in league with her—hoping to get rich, too. When she learned about the boys and girls born in the year of the comet and the supernatural gifts they'd develop, she traveled to towns and villages to find them. Sometimes she abducted the kids. Sometimes she bribed mothers and fathers to give up their children saying they'd be taken to a good school, learn a good trade, and then returned to their families." Tumla reached for a roll of leather and spread it before me.

"All rubbish!" He said as he began cutting a strip from it.

I stroked the leather. "This doesn't look like rubbish to me. It looks good and strong."

Tumla laughed softly. "Not the leather. What she told the parents when taking their children. That's rubbish. In reality, she sells them to the highest bidder. The bidder gets someone they think will make them rich. Actually, Harmonia is the one who gets rich."

I was thoroughly frightened especially when he added, "Be careful." He looked over his shoulder to the door. "She has watchers everywhere. She might put you in the sanctuary and sell you. She won't care if you were comet-born or not. Last year, she sold two boys who helped me in the shop. She lied about them having supernatural skills. They'd been born right here! In the year before the comet passed over!"

I had been right. Harmonia might put me in the stockade just to have one more person to sell. Chills goose-bumped my whole body. My heart raced, my throat tightened, and I trembled. I remembered Huldor's story of how she and my mother had been sold. Even though my mother had a lame leg, the seller had said she was worthy to bid on because she of the age to bear children of the comet. Now Harmonia was selling the comet-born children. I was one, and

I was in danger of being kept in the stockade and sold. I had to make sure that didn't happen.

"The Festival for the Night Sky Dancers is tomorrow. If I help," I said to Tumla, "will you be able to get my boots finished so I can sneak off when Harmonia is busy there?"

Before Tumla could answer, Harmonia burst through the door.

CHAPTER 10

"Bed time!" Harmonia said, then harshly added to Tumla, "That's for you, too. All lamps must be snuffed in fifteen minutes."

I looked back at Tumla as Harmonia grabbed me by the arm and pulled me toward the door. He gave me a slight nod of the head before slipping his mask back on.

The street lamps outside were already dark. Clouds covered the moon, giving off a hazy glow. "Hurry, now," Harmonia said, yanking me along. I almost had to run to keep up to her. I was eager to find out which of the neat little houses we were going to, where I'd spend the night.

When we got to one of the little stone buildings at the foot of a pillar, she lifted the wooden bar and opened the door. Inside, a lamp glimmered giving enough light for me to see a small cot. "You should be comfortable for the night," she said pointing to the cot and then to a bucket. "Don't bother trying to get out. The watchers will stop you before you destroy the harmony of the night sleeps."

My heart sank. I'd hoped to be in one of the little houses. I thought I'd be with Neoma and Ayla, or at least, not alone. Neoma entered carrying a small tray with a sweet bread and mug of something that smelled spicy. My hopes lifted a little. Harmonia took the tray from Neoma saying, "Hurry to your quarters before all lamps are out." I wished she could have stayed with me, even for a little while.

"Enjoy your bedtime tea. Then blow out your lamp and get a good night's sleep. Tomorrow's a busy day. Breakfast is at daybreak. Then cleaning and scrubbing chores for everyone. In the afternoon, the great Festival of the Night Sky Dancers starts."

I was glad when Harmonia turned to leave, but then I heard the heavy thud of the bar locking me in. That thud, thud, thud of the bar echoed and resounded, scaring me. I was locked in. Doomed. A prisoner. Just like the ones the triplets had said. I knew I'd be going nowhere, but to bed. And then to the stockade. Maybe sold on an auction block. I was alone with no one to help free me. Tumla didn't know where I was. And Shadow must be worried about me.

I calmed myself by thinking about the coming festival and hoping my sister Selene would be there with Lady Magda. I could leave with them. Harmonia couldn't stop me. Could she? The thought that I could be with my sister again comforted me enough so I sipped the tea. It was deliciously fragrant.

With each sip I took, the spices wafted and tickled my nose. I tasted chamomile and cedar. Then I detected ginger, and something else. Something I'd never tasted before. I ate the sweet bread and sipped more tea. A sudden weariness overcame me—unnaturally so. My eyelids drooped. The tea! I tried to stand, but couldn't. Harmonia's words came back to me, reverberating in my head. *Then we'll find out who you really are.* I threw the mug and tray to the floor. Crack! Splinters flew everywhere. Then another sound. Slowly, the bar was lifted and the door creaked open.

In a dream, I floated down a rippling river. The sun shown on my shoulders warming me. Ossi and Huldor were there holding hands.

Bees gathered honey and packed it into my ears. A flower bloomed from my belly button.

Dim sounds echoed. The sounds came closer. Booming. Rumbling. Thundering. Exploding!

I cried out. "Ossi! Huldor!" They were no longer to be seen. "Help me!"

A crow pecked at my ears.

Caw! Caw! What's your name?

I tried to think. What was my name?

A weed? Was it a weed? Or was it the moon? Moon or weed?

I couldn't say.

The pecking wouldn't stop. I tried to shake the crow away.

Caw! Caw! What's your name?
Was I weed child? Was I moon child?
I swung at the crow. The crow fluttered.

Caw! Caw! What's your name?
I retched. I gagged. I spewed.
Tea and sweet bread swirled in the river.
The crow pecked harder.
The sunny rippling river became
A roaring rocky tumbling torrent.
The crow pecked again and again.

Caw! Caw! What's your name?
Luna! My name is Luna!
The crow melted. The pecking stopped.
Not Purslane. Not weed child.
Luna, child of the moon. Child of the sky.

Caw. Caw. The crow was back.
How old are you, Luna, child of the moon?
I floated above myself seeking the answer.
The roaring rocky tumbling torrent returned.
The crow pecked again.
The hewn logs of a hovel rose in front of me.
In pain I tried to count the marks on the wall.
Gashes made by Father to remember the day
Mother died giving birth to me.
How many? How many? Insisted the crow.
The moon whispered to me. Don't tell. Don't tell.
Thirteen. I lied.

Caw! Caw! Or maybe fifteen.
Are you comet-born? Fifteen.
Are you fifteen?
Child of the comet. Child with gifts?
No! No! No!

The river slowed to gentle ridged ripples.
I'm just a poor orphan child looking for family among the Ice People.

Who did you live with?
Father. My Father.
And what about your mother?
She died when I was born.
What was her name?
Alcyone.
What was your father's name?
He called himself Polaris.

Caw. Caw. Star people with moon daughter.
Star-sky people. Maybe comet girl.
Why isn't your father with you?
He flew to the Pleiades.
The crow tilted its head. Its eyes gleamed brightly.

Caw. Caw.
How was he going to get to the Pleiades?
He catapulted himself into the sky.
He swam through clouds and stars to reach the Seven Sisters.

The crow clicked its beak and pecked my ear sharply. My whole body felt hot. I wanted the crow to melt away. Bees stung me. A spider dropped from the ceiling. It broke into dozens of little spiders that crawled all over me. My face. My nose. I screamed. Thunder and lightning roared and slashed above the river. Rushing water filled my ears. The canoe spun. The roaring rocky tumbling torrent seethed and simmered. Dizzy. I was so dizzy. Father stood on the shore. I reached out to him. He didn't reach out to me.

Caw! Caw! Fairy tales! Falsehoods! Fabrications! All lies!
The crow flew away. A door slammed. A bar dropped.
I tried to stand. My knees buckled. I fell.

Dimly, I heard the door creak open. Harsh sunlight stung my eyes. "Time to be up and about," Neoma said. Then she stopped short. "What a mess you've made."

My head pounded; my vision blurred. Neoma sat next to me holding a tray with steaming oat cereal and an apple. My stomach churned. I remembered my dream. Dream? Or had it really happened?

Little by little my head cleared. The tea. The tea, of course, had been drugged. By Neoma? She'd brought it to me, but she hadn't questioned me in the night. The crow. I was sure Harmonia was the crow of my dreams. "Did you make the tea last night?" I asked.

"No, Harmonia made it. Is that what made you sick?" Neoma looked at the floor and wrinkled her nose. "I'll bring a mop. We'll clean this together. Harmonia has demanded that Ayla, Elio and I be with you all day. We have chores to do before the festival. We'll get done fast with you helping. Then we'll have time to twist our hair into fancy curls."

I sniffed the oat cereal. No strange spice. No spice at all, so I spooned a bit into my mouth. It was soft and buttery and tasted just like Huldor's oat cereal. As I ate, I asked Neoma about the children of the comet.

"How do you know about them?" she asked.

"The big sign above the gate says this is a sanctuary for children of the comet. Is that what you and Ayla are? Children of the comet?"

"Ayla, Elio, and I were not born when the comet was above. Our parents live here among the exotics. And I pray to the gods of Callisto, that we'll never be mistaken for comet-born children. If we behave and obey Harmonia, she won't make us live in the stockade with them."

"Why, is that bad?" I asked.

"Bad! Where have you been? You don't know? The comet was an omen. Part bad and part good. The good part was you could be born with a mystical gift. The bad part is that if you were, people like . . . people like. . . ." Neoma stopped and looked at the door. Then she whispered, "Well, some people would want to lock you up until you showed signs of your gift. Then sell you like a slave to a highest bidder."

It was what Tumla said. He'd been right. Now I was sure that Harmonia was the crow in my dream. What had I told her after I drank the tea? I had tossed most of it when weariness overcame me. Had I been able to resist and not tell? Not tell how old I was? Not tell my Luna name. Luna, a name of the moon and of the skies, just like the comet. If in my dream, I had told, Harmonia would know I lied about my name when I first came. She would doubt I told my right age, too. Tumla had warned me, and now Neoma, too.

When Neoma and Ayla returned with a broom and mop, we dusted and scrubbed the little room. I folded the blankets on the cot. Elio came just as we were finishing. "Harmonia said we're to pull weeds and rake all around the pillars. We need to get done before the mid-day meal."

Elio did not look anything like his sisters. The girls were like twins with dark hair. Elio was red-haired, freckled, and his ears stuck out. One would never guess they'd all grown in their mother's womb at the same time. As we pulled weeds, they teased each other. Ayla said, "You should have heard Neoma snore last night."

"I heard her," Elio laughed, then told me, "I slept in a cave way out by the sheep pasture last night and was wondering why thunder was rumbling and roaring all night when there wasn't a stormy cloud in the sky. Now I know it was Neoma snoring!"

"You slept in the cave? With sheep? No wonder you smell like an animal barn!" Neoma teased back.

"No, no sheep. Harold and Otis and I wanted to camp out one more time before the Snow Maker comes."

Even though I liked listening to them tease each other, I still worried about Shadow and hoped he'd catch a squirrel to eat. Soon, we finished weeding and raking around one tower so went on to the next.

CHAPTER II

The morning hours flew by as the four of us cleaned the small stone rooms at the base of each tower. The triplets called them *keeps*. I hadn't heard the word used that way before.

When I told them, "Harmonia locked me in and kept me like a prisoner last night."

They looked from one to the other. Ayla finally said, "No, I don't think she did that to keep you from running away. I think she barred you in to keep you safe."

The others nodded their heads vigorously while looking around. "Yeah! She kept you safe."

I doubted it. I told them, "And I think Harmonia put something in my tea. There was something in it I had never tasted before. After drinking some, I got drowsy. I couldn't even stand so I threw the tray to the floor. I fell onto the bed as I heard someone unbarring the door. It had to have been Harmonia. I was in a dream-like state. She questioned me—wanting to know if I was born under the comet. Whatever was in the tea made me vomit. I wanted to get away, but couldn't sit up. My tongue was thick. I could barely talk." I wrung my hands feeling agitated. My stomach churned as I remembered the dream. A river roaring. Bees buzzing. A crow cawing—insisting I answer its questions.

"I don't know what I told her. I was seeing things that weren't there. I couldn't shake them. I didn't wake up until Neoma came this morning."

"Scary," Elio said. "You'd have been better off sleeping in the cave with some sheep. Harmonia can be difficult."

"That's putting it nicely," Ayla said. "I'd say she's demanding and a challenge to please."

"Pffft. Say it like it is. She's like a pendulum. Swinging one way, she's smiley and nice. She was good to take in our parents and all the other exotics. But watch out when it swings the other way. She can be darn right merciless. Says she has the right because she's royalty." Neoma looked all around, then whispered, "Worse yet, when she's being nice, you know some harsh task or punishment is coming next. She demands harmony, yet she causes the discord."

"If you stay here, you'll find out. You'll be saying all these things and worse."

"I don't want to find out, and I don't plan to stay. I'm just traveling through—on my way to find a village of my mother's people. I stopped here hoping to get some warm clothes and boots before the snows came. I stayed because I was curious when I saw the signs about the comet-borns and exotics. I'm only staying now to go to the festival."

"If Harmonia wants you to stay, she'll make sure you do." Elio frowned as he talked. I shuddered. I decided to leave right after the festival. Hopefully, it would be with my sister. I didn't want to have anything to do with Harmonia anymore.

We finished raking leaves and dead grasses from around all four keeps. When Harold and Otis finished their work, they came to see if Elio needed help. They carted all the debris to the woods. When the noon meal bell sounded, they hurried back.

After eating, Harmonia assigned me, Ayla, Neoma, Elio and his friends to take down and wash all the lamp globes from the along the stone path. "Don't break any," she warned. Then I heard her whisper to the girls, "Don't let her out of your sight."

I winced when I overheard that. I wanted to go to the festival hoping Selene would be there with Lady Magda, but I also kept thinking of a way to escape. The boys climbed a ladder and passed the globes down to me, Neoma, and Ayla. We washed the soot and dust from them before passing them back up the ladder. I worked with Elio while Ayla and Neoma worked with his friends. Everyone grumbled, but not when Harmonia was within hearing distance.

"Why did she have us do this now? It could wait until tomorrow."

"Yeah, we should be getting ready for the festival."

"I hate climbing ladders and handling these. Harmonia would break me if I broke one."

I even joined in the grumbling. "I want to check with Tumla to see if my boots are ready, but here I am with my hands and fingernails getting grimy and sooty." I wanted to do more than see Tumla. I wanted to go to my canoe. At the noon meal, I had stuffed a chunk of meat from the stew and a slab of buttered bread for Shadow into my pocket. I'd been away for a long time. I imagined he was worried about me. I wanted to pet him and assure him that we'd soon be on our way.

"I want to fix my hair in long curls. I'll probably barely have time to brush it!" complained Ayla as she dusted a globe.

The more I thought about leaving, the sooner I wanted to be on my way. I was nervous about staying any longer. The triplets were supposed to keep an eye on me. I wanted to go to the festival. Hopefully Selene would be there and I could leave with her, but I feared Harmonia had another plan for me. One that I wouldn't like—not letting me go with Selene, locking me in a keep, putting me in the stockade, and being sold. She had told the triplets not to let me out of their sight. I didn't like that. I was so confused, but I finally decided I didn't care if I had to leave without new boots. I just had to get away, then I could look for Selene at other festivals.

We were on our last lamp globe when I said, "I've decided not to go to the festival. It's best if I leave now."

The triplets looked back and forth at each other. Elio finally spoke, "We're supposed to stay with you—making sure you don't leave."

"Yeah," Neoma said, "More than *supposed to*. Harmonia demanded we were not to let you out of our sight."

"She said it stronger than that," added Ayla. "She said she'd make us very sorry if you got away from us."

"Just imagine how many welts there'll be on our behinds if we let you go. We wouldn't be able to sit for a week."

"And she'll probably make us clean the shat houses for the rest of our lives," Ayla groaned.

"Who knows? She might even have Tumla make boots from the skin off our backs. Boots she'd proudly wear to remind everyone not to upset the harmony of our village." Elio shook his head as he repeated, "Harmony."

"Come to the festival with us. We'll make it fun. You can leave tomorrow. When it's daylight. Then Harmonia'll probably be so excited getting some of the comet children ready for the auction block that she won't notice you slipping away. We'll even help you."

"I have an idea," Harold said. "After Harmonia locks you into the keep and turns in for the night, Otis and I'll sneak and unbar the door. Then you can leave without a big fuss."

"You'd do that for me? Get into trouble for me?"

"If you want to leave tonight, that's what you'll have to do. Besides, Otis and I sneak out every chance we get to go camping in the cave or the woods," admitted Harold. "Elio does, too. We've never been caught."

"Great. You've just ratted us out," groaned Otis.

"All right. Tonight, after everyone's asleep, you'll open the keep door for me, and then I'll leave."

Neoma nodded saying, "Maybe you shouldn't eat or drink anything at the festival if Harmonia gives it to you."

"I won't," I promised.

"Secrecy pledge," Elio said.

"What's a secrecy pledge?" I asked.

"Watch and you'll see."

All five of them put their right fists into a circle, raised them three times, spit into the circle and chanted all together.

Secrecy!
If I tell, my face will scab, I guarantee.
Secrecy!
If I tell, my toes will rot, I warrantee.
My breath will stink.
Shunned, I'll be.
Nobody'll marry me.
Forever and ever.
Secrecy!

CHAPTER 12

The secrecy pledge brought a big smile to my face. I said it over and over to myself. I was in a strange place, with strange people, with a threat of being locked in a stockade and sold to the highest bidder. I'd never had friends. I'd never even spent time with others my age, but now I had friends eager to help me. Tumla, the triplets, Harold, and Otis were not born of the comet, but were willing to help in spite of the punishment that would follow if they were caught.

I slipped my hand into my pocket and felt for the moonstone. I was sure it would be warm and comforting, but it was not. It was cold to touch. I didn't even pull it out to look. The soft yellows, pinks, and blues would not be gently swirling. The secrecy pledge! Maybe it was not what I thought it was.

Neoma, Ayla and I scrubbed our hands to get all the soot off. I was nervous as we pinned each other's hair this way and that. They were fussing over how they looked. I was beginning to question everything. What was in store for me? What if I couldn't trust the triplets, Otis, and Harold?

"I'm putting my hair up. It'll make me look older," Neoma said as she pinned curls around Ayla's face.

Together, they braided my hair. Ayla had just tied bows at the ends of my braids when a bell tolled. "Hurry now," Neoma said. "It's time for us to meet in the square. Everyone gathers so we can walk together to the sanctuary for the festival."

I found myself getting excited. I said, "I hope my sister will be at the festival."

Ayla shook her head and said, "No outsiders are allowed. It's not that kind of festival. It's amazing Harmonia is letting you go because she forbids strangers at any time, especially for the festival."

My chest clenched. *It wasn't that kind of festival!* No Selene. I would not have the chance to leave with her and Lady Magda. My hands felt clammy as Neoma grabbed one and Ayla the other.

From every direction, the townspeople came to mingle around the big bell. Harmonia climbed three steps onto a raised platform. She raised her hands for the assembly to be silent. Immediately all chatter stopped, and everyone looked to her. "Today we gather to celebrate the Coming of The Night Sky Dancers as they announce the convergence of the stars, the moon, earth and a multitude of comets. They assure us we are part of the great cosmic balance by living in harmony with each other. The Night Sky Dancers come only after the lamps are snuffed and we huddle under our blankets. When a night watcher sees the dancers, he pulls the bell's rope seven times, tolling it to awaken us so we can join hands and dance in the night with the sky spirits who have come to praise us for our work here."

Everyone applauded.

Harmonia continued, "The Night Sky Dancers remind us when we are in spiritual harmony with each other, life will be pleasant and peaceful as we work together. Bow now, for it is I—the royal emissary from the Pleiades—who brings this village the gift of harmony to honor my name."

Everyone bowed. Everyone, except for me. I would not bow to Harmonia. Ayla scowled at me and pulled on my arm until I was almost in a bow position. When I straightened, I looked around to see if I could find Tumla, but couldn't see him in the crowd packed around me. I wanted to thank him and then get out of the village as fast as I could.

"And now, let us hum our way to the Sanctuary where the blessed children of the sky comet live in happiness and joy."

Neoma and Ayla still held my hands. Elio and his friends followed. They began to hum, along with everyone else. *Hmmm, ahhh, aaa, hmmm, hmmm, ahhh, aaa humm.* Walking shoulder to shoulder with the girls, we swarmed out of the village, into the pasture, past the sheep field, humming the whole way. It was the same as had been at the dinner table. I felt the vibration of their humming to my deepest core. But this time, instead of relaxing me, it made me fearful. I worried if I should be going to the festival at all. There was so much I didn't understand. I tried to shake my hands loose, but Neoma and Ayla held on tightly.

In the distance, with a steep hillside arising behind it, I saw a long line of tall wooden walls made of logs stuck vertically into the earth. Each log was sharpened at the top to form a formidable peak. The stockade! Where the children of comet were kept. It looked more like a terrible prison than a sanctuary.

Looking at the stockade, my heart squeezed. My breath came quickly and shallow. Drops of sweat rolled from under my arms.

"What's wrong? Don't you feel well?" Neoma asked. She held my hand out. It was damp and beet red.

"The stockade doesn't look like a sanctuary," I said. "It's scary. I don't want to go."

"You'll be all right. Neoma and I won't leave your side," Ayla's voice calmed me a bit.

She squeezed my hand. "We won't let anything or anyone hurt you."

I looked from one to the other. *Secrecy, secrecy* rolled through my mind. What if they had other secrets? Secrets they were hiding from me? Secrets Harmonia wanted them to keep? I shivered at the thought. *Could I trust any of them?*

I entered the stockade through the guarded gate along with everyone else. My mind buzzed, and my fingers pricked. I remembered Father telling a story about a king of Scotland. In the story three witches stirred up a brew. One of them warned that pricking in the thumbs foretold of a coming disaster. I thought it was a terrible story, but Father had enjoyed the telling. Everyone was killing everyone else, just to be king, or something like that. What was the pricking telling me? I was sure it was something bad. I wanted to get away, but Neoma and Ayla held my hands tightly and smiled with excitement.

Great bonfires blazed inside the stockade. Flaming torches hung along the walls of the interior yard giving the whole area a smoky and eerie glow. A group of musicians blew melodies on flutes. After a while, a silver-haired man in a long robe intoned words that made no sense to me, but sounded like *Uum baa yai maa lah*. He said them twice, then everyone repeated them several times swaying back and forth. Drums beat along with the *uum baa yai maa lah*. They slowly increased to a resounding beat and then softened to gentle thrum while the flutes faded to a whisper. It was a festival unlike those I'd gone to with Father. This one was scary.

I slid my moonstone from my pocket. The pearly translucence brightened, then faded. The blues faded. Yellows and pinks paled. Then the stone turned cold again. Warned, I slid it back into my pocket.

The silver-haired man announced, "And now it's time to partake of the sustenance we've gathered from the bountiful and glorious Earth—our primordial goddess who offers us life and nourishment."

People dressed in white carried tables and set them around the yard. Others carried platters of roasted chickens, goats, and pigs. Roasted rutabagas, potatoes, carrots, beets, and mushrooms filled other tables.

I scooped rutabagas and carrots onto my plate. I gagged as I walked past a whole goat that'd been skinned, gutted and roasted. I thought about the lively goats prancing and running at Huldor's. At a table laden with roasted chicken, I pulled a wing and a leg and thought of Lamb-i-kins who'd traded bits of her "borrowed' chicken for my boots so long ago. My stomach seized when I saw Neoma and Ayla tear meat from the ribs, haunches, neck, and legs of a goat. Elio and Harold were pulling flesh from a roasted pig with their fingers.

"Where are the children of the comet?" I asked as I sucked all the last flavor from a chicken wing.

"They're having a feast just like this in their enclosure."

"Enclosure? Why aren't they allowed out here?"

"Not during the festival. It'd be too easy for them to slip away when no one was paying attention," explained Ayla.

"So, they're like prisoners?" I asked. My stomach churned. I looked at the food I had left on my plate. I quit eating and slipped a chicken leg into my pocket for Shadow.

Neoma gave Ayla a poke and a slight scowl. "They're not really prisoners," she whispered to me. "It's only this once a year during the festival."

"I want to see them," I said.

"You can. When we're all done eating, and the night darkens, the dancing starts. Then we form a long line and dance by the fencing so they can see us, and we can see them. Some of us bring handfuls of candy that we pass through the openings. They cheer us, and we wave to them. It's what we work for so hard all year. And, I'm sure they love it, too, although most of them pretend not to."

The poke and scowl Neoma gave Ayla had not escaped my noticing. The hair on the back of my neck bristled. I had thought of them as friends. I enjoyed being with them, but I couldn't trust them. They shrugged their shoulders and didn't seem to care a bit about the comet-borns. I was sure they would do what Harmonia told them so they wouldn't get punished. It was then I realized I couldn't even trust Harold and Otis to unbar the door for me that night.

I stood on tippy toes looking for the enclosure that held the comet-borns. Ayla went to fill her plate again. Neoma was standing in a circle of laughing people when Tumla came to stand by me. He wore his silver disc. I wished I could see his face and his reassuring smile.

Pulling his hat low, he whispered. "You need to leave tonight."

I looked at Neoma. She wasn't paying any attention to me like she was supposed to. Instead, she was listening intently to a tall woman who had a very large lower jaw. I stepped back, closer to Tumla. "Harold and Otis say they'll let me out of the keep tonight."

"You can't trust them. You have to leave sooner. After the sun sets completely, they'll open kegs of wine and brew. Don't drink any. When the music for the dancing starts, find some excuse to get away from the triplets, then convince the gate keeper to let you out. Once outside the stockade, make your way toward the main gateway. Hide in the deep shadows. I'll find you."

CHAPTER 13

Night fell and the stars came out. Only the hazy moon, bonfire and torches lit the darkened area. Neoma and Ayla drank mug after mug of the *spirit water* as they called it. They refilled my mug each time, too. I pretended to drink, but when they weren't looking, I poured it on the ground. It wasn't long before they joined a crowd surrounding the kegs. They sang, laughed, and soon forgot to watch me. Free of Neoma and Ayla, and not seeing Harmonia anywhere, I headed toward the steep hill at the far side.

A heavy chain enclosure held thirty or more boys and girls standing and holding onto the fence. They watched the festivities going on outside their penned area. They didn't look like they were enjoying the festival or any merriment. They had no tables laden with food. There were no musicians. Each wore an identical drab brown shirt with long swoosh of white trailing a blazing ball of yellows, oranges, and red—the comet.

When I got closer, a girl who was taller than I was, pushed her way to the fence. She beckoned to me. Her dark hair shone in the dim light. It was braided into a crown around her head. Her dark eyes gleamed. When I got up to her, she looked around then whispered in a rasp, "Escape! Climb the stockade if you have to. Get away before it's too late. Go now! Run!"

"She's crazy," the boy next to her said. "She says she can capture everyone's thoughts, know their plans, and pass messages just by thinking them. Absolutely crazy!"

The girl gritted her teeth and wove her fingers into the chain links.

59

"Maybe she can. Maybe it's her gift from the comet," I said.

"That's no gift. I can make myself invisible. That's a real gift."

Another boy joined in, "What good is being invisible, if you never get out of here? And if you do, you're still not free?"

"Remember when Harmonia was so afraid I'd escape that she put a rope around my neck and tied me up like a sheep? I had to beg her to untie me. I had to pretend I liked it here. I know I'm not free yet, but I will get out of here some-day after I practice getting invisible more. Crazy Girl even said so." He laughed a laugh that didn't sound like a real laugh.

Not knowing what to do, I asked the girl who'd told me to run, "What's your name?"

She squinted her piercing black eyes, then said, "Liida. But listen. Harmonia plans to keep you. Sell you. Maybe worse. Go now! It's the only way to save your-self—and me. Run!"

Shivers ran up my back. My thumbs pricked. I wished I could make myself invisible.

I didn't run, but walked slowly back to the crowd, mingled for a while keep-ing an eye out for Harmonia, Neoma, and Ayla. Assured that they were too busy drinking and having fun and weren't watching me, I slowly headed toward the gate. The guard watched me approach, so I bent over and coughed. I stood. Held my head. Held my stomach. Pretending to spasm and retch, I hurried to the gate saying, "I'm sick!"

The gate guard lost no time opening a gap for me. I faked gags and stumbles as I squeezed through. I heard the gate close behind me. I was out!

Still pretending to retch and spew, I slowly made my way to the keep where I'd been held. I grabbed my pack and headed toward the entry gate, bending over, pretending to spew in case anyone watched.

In the shadows of a tall tree that hadn't yet shed all its leaves, a night owl hooted. Leaves on the ground rustled in the breeze. I thought about Liida. She'd said the only way to save myself and her was to run. What could that possibly mean? Could she really read other people's thoughts? Or was she crazy as the boy had said? If I were to believe everything I'd heard, Harmonia and others really sold the children of the comet to people who wanted to enrich them-selves through their gifts. I was in danger. I needed to leave right away! Father's wish was that I'd enrich him with an extraordinary gift. Now I wished I'd never been born when the comet blazed overhead—or that I'd even heard of it. Did

I even have a gift? I had entered portals to the dead, and sometimes I thought I heard the breezes bring me messages. Were they real? Or was I crazy like the boy had called Liida?

Shaking all those thoughts away, I crept among the bushes and listened for Tumla. Every noise. Every rustle of leaves. Every snap of a twig brought me to full attention. Was it Tumla? Harmonia? Neoma and Ayla looking for me? Afraid I'd get away? Some other danger? Finally, Tumla came to crouch beside me. "Shhhh."

Whispering, he told me, "This morning I walked along the river, thinking and planning a way for you to escape. I found your canoe. Your dog was hungry and pacing, looking for you. I fed him, then pulled some clover and grasses for the rabbit. Later, I went back to the canoe. I put a new pair of boots and some food there for you."

A burden lifted from me. Excitement filled me, and a bit of anxiety. I would be leaving, but it was night, and I still didn't know what direction I should travel. "Thank you, Tumla." Without a thought, I reached for his face. He wasn't wearing the silver disc.

He held my hand to his face. "You are the only one who has touched me for years. Thank you. Now we must go."

Tumla led the way. We climbed a fence that was shrouded in bushes. There was no path, but he held branches for me to pass under. There was only a cloud-covered moon to light our way. Soon, I heard the rippling of the river and a soft whining. Shadow! I called out ever so softly, "Shadow, I'm coming."

Tumla knelt to one side as the dog bounded though the brush to us. Shadow licked me and whined softly as I held him, stoking his back, his ears, his head. "You have a good dog there," Tumla said, "but now it's time to be on your way."

When we got to the canoe, I hoisted my pack in. Shadow jumped in. Tumla pushed the canoe into the shallows and said, "You're next."

"One more thing," I said, then turned to find the rock where I had buried my coin pouch. I checked rock after rock, but in the darkness couldn't find the right one. I was getting exasperated when Shadow jumped out of the canoe and began digging next to a rock further up the bank.

"Looks like your dog knows where to find what you're looking for," Tumla chuckled.

In a moment, Shadow came to me holding the pouch in his mouth. He dropped it at my feet and then ran back to the canoe as if to say, "Time to get out of here!"

I turned to Tumla and opened the pouch, "How much do I owe you for the boots and food?"

He held his hand over mine and said, "Your thanks will be enough. I have not had the pleasure of doing something as wonderful as meeting you for a long time. You listened to my story. You didn't mind looking at my face, even touching it. It is I who should thank you."

"You have. You've been a friend and now you're helping me get away from Harmonia and whatever plans she has for me. I *was* born while the comet flew the skies overhead. Without you, I would probably wake up tomorrow in the stockade with the other comet-borns and end up being sold to the highest bidder."

"I suspected as much about your birth. Now, you really have to be on your way. Let the river currents carry you through the night. Let them guide you to the family you seek."

I gave Tumla a big hug and turned to the canoe before I started to cry. He gently pushed the canoe into the currents. As the canoe floated away, I heard his soft voice, "Fare thee well."

CHAPTER 14

I couldn't sleep. I missed Tumla already. I worried about Liida and the others imprisoned in the stockade. I was afraid Harmonia would send someone to capture me. I worried she would punish Ayla and Neoma for forgetting to watch over me.

The night air was unseasonably warm. Mists rose from the waters. The woods along the river were alive with little blinking lights. I hoped they were fireflies and not the night creatures Father told me about. One night, as we had sat around a fire while steaming cattail roots, he scratched his forehead and counted off, "Night fairies, pixies, nisses, sprintes, tonttus, and haltijas. Some protect us and keep us safe while we sleep. Others are tricksters and shapeshifters. Watch out for those."

"How will I know them, to watch out for them?" I'd asked.

"Most look like squat, wrinkled mushrooms with faces. Others look like withered leaves—all full of veins with drab dappled colors."

I'd laughed. Father's stories were always amusing and full of exaggerations.

"Easy to spot those," he had said, "but when they shapeshift, you never know until the mischief starts."

I wasn't comforted thinking about the night creatures he'd described. The rabbit and Shadow both slept soundly. I felt all alone as I peered into the darkness looking for a mischief maker who might make my canoe crash into a river rock, or worse yet, cascade over a waterfall into a whirling eddy. I wished for the comfort of Ossi and Huldor's arms around me. They'd made a home for me.

Joined themselves together and made me their daughter. It had lasted only a few hours and then they were gone. Why? Why did that happen just when everything was so good? So right? Had I brought bad luck to them? If so, being born with the comet overhead was not a blessing. My eyes filled with tears blurring the tiny flashing lights. My chest seized. I could hardly breathe. A torrent of tears broke loose.

A wolf howled in the distance. Other howls joined his. A pack. A family. I howled to the sky, too. I was a lone wolf looking for a new family. I howled again. And cried.

Back on the river the next morning, I let the current decide my direction. I searched the horizon constantly, looking for a town, a village, a farm, anywhere I could find people and a shelter. Besides that, I constantly looked behind myself, looking to see if someone from the sanctuary was following.

On the third day, after escaping Harmonia, I pulled the canoe onto a sandy shore and got out to stretch. Shadow headed into the woods sniffing a trail. I followed him on tiptoes so I wouldn't alert squirrels or grouse, or whatever he was following. His search ended at the base of a tree. He and I both looked into the high branches and saw a squirrel looking down at us chattering. "Not today," it was saying. "Find something else to eat." It held an acorn in its paws and chattered until we left.

Shadow had no luck finding anything to chase, catch, and eat, so we headed back to the canoe. When we got close to the river, Shadow ran ahead barking. "Shhhh," I warned. "It's just the rabbit. Don't scare her." I hoped it was the rabbit and not Harmonia.

When I reached the river, I gasped. The rabbit and her cage were nowhere to be seen. My food had been ransacked. Apples were strewn everywhere. The loaf of bread and cheese from Tumla were gone. Heat rose within me. I quaked with fright. Had a shape-shifting light-blinking trickster stolen my food? A bear or fox? Was it Harmonia? Or someone else?

I pulled every ounce of bravery out of myself and shouted, "Show yourself, Thief! Bring back my food. And my rabbit!" Shadow ran along the river bank, nose to the ground. I followed carrying a big stick. Growling and snarling, Shadow disappeared into an undergrowth of thick bushes.

A rough voice rang out, "Git! Git you dog offa me!"

I stumbled. Shadow kept growling. When I got close, Shadow was trying to drag a dirty and smudged girl out of the thicket. She tried to hold onto the food she'd stolen, and at the same time pull her ragged dress out of Shadow's teeth. Shadow was winning.

The girl scowled when she saw me. She glared through her tangled her. She shouted, "You gettin' this monster offa me or I . . . I pluck his eyes out! An' I toss you in river."

I couldn't help it. I laughed. There she was. Skinny as could be. Dirty. Torn clothes. Hair as tangled as the thicket she tried to hide in. Trying to sound tough. Probably hungry as a bear coming out of hibernation. I laughed and said, "Lamb-i-kins. It is good to see you again. Or maybe not."

It was Lamb-i-kins. There was no doubt about it. Lamb-i-kins who'd left me tied to a tree. Who'd agreed to trade neck bones, rib meat, burned skin, and other chewing bones from the chicken she'd "borrowed" for my boots. I'd been hungry and out of food when I stumbled upon her camp among the boiling and bubbling mud pots in the Land of Lucifer. I'd agreed to the poor trade because I'd outgrown the boots, and they were pinching my toes.

"Lamb-i-kins," I said again. "This time I get to decide what *you* eat."

Apples tumbled out of her arms as she tried to pull her dress out of Shadow's mouth. Shadow growled and tugged. Lamb-i-kins dropped the bread and cheese. She strutted toward me as if I were the one caught stealing *her* food. She brushed tangled hair from her eyes. "You," she said, "you girl called Luna?" She wore the boots I'd traded for bones and a little meat so long ago. She looked at my new boots made by Tumla. "Where you get good boots?" she asked.

"A good man," I said. "But if you steal or 'borrow' them, I'll tie you up and leave just like you did to me. But never mind that. Where's my rabbit? Bring it back to my canoe, and we'll eat together." I began picking up the apples, cheese, and bread she'd dropped. Shadow followed her into the thicket.

"You borrow canoe?" Lamb-i-kins asked as she came lugging the rabbit and its cage.

"No, I don't borrow things like you do. And I'm still mad at you for tying me to a tree for days on end, not caring if I lived or died or dirtied my pants while you went off by yourself somewhere having a good time borrowing things." I reddened as I thought of it. I still seethed thinking back to when I thought I'd die alone tied to a tree and there was nobody who'd ever know or care.

"I do be sorry fer tyin' you up. I kinda run inta trouble meself an' not be gettin' away fer a while. Else, I woulda gone back an' untied you."

I was surprised at her apology, but reminded myself to keep an eye on her so she wouldn't find a way to tie me up again. "Gather some wood. We'll make a fire to roast a squash. You can tell me your adventures while we eat." I felt sorry for her. She'd had a Grammy who was good to her, but her pap had been cruel. She'd never talked about her mam. I didn't know if she still lived or if she'd died. Grammy had cared for her, but she was probably dead by now. Lamb-i-kins herself looked like she'd been starving for days without anywhere to live but under sheltering trees. Winter was coming. I wondered if she was headed back to the warmth of the bubbling mud pots—the Land of Lucifer.

CHAPTER 15

Shadow circled Lamb-i-kins sniffing her. Finally, he lay down next to her and began licking his paws. I stacked the food I had recovered while Lamb-i-kins began telling why she hadn't come back to untie me from the tree.

"I bashed you on da head. Tied you up good. You helpless, useless, but someone talk to.

"Thinkin' you not so bad fer big person. Meybe keep you fer while. Grabbed me carryin' sack. Went lookin' fer garden diggin's. Rooties an' such. Wearin' yer nice boots I traded fer bones.

"I laughin'. Such good trade."

Lamb-i-kins stopped long enough to help me dig a hole in the sand.

"Got to village, lookin' roun'. Meybe borrow 'nother chicken. Gang rowdy boys attack. Steal sack. Steal boots. Leave me on ground with punch in belly. Leave me bleedin' nose. Leave me black eye. I got me hits an' kicks in on them, too. Like wild cat clawin', I was."

Lamb-i-kins paused in her telling to break dried twigs for fire starters while I gathered fallen birch bark. She watched as I rubbed my two fire-maker stones together. When a little spark caught and glowed, she added more bark, then small twigs. We worked together without talking. Our fire grew. I added bigger wood that we gathered along the edges of the river bank.

When the flames died to embers, I wrapped the squash in cattail leaves Lamb-i-kins collected. While we waited for the squash to roast, we ate an apple and lay back listening to the birds and the rippling of the waters. Shadow ran back out of the woods and proudly showed us the squirrel he caught. Together we laughed and patted him on the head, "Good dog. You wouldn't have liked squash very much."

"You not useless like I thought," Lamb-i-kins said. "Good fire maker."

From her, that was a great compliment. Curious I asked, "What happened then? Did you go back to your camp at the bubbling mud pots?"

"I hurt much. Big owies. Lookin' fer food. Beggin'. Pocket pickin'. Nothin'. Hurtin' more an' more. Went house where Pap lived. Gone. No Grammy. No one. Got chased by dogs. Geese. Peoples. Everyone name-callin' me *Trash! Thief!* Even got hit by rotten stuff. Constable man catch me. Bit him. He box my ears an' drag me to place called Orphan House. Worried tiny bit 'bout you all tied up. An' not gettin' away."

I looked at the boots she wore. She'd just said a gang of boys had stolen them, so I asked, "How did you get those boots back?"

"Oh," Lamb-i-kins started, "at Orphan House, ugly boy there wearin' my boots. Not fer long. I ask all nice like they teach me at that place. Even said *please* afore I toll him or else. He give 'em easy not wantin' busted teeth. An' then I toll him *thank you.*"

I tried not to laugh. "If you're going to eat my food," I said, "the *please* and *thank you* are good, but I don't want to hear any *or else*. And no more threatening my dog with plucking his eyes out and throwing him or me in the river."

"I be good. An' say *please* an' *thank you* to eat your food." Lamb-i-kins' voice had gone soft. No more growl or hollering. Her face, too. No scowl.

Looking at her, my breath caught. Had I ever been that skinny, dirty, and ragged? I'd felt that way at times, but I'd found kind people like Ossi and Huldor.

"C'mon," I said, "Let's get cleaned up some before we eat."

She brushed aside a tangle of hair that hung across her eyes. Instead of frowning, a smile broke out on her face as she followed me to the river. We washed our hands and splashed the chilly water on our faces. An otter swam downstream and climbed onto the opposite bank. Shadow woofed at it. Lamb-i-kins pointed and asked, "It good eatin'?"

"No," I said. Father and I never, not even when we were almost starving, tried to catch an otter to eat. I remembered entering my mother's portal when she told me the story of how an otter came to her one day and dropped the moonstone on her lap. I pulled the same stone out of my pocket now and held it out for Lamb-i-kins to see.

"How you get so pretty rock?" she asked.

"Long story," I said.

"Tell. Squash not ready yet. Sun still up. Tell."

"I will if you tell me your real name." When I happened upon her living alone among the bubbling mud pots, I'd asked her the same thing. She'd told me her pap had always called her *Dirty, Rotten Ugly Gap-toothed Brat*, but Grammy had held her close, rocked her, and called her *Dear, Sweet Lamb-i-kins*.

"Almost don' remember. So long ago," she started out, "but I reckon it coudda been somethin' like Ahni. Ya, some people called me Ahni. Sounds strange to me ears an' feels strange to me tongue."

"Is it all right if I call you Ahni? My father named me Purslane. Purslane is a weed. An unwanted weed. A curse to gardens. That's how I felt with that name. Unwanted."

"You? You felt that way?"

"Yes, until the day I learned my mother had wanted to name me Luna."

"How that come about?"

I told Ahni my story as we each ate some cheese and waited for the squash to soften over the embers. I told her my father said my mother died giving birth to me, but I found out later that she'd lived and a second child had been born on the same day, my twin sister Selene. I told her about my life with Father in the hut along the shores of Kawishami and foraging for food.

I had just finished telling about the Harvest Moon Festivals we'd gone to every autumn when Ahni poked a stick into the squash and said, "Soft an' done. Time we eat."

CHAPTER 16

An owl hooted; a wolf howled. The moon was but a sliver. Ahni and I slept on a bed of cedar boughs under the low branches of a fir tree. Shadow snuggled on one side of me. Ahni, on the other, held the rabbit close.

I couldn't sleep right away. Every snap of a twig. Every rustle in the breeze kept me on alert wondering if Harmonia was after me. I tried to plan for the next day, but no thoughts came. Pressed between Ahni and Shadow, I felt a strange comfort when a wolf in the distance howled again. I wasn't so much a lone wolf when I felt the warmth, heard the breathing, felt the heartbeat of Ahni next to me. Memories tumbled one by one as I tried to sleep—the children fenced in the stockade, Tumla and his kindness. Ossi and Huldor. I wept silently until I finally fell asleep.

In the morning, Ahni stretched, yawned, and said, "Tummy's howlin' like wolf that howl in night. Time we eat."

I groaned to myself. I'd already taken stock of the food. One squash, several withering apples, half the cheese and bread Tumla had given, and one rabbit that Ahni was hugging and petting. To Ahni it must have seemed like a lot, but to me, I knew it wasn't enough even for me alone while I traveled looking for a village. Would Ahni be staying with me? Eating with me? I was worried to think the snows were coming soon. There'd be nothing to forage.

"We can each have an apple." I handed her one along with a bit of cheese and a chunk of bread I tore from the loaf.

"That all?" Ahni frowned.

"That's all. I'm trying to find a village of the Ice People, or any village—somewhere I can spend the winter. I don't know how many days I'll be looking so we need to be careful with what little food there is."

Ahni looked at her meager meal. Her tousled and matted hair fell over her eyes. "I go with you," she said.

It was what I feared—and in a little way—hoped for. I wouldn't be alone. Good and bad. I looked at my pile of food and scratched my head. I still hoped—and yet dreaded—that she might change her mind and not go with me. Sharing food might mean we'd both starve or freeze if we didn't find a place to spend the winter. "I'm not headed toward the bubbling mud pots where you'd be warm for the winter," I said. "Where I'm going, it might be cold all the time."

"I know place good for winter. Shelter. Food to borrow. Only scary thing be Ghost Man."

"Good place? Shelter? Food? Ghost man?"

"Ya, Ghost Man. He walk aroun' talkin' to peoples not there. Seein' things not there. Hearin' things not there. I be careful he not see me. Borrow his food now an' then."

Curious now, I asked, "Where is this Ghost Man? Far from here?"

"Not so far walkin'. Two three days. River bend away, then back, so longer on river."

Should I believe her? Ghost Man? With food? And shelter?

"How do you know all this?" I asked.

"After runnin" from Orphan Home, I find good spot an' start livin' roun' there. Lookin' fer food, hidin' from constable an' other people, an' spyin' on Ghost Man."

"Well, we can't drag the canoe over land for two or three days, so we'll take the river. Maybe we'll find a real village without Ghost Man."

I was eager to find a place to shelter for winter. Ghost man or no Ghost Man.

When we got to the canoe, a raven perched on the bow. He fluttered to a tree across the river when he saw us. He preened his feathers and watched while we loaded the canoe. I rearranged the tools, pots, sacks of food to make room for Ahni next to the rabbit in his cage. Shadow jumped in. Shadow curled into a spot next to my feet and woofed at the raven.

"Is this the way we go?" I asked Ahni pointing downstream. I hoped she'd say yes because I didn't want to paddle against the current. Or paddle upstream passing anywhere near the Sanctuary for the Exotic and Comet-borns. I didn't want to fall into the clutches of Harmonia again.

"Yeah, but I need somethin' afore we go." With that she grabbed the saw and ran into the trees lining the shore. After a while she returned with a long straight branch. She tore smaller branches from it as she hurried back to the canoe.

"Pole," she said scrambling in. Then she used the pole to shove us into the current.

"You're smart," I said. "You know how to figure things out even though you've never done them before. How old are you? Ten? Twelve?"

"Maybe ten. Maybe eleven already. Dunno fer sure. I remember some things about when I was eight, jest turnin' nine. You really think I smart?" She turned to me, beaming. "No one ever say that afore. Jest call me things like *stupid* an' *dodo*. Pap say I born scary-bad cuz I born durin' a 'clipse."

"You're not stupid or a dodo," I said. "And no one is born bad. What is this *'clipse* you say you were born during?"

"Forget I said that. Maybe the 'clipse is somethin' I made up. Cuz how could it be dark durin' day when I born?"

"Oh, you mean eclipse! I've never heard someone born during an eclipse is born bad, so I don't think you were either. In fact, I think you're very smart. You've scrabbled out a living on your own for a long time. Even though borrowing things you're not going to return isn't nice, you still are smart."

"And you not bad for big person. You give food an' me not havin' to borrow or even ask. You don't even care I be born bad like Pap say. We together now. I help you." She paused, then added, "Not borrow anythin' from you. That a promise."

I chuckled to myself. Ahni was turning into a different person than what Lamb-i-kins had been—had to be. We were together now. Like it or not. Whatever happened, we were together. I was no longer a lone wolf, but a pack of two.

CHAPTER 17

Ahni sat in the front of the canoe. She used the pole to push us from crashing into rocks and guide us back into the current. We both were escaping from someone or something. Me? I was escaping, not only from the memories of the fire that took Ossi and Huldor, but also from Harmonia and the stockade that imprisoned the comet-borns. Ahni? I was more convinced than ever that she was escaping from people who'd been cruel to her as well as the Orphan House. I took deep and strong pulls on my paddle and was thankful for the current that carried us both further from the somebodies we were escaping.

As we zigzagged around a rocky bend in the river, I thought about the changes coming over Ahni and then about myself. After escaping the farmer Father sold me to, I had shed the name Father called me—Purslane. I was thrilled when I found out my mother had not wanted me to be named after a weed, but after Luna, a moon goddess.

In the middle of our first day together, we pulled the canoe to the shore to eat and rest. Ahni asked if I'd write in the sand so she could practice reading. It was a good idea. We could do that each time we stopped. She surprised me by how much she already knew.

"Did your Grammy teach you letters?" I asked as she learned to recognize more of the squiggles and the sounds that went with them.

"Some. Most I learnt from Mam. She wrote on my hand an' teached me. Some I learnt from others."

"What others?"

"No more askin'. I no talk about them or Mam."

It was the first time she'd mentioned her mam. I asked her to tell me more, but she pursed her lips, folded her arms across her chest and said, "No talk! Now, you teach me numbers!"

I wondered why she didn't want to talk about her mother. Had her mother died and she didn't want to remember? Were memories of her mother filled with so much sorrow that she wanted to forget them? What else could it be? After a while, I tried teaching Ahni how to speak in full sentences. Tried. Changing how she spoke wasn't as easy for her as adding numbers that I wrote on her hand or in the sand.

"Why?" she asked. "Why does *grow* become *grew*, and *know* become *knew*, but *snow* becomes *snowed* instead of *snew*?"

I wished I had good answers, but could only marvel at how smart and curious she was. I felt inadequate as I answered, "Words are like the leaves on a tree, or flowers on a plant, sometimes one is different. Even people could look different. That's just how things are. Even words in a language."

When I said that, she gave me the look I remembered the *old* Lamb-i-kins giving me long ago. I imagined her thinking *Big person dumb after all!* I deserved that look. I'd given her a terrible explanation because I had no idea why words seemed to change without any good reason. Why hadn't I just told her I didn't know?

When we stopped for the evening, I insisted Ahni wash her hair while I washed mine in the river. "Why?" she asked. "Water cold."

"We can warm up by the fire. We have enough wood to keep it going. Besides," I said, smiling to myself, "You'll want to look good for Ghost Man when we get there, don't you?"

"You is . . . you are foolish. I not be gettin' all fixed up to see any Ghost Man."

Despite her fear of the ghost man, she did splash into the river and wash her hair. Afterwards, we sat by our evening fire. Remembering how Neoma had run her fingers through my hair, untangling snarls, I wanted to do the same for Ahni. I wanted to be kind to her, so I started unsnarling her hair with my fingers.

"Ouch! No pull so hard!"

Poor Ahni. She complained more than once as I worked on her snarled hair that was almost beyond untangling. My arms and fingers got tired before her hair was ready to braid, but it was smoother now. I could run my fingers through most of it without hearing, "Ow, that hurt me."

I held the untangled hair in my fingers, letting the warmth of the flames dry the smooth strands. After what seemed forever, all her hair was untangled and dry.

As I thought of Neoma smoothing and braiding my hair, my heart took a leap. There were comet-borns locked in a stockade. A tightness grew in my throat. I didn't want them sold as Huldor and my mother had been. I wanted them to be free. Maybe if I hadn't run, I could have helped them, but Liida had told me to run to save myself and her. I regretted not helping them all escape. Maybe someday I still could.

Taking a deep breath and shaking off the memories, I told Ahni, "Feel. Run your fingers through your hair before I braid it. See? No snarls."

She did. "Nice. An' no more itchings." Then she added, "Thank you. It good when you fix my hair."

I braided as gently as I could. I wanted it to feel good. No more ouches!

Hair done, Ahni smiled as we sat around the fire with the rabbit and Shadow next to us. No more tangles hung over her eyes. No scowl stormed onto her face. We steamed clams we'd picked in the river, and shared the last of the cheese and bread. We needed to keep moving toward Ghost Man and all the food Ahni said he had. I hoped she wasn't exaggerating about the food. I did hope she was making up someone she called *Ghost Man*. The rabbit snuggled next to Ahni as she petted it. I could no longer think of it as food, but if things got desperate, we would have to eat it.

The next day, while Ahni paddled and I poled, she pointed to a majestic pine that had a huge gash along one side where no branches grew. Gobs of sap hardened along the gash to heal the wound.

"I wonder what happened to that tree." I pointed.

"Lightning. Lightning strike. Crack. Boom. Thunder. But tree strong. It live. I be strong like tree. Like rock, too." She pulled out a pouch that was strung around her neck and stroked whatever was in it.

"What do you have there?" I asked.

"Nothin' but old pouch," she said tucking it back under her shirt.

"Where did you get it?"

"Good big people. No talk about it."

Again, the not talking about something bothered me. Something that I was sure would help me know where she'd been and what she'd done before going to live by the bubbling mud pots.

Even though there were things she didn't want to talk about, Ahni never ceased to amaze me. She took notice of everything and knew so much more than I expected. "How do you know lightning hit the tree and so much more?"

Ahni patted the pouch hanging around her neck. "At logging ca. . . ."

She stopped short. No matter how much I persuaded her, she would not tell me anything about a logging camp or the pouch she guarded around her neck.

Finally, she changed the subject. "Gashed tree tell me we gettin' close to where Ghost Man be," she shivered a bit. "Tomorrow, we get even closer to Ghost Man. I scared."

"I am scared." I said correcting her.

"I knew you scared but not say so."

At night we ate sparingly. Our food was running low. If Ghost Man didn't have food to share with us, the rabbit would have to be roasted.

CHAPTER 18

"Quiet. No noise."

After we pulled our canoe onto the bank of a small tributary, Ahni led us through the woods toward the Ghost Man. I followed as she snuck from tree to tree always hiding before peeking around and creeping toward the next tree. Dried leaves crunched under our feet. We tip-toed as much as possible trying to be quiet.

Not knowing what or whom to expect, Ahni's warnings made me nervous, looking around, and half-expecting a ghost to jump out at us from behind any tree or rock. My heart beat furiously, but my thumbs did not prick or tingle. I reached for my moonstone. Its colors swirled gently, and it was warm to the touch. I kept my hand on it in my pocket wishing with all my might that we would be safe. A raven flew from tree to tree ahead of Ahni. The whirring of its wings was lost in the gentle breeze.

When I saw Ahni buckle her knees and sink to the ground behind a big tree, I knew we were close. I crept my way to her.

"Sssssh!" she warned. "See him. Ghost Man. There!"

I peered around the tree. I saw him, too. I whispered to Ahni, "I'm going closer to get a good look. See that big rock? I'll hide behind it."

She held onto my arm. "Careful he not see you. Not hear you. Capture you. Prob'ly eat you."

Heeding her cautions, I brushed leaves from my path as I crawled so they wouldn't crunch and rustle, alerting the Ghost Man. At the rock, I pushed branches aside and saw a man who didn't wear rags, but animal furs hung loosely around him. A large bear pelt encircled his chest and hung to his knees. On top of it, rabbit and raccoon furs draped from his shoulders. A fox tail encircled his head. He'd swathed birch bark around his legs from his knees down. Skin boots covered his feet.

The man reached out to a bird at that very moment. It landed on Ghost Man's outstretched hand. I heard a little melody. The man singing? The bird?

Amazed, I signaled for Ahni to come to me. She shook her head so furiously that one of her braids came undone.

I looked right and left. Small trees grew here and there. Cairns of carefully piled rocks were everywhere. When Father and I came upon a cairn once, he'd told me that people made them to mark important places, burial grounds, or sacred grounds for ceremonies. I counted up to thirty before I lost count. So many! Burial grounds? I shivered to think so many had died. Was the man a ghost or a real man who had killed all those buried beneath the cairns? The hair on the back of my neck stood up when I thought about the possibilities. Or, as I hoped, was he a forest spirit protecting those who'd died?

Way off to my right I saw one small round-topped dwelling. Further on, I saw another man-made structure. A small log hut perched atop four tall tree trunks. I wondered how anyone could climb that high and what it was for because it looked too tiny to be anyone's house.

Ahni crept up to me. "I afraid. No go closer. I scared Ghost Man see you. Come. Now, I show you good sleepin' place."

Back at the river, Ahni followed the shore quite a distance before she entered the woods again. At the side of a hill, a huge tree had fallen over. Its root mass had pulled up an enormous amount of earth when it fell leaving a hole in the earth.

"Good place for sleep," Ahni said with a big grin on her face. "Found it last time I come this way an' spied on Ghost Man."

I stepped down into the hole made by the root mass when it pulled from the earth. Amazed, I said, "It is. And the tree's roots make half a roof."

"I find good places. Snug places. Away from cold."

"You do. We could cut some branches from those fir and cedar trees," I said pointing. "Then we wouldn't have to lie in the dirt. We'd have a nice bed."

"An' more branches to cover us."

"I wish I'd brought one of Ossi's shovels. We could dig further into the hill side and have a really good place."

"You have saw to cut branches. Together we make roof-like thing bigger. Cover whole opening."

I looked past the river banks and saw a swampy area full of cattails. "Look," I said to Ahni. "Cattails. We can weave their long leaves into mats to lie on. They'll be better than branches for keeping us off the ground. We could even make a big mat to use like a roof to cover this opening. Best of all, we can dig out and gather the cattail roots to cook and eat."

"That plant be good fer all those things?"

I nodded, "Lucky for us, the roots—*rhizomes* is what Father called them—are best eaten in the fall or winter. We won't starve. And the fluff from those brown things on top are good for catching sparks for fire and stuffing into boots to keep our feet warm."

"You smart, too." Ahni smiled.

"And you, too."

"Now we get our smarts busy so we have good place to sleep."

I gathered cattail leaves and roots while Ahni used the axe to dig further into the tree root cave making more room. I built a small fire and peeled the rhizomes down to the edible parts like Father and I had done so many times. While they boiled in the pot I'd taken from the burned inn, I began weaving and tying the long cattail leaves together.

We ate as much of the cattail root as we wanted. The sun was starting to set so we laid branches to make a soft floor for sleeping. In the dimness of the evening, I showed Ahni how I was weaving the leaves to make a large covering to close the opening of our root cave.

"I help do that," she said.

We wove as I taught—or tried to teach—Ahni about the little words used to show action. I had her repeat after me. "I can wash my hands. I did watch the fire. I will eat."

"Silly words," she said. "You know what I mean when I say, *I wash my hands.* Why I need other words?"

I sighed wondering if she'd ever catch on. It was so much easier teaching her how to add and subtract. Thankfully, it was quite dark already so we quit the lessons and washed at the river's side, snuffed our little fire and crawled into our root cave for the night.

It took us a little bit of shuffling around to find comfortable spots for us to fit with the rabbit and Shadow snuggled in, too. We pulled cedar branches over us.

Ahni was soon breathing deeply. I thought about the Ghost Man. He reminded me of Ossi. So alone. So gentle with the birds that landed on his hand. I fell asleep missing Ossi.

The raven settled on a branch nearby.

CHAPTER 19

I dreamed. Dreamed dream upon dream as I hadn't since before the fire took Ossi and Huldor from me and changed my life. The dream started with a cloudy swirl. Ossi and Tumla both emerged from the miasma to measure my feet, cut leather, weave bark, and make me boots. After they disappeared into the hazy whirl, Huldor simmered pork hocks and cabbage in a big pot for my supper. She, too, evaporated into a fog as Ghost Man arose in my dream. He walked from stone cairn to cairn. At each, apparitions and phantoms, tall and short, old and young floated around him. He nodded and talked to the wavery figures surrounding him.

Ahni and I awoke in the morning to lightly falling snow. Even the rabbit and Shadow seemed reluctant to get out of our cozy cave to look for food. Ahni used some cattail fluff to catch a spark as she rubbed my spark stones together. I helped by adding small pieces of birch bark and then twigs. When our fire was burning nicely, we put cattail roots into the pot with water to boil for our breakfast.

"Today we'll finish weaving the big mat to cover the opening and if we have time, we'll start smaller ones to sleep on. They'll keep us even warmer if we put them on top of the boughs we used last night."

I cut two more armloads of cattail leaves and dug rhizomes to cook later. Ahni and I dragged it all into our shelter and started weaving. We spent the whole morning finishing the large mat. We lay it over the opening of our root cave and figured out how to poke some of the smaller tree roots through the woven edge to hold it in place.

"Good! We make good home." Ahni proclaimed. "Look how it roll it up to open an' roll down to close. An' still one little openin' here fer Shadow an' the rabbit goin' in an' out."

We admired our work. We had a home for the winter.

"We have sleepin' place. Now we need more food," Ahni said. "We get from Ghost Man's hidin' place. We be quiet. He not catch us."

"I don't like *borrowing* food like you do," I said. "Maybe we should just spend our time digging more cattail roots. And try to catch fish. Maybe we'll even find clams in the river." I shivered. The weak sun barely gave off any warmth even at its highest for the day. "And we need to make sleeping mats. And figure out a way to use the cattail fluff to help keep us warm."

"You scaredy cat of Ghost Man. Me, too. But he have good food. Fish. Meat. Berries. Nuts. Rootie kind of things, too."

"How do you know that?"

"Easy 'nuff. I tol' you I been here afore. I spy on Ghost Man. He be huntin', fishin', makin' garden. Pickin' an' storin' food every day."

"Maybe if we just make friends with him, he'll share." My mouth watered to think of all the different foods Ahni talked about.

"Come. You see. He have tiny little house way uppity high off-a ground. Just fer food."

Tired of her nagging me, I finally agreed to see what Ghost Man had. Ahni led me in a big circle. We stayed hidden in the trees. "There." She pointed.

It was the small log building perched atop four tree trunks that I'd seen the day before. It was perfect for storing food. Off the ground, no animal could get to it, but there was no way up that I could see. How could the man even get to his food?

"Now when man way far on other side over there," Ahni pointed again, "we be safe gettin' some food."

"But how do you climb up there?" I asked. I was curious, but still didn't want to snitch anyone else's food.

"See log on ground? Got cuttings like steps. Jest hoist it up. Lean it by little door. An' go uppity up as fast as squirrel. Snatch food. Down fast. Push log over. Run to woods. Easy." Ahni's eyes beamed. Her cheeks crinkled with her smile. "Lotsa food easy fer the takin'."

"Oh, no," I said. "I will not uppity up as fast as squirrel on a log to steal any-one's food."

"Just go an' lookie-see what you see. No borrowin' any an' we eat mushy cat-tail every day." She wiped her mouth.

It wouldn't hurt to just look. Would it?

Ahni pushed me forward. "Go lookie-see. No take if not want—maybe jest take a few dried berries."

We watched the man walk to the far side of the clearing away from us. I ran to the building. The log was heavy, but I got it up. I didn't scamper like a squirrel, but carefully inched my way up the notched steps to the door. I turned the wooden latch, pulled on the deer antler handle, and stooped inside. Woven baskets on shelves were heaped with cranberries, raspberries, and blueberries. Dried fish heaped in other baskets. A whole deer, all gutted and skinned, hung from the ceiling. Rabbits, too. In a corner were heaps of rutabagas, potatoes, carrots. Baskets of apples and nuts were everywhere. Bunches of dried herbs and grasses hung from the ceiling. My stomach rumbled. My mouth watered. I was tempted, but Ahni and I had food—cattail mush. I backed out and closed the door. On the ground, I pushed the log back down. As I scampered to the woods, I followed my own footprints in the snow. My heart sank. They were evidence I'd been there. I hoped more snow would come before the man saw my footprints.

When we got back to our huddle beneath the massive tree root, Ahni talked incessantly about the good food stored by the Ghost Man. "Did you see the berries? Fish? Nuts? We could jest borrow itty-bitty bit."

My mouth watered as she talked about berries and fish. We settled down to eat cattail mush. The whole time, she did not quit talking about all the food in the little high up building. "Even rutabeggies be good cooked up nice an' tender." Everything she said sounded more and more tempting as I ate my mush and thought about eating it day after day.

When Shadow brought a squirrel in his mouth to show us, I had to tell myself *It's his*. He caught it. I would not take it away, but the thought of roasted meat brought a flood of saliva to my mouth. I could tell Ahni thought the same thing as she watched Shadow toss the dead squirrel into the air playing before he tore into it.

The day turned colder after the snow quit. The wind picked up, so we stayed inside our shelter and worked on weaving sleeping mats. "Roof weavin' good fer keepin' wind out," Ahni said.

While the wind gusted and howled, the rabbit and Shadow poked their way in through the small opening on one side. As soon as we finished one mat, they both settled on it, claiming their bed for the night.

"Lookee them. Thinkin' that's fer them." Ahni laughed. She gave them pokes. "Shoo. People mat, not animal mat."

"Looks like we'll have to make mats for them, too," I said watching Shadow's paws twitch in his sleep.

The wind continued whipping, so we pulled the roof mat over the opening and tried to settle for the night. Tried to. The sleeping mat was only big enough for one person. Ahni said, "How abouts we stuff your old dress with cattail fluff? Then we each will have good place to sleep an' animals ken snuggle next to us. Keep us warm. See, I used the word *will*. Maybe little words useful."

"You are smart," I said. I liked to tell her that because she beamed and smiled when I did.

"We good doin' things together," she answered. "Maybe I not be bad if I with you. Maybe nothin' bad happen anymore."

After tying a knot at the neck of the dress, we pulled the cattail heads apart and stuffed the fluff in through the arm holes. It would keep one of us warm and off the ground.

As soon as we finished Shadow jumped on it, circled three times, and then curled up to sleep. "You have to share," I said boosting him over so there was room for me.

Ahni lay next to the rabbit on the woven leaf mat and covered herself with cedar boughs. "Tomorrow, we make big mat, fold it over an' stuff it with fluff. Be good and warm."

"Good idea. We can make more than one of those. Maybe cover the whole ground area to keep us warm all winter." My back already felt warm and comfy on the fluff cushion we'd made out of my dress.

"An' we be gettin ourselves some good food," said Ahni.

I didn't want to encourage her stealing from Ghost Man, but I knew what hunger was, and he had so much food.

CHAPTER 20

I awoke not knowing where I was. Shadow snored lightly beside me. His paws twitched. I looked at the root ceiling and remembered. During the night the wind had softened and lulled me to a deep sleep. Little by little I wiggled my way up to sitting. Ahni was gone. The rabbit, too. *Good.* I hoped she was building a fire.

Shadow woke and woofed. He looked at me and then at the empty space where Ahni had slept. He woofed again asking *Where did she go?*

"Go find her," I said. He ran out of our shelter.

I stretched. I didn't want to go into the cold. We'd have to catch some fish before the river froze over. Find clams if there were any. Dig for more roots. Cut more cattail leaves and weave another mat. It would be a busy day. Ahni was already up so I needed to face the cold and get to work, too.

Outside, I couldn't see Ahni anywhere. She hadn't gathered wood or even gotten cattail heads and kindling ready to catch a spark. I was annoyed. I knew I shouldn't be. I should be worrying if she was safe, but reminded myself that she'd fended for herself since she was a young child. She was still very young. Maybe only about ten. Where had she gone? Digging more roots? Cutting leaves we'd need for another mat?

I looked for her footprints. The wind had blown and the cold had crusted the snow, but I finally found her blurred prints. They headed, not toward the cattails in the boggy area, but toward Ghost Man's camp. I grew anxious. Was she going to "borrow" from his food stores?

Part of me hoped so. He had a lot of food for the winter, and I was already growing tired of peeling and boiling roots. Another part of me was afraid of what he'd do to Ahni if he caught her. And me, too. We should have moved on, further away from him, found somewhere else to build a shelter. We could fish. Snare rabbits. I thought of the whole deer carcass hanging in his food store. Maybe we could even a take down a deer if we were clever. We'd skin it and have its warm pelt to wear in the coming cold.

I was deep in thought about how useful the tools from Ossi's shed would be as I got a small fire going. We could make spears for fishing. I had an axe, a saw, hammer, and a knife along with some other tools. I wanted Ahni to come back so I could tell her how we could dig a trench and cover it with branches. Then we'd camouflage ourselves in a bush, lying in wait for a deer to come by. We'd jump up and scare the deer so it would leap and run into the trench. Maybe break its leg. Or be stunned enough so we could smash it over the head with a hammer. My stomach revolted as I thought of what we might have to do. I didn't like killing animals. Not even fish, but if we were to survive the coming winter, we would have to do those things.

Shadow woofed bringing me out of my reverie. The hair on his ruff stood straight up. He sensed danger. The hair on my nape prickled, too. I looked toward the woods. That was when I heard Ahni.

"Lemme go! I do nuttin' wrong. I hurt nuttin! Lemme go!"

She emerged from the woods kicking and screaming. Ghost Man held her half off the ground by the back of her dress. She flailed and struck out at him, but he held her away from himself so her blows couldn't strike with any force. "I say lemme go! Now! Or I scratch you eyes out an' toss 'em to weasels."

Ghost Man paid her no attention; he just kept holding her and marching closer and closer to me. Her other braid had come undone. Her hair hung over her eyes. She was as mad as a hungry wolverine.

Shadow woofed again. I hid behind our shelter trembling. What had she gotten us into? She sounded like the Lamb-i-kins of old again. Shadow's woofs turned to barks and growls. He pawed the ground. "Shhh," I whispered to him.

"I pluck you like chicken if you no let me down." If I hadn't been so scared, I would have laughed. There she was, feet barely touching the ground, with wild hair in her eyes, arms thrashing—yelling threats at the Ghost Man who had her firmly in his grip.

Anxious and almost in a panic, I looked for something I could use as a weapon if I needed one. Everything I'd taken from Ossi's shed was in the shelter. I just had the fire. I poked a long stick into the flames and hoped the end would catch and be hot enough before Ghost Man dragged Ahni closer and did to us whatever it was that he intended.

"Luna, help me! Ghost Man! He mad man! He no let me go!"

They were closing in now. The stick barely had a bit of fire catching at the tip. It wouldn't be enough to scare the man into setting Ahni free. I grew panicky. I looked around. Nothing! Nothing! I dove into the cave to grab the hammer and axe.

I was crawling out when Shadow set up howling, growling and snarling. Ahni yelled cuss words I'd never heard her use before followed by a whole string of threats. "I boil yer liver! Let birds peck yer brains! Throw yer fingers and toes to the fishes!"

I trembled. Ghost Man stood only two steps away. Ahni still dangled from his hold. The hammer and axe were on the ground where I'd pushed them ahead of me. Shadow had quit barking. He was sniffing Ghost Man's boots, circling his feet, not growling, and the fur on his ruff wasn't raised. I took a deep breath and stood. My knees shook, but if Shadow thought the man was not someone to growl at any more, maybe he wouldn't harm us. Ghost Man put Ahni down. She ran to me and put her arms around my waist stammering, "Ghost Man! Bad Ghost Man!"

The hammer and axe were still on the ground. The Ghost Man looked at them, then he bent to pet Shadow.

"Good dog."

His voice was gentle. Shadow wagged his tail. I brushed the hair out of my eyes. Ghost Man patted Shadow on the head again and repeated, "Good dog."

His voice was soft and melodious like Ossi's. Could it be that Ahni and I were at the village of the Ice People? Ossi and Huldor's people? My mother's home? The village the marauders burned? Could the cairns be for my grandparents and others?

I thought back to the words Ossi had used as a greeting. Trembling, I said, "Aa-vi-ap. Hello."

The man smiled and pet Shadow some more. "Aa-vi-ap," he said as he nodded to me. Then he bent and added more wood to my fire.

"No be nice to him," Ahni let go of me, stomped around, then picked up the axe. "He grab me. Scare me. Not put me down. Drag me here."

"He knows our language," I said as though that was a good explanation.

"No care about language. We chop him up. Have plenty to eat from his little house." Her eyes glinted fiercely in the morning sun. She brushed the hair from her eyes as she handed me the axe. "You bigger. Stronger. You chop him up."

"I'm not doing any such thing," I said tossing the axe a distance away.

"You dumb big person!" She said picking up the hammer. She was ready to throw it at Ghost Man, but I caught her arm and took it from her.

All the while, the man kept an eye on us as he built up the fire. Shadow sat by his side chewing on a stick. "Look," I said to Ahni, "Shadow trusts him."

"Him dumb dog. Dumber than I thought," she scowled. Just then the rabbit came hopping out of the woods, stopped short, then sat by the man who scratched her ear.

"Dumb bunny. Dumb everyone." The fight had gone out of Ahni's voice. She sat by the fire and pulled a handful of hair over her eyes.

CHAPTER 21

Ahni's Ghost Man stood right in front of me. He was dressed all in furs. Mostly bear, wolf, and rabbit, but weasel and squirrel fur wrapped his arms. Little tails hung from them, swinging as he piled more wood onto our fire. A fox tail circled his head. Deer skin and birch bark wrapped his legs. He looked part of nature. He could stand next to a tree and blend in.

Strange as he looked, I wasn't afraid. "My name is Luna," I said. Pointing, I added, "She's Ahni. The dog is Shadow, and the rabbit is Bunny."

He straightened up from his fire building. His eyes were as clear blue as a summer day. They reminded me of Ossi's. His brows were an ash-gray color and bushy. The rest of his face was hidden behind a gray beard. He smiled and said, "Luna. Ahni. My name is Gromske."

"Gromske," I repeated and then I remembered where I'd heard the name before. "Gromske!" I almost shouted. Gromske had been Ossi's friend who'd been on his separation journey at the same time Ossi had. Then I said, "Ossi. Oriina." Oriina had been Huldor's name before the awful man bought her, tied a rope around her neck, and took her to be his wife.

A big smile spread on Ghost Man's face. "Ya. Ya. Ossi. Oriina." He looked around as though expecting them to come walking through the trees to the river's edge.

"Are you Oriina's brother?" I asked, then added, "Gromske?"

"Ya. Gromske," he repeated pointing to himself. Ghost Man was no longer ghost man. He was of my people. The Ice People. He tapped his chest smiling and saying, "Ya, ya. I'm Gromske. Brother of Oriina. Friend of Ossi."

91

I said to Ahni. "Everything is good. Your ghost man is real. A real person. You don't have to be afraid of him."

Ahni slowly came to stand by me. "You sure he not ghost?"

"Not ghost for sure. He's real. Remember when I told you about Ossi and Huldor? He knew them when they were young and lived all together. That was maybe right here before their village was destroyed by marauders."

"Not people ghost? Lookee him. All animal like. Animal ghost with dead animals hanging all over from him. An' he drag me like wild beast even when I yell put me down."

"He's not a ghost of any kind. He's one of the Ice People. One of my people," I said as I turned to Gromske. "Ossi told me about you. How you and he had been away on your separation journeys when your village was burned."

Gromske looked at me. His eyes blurred as though filling with tears. I continued before my eyes blurred also, "When Ossi came back, the village was destroyed and no one was here. He built cairns for those who'd died while he waited for you to come back. But you never did. He was filled with so much sadness and so many memories that he finally left and made a life for himself on a high rock ridge where the wolves sang to him."

Gromske wiped his eyes and asked, "My sister—Oriina—did she live through the destruction of our village?"

I hesitated. Gromske had been alone for a long time with just his memories. He needed to know what happened. Finally, I told him, "When you and Ossi were on your separation journeys, Oriina and Etta Carina were taken by the marauders that burned their village. The marauders sold them to the highest bidders. Oriina was bought by an awful man who kept her tied on a leash. He never even asked her name. Just called her Huldor. My father traded his horse to buy Etta Carina."

"Etta Carina? Your mother?" he asked.

"Yes," I said, "My father was poor, but he was able to trade his horse for my mother when no one else bid on her at the auction because she had a lame leg."

Gromske shook his head. "I remember she was lame, but so smart and kind. Where are they? Oriina and Etta Carina? And Ossi?"

Shadow nuzzled my leg as though he knew what I had to say next would be hard. "Father told me my mother died giving birth to me. But it wasn't so. I found out later that a great storm had separated them after I was born. Father and I had been flung to a far shore of Lake Kawishami, while Mother had been blown to an opposite shore where she gave birth to my twin sister, Selene. Mother died years later."

All that had been hard to tell. My voice had cracked and tears ran down my cheeks as I talked, but I wasn't finished. Gromske had to know it all. "Ossi and I were saved from freezing to death about twelve moons ago when we found Oriina at her inn. We lived together as a family through the winter, spring, and fall. One day they joined together as husband and wife and took me as their daughter." I struggled, but I had to say the last words. "That night the inn burned. Huldor, as your sister Oriina was known, died in the fire. Ossi did, too."

Gromske and I both let silent tears run down our cheeks. The only sound was the river rippling beside us. Even Ahni was quiet. Shadow, too, as though he knew we were remembering a great sadness.

Our reverie was broken when Ahni's stomach howled loudly, and she tugged on my arm.

"Ya. Ya." Gromske said wiping his tears away. "We eat."

"We'll eat now." I said to Ahni as I rubbed my sleeve over my face to dry my tears. I picked up my cooking pan, dipped it in the river, set it on the rocks around our fire circle.

I was adding some cattail roots when Gromske repeated, "Ya. We'll eat." Then he turned and headed back into the woods.

"Where he goin'?" Ahni asked. "Maybe he goin' get somethin' to skin us alive an' hang us—without our skin—in his food store."

"No," I said. "I think he's getting something to eat!"

"How you know? Maybe he jest go get big pot to cook us in."

Ahni would not let go of the idea that Gromske was a ghost. People ghost. Animal ghost. Woods ghost. Ghost who ate little girls. She shivered when she talked about him. "Now he know our names! Ghost do terrible things to peoples they know names."

I was getting tired of explaining to her how I knew he wasn't a ghost. She pulled her hair out of the last braid saying, "An' you. You talkin' to him about people you know, an' tellin' our names. You some kinda' spook or witch, too? I be gettin' away if you be." She looked even more like the wild Lamb-i-kins I'd first met so long ago as she scowled from beneath her tangled hair.

How do you convince someone when they don't want to be convinced?

"Pap tell me all about evil kinda beings. How they dance on you when you sleep. Conjurin' up mischief. Give you scary dreams. An' all that. An' how do I know *you* not brewin' up somethin' potion-like with those things?" She pointed at the pot full of cattail roots. "How I know *you* not a mixin' up spells an' such? Maybe Orphan House better than be with you."

Tired of arguing, I just said, "You don't. Now get more twigs for the fire."

Just then Shadow went running to the woods. Then he came back romping next to Gromske who swung a burlap bag at his side. Shadow sniffed at the bag as he danced along.

When Gromske got to the fire, he knelt, opened the bag, took out a chunk of meat, a squash and a basket of berries.

Ahni—suddenly not worried about ghosts, evils and spells—brushed the hair out of her eyes and knelt right next to Gromske to check what else he had in the bag. He gave Ahni the knife he slid from a pouch at his side. Pointing to a tree he said, "We need three long sticks."

"What fer?" she asked brushing the hair from her eyes again.

Gromske explained, "We will spear the meat on the sticks and hold it over the fire for roasting."

Ahni licked her lips in anticipation while saying, "I go make three sticks." Then she took the knife and dashed into the woods. I wouldn't have given her anything sharp knowing the mood she'd been in. I hoped it wasn't a mistake.

Keeping an eye on Ahni, I got busy soaking the long leaves from the cattails. I wrapped them around the squash and set it among the embers. Gromske watched as I did it and smiled. He poked more embers over the squash and then pushed the flaming pieces of wood off to the other side.

When Ahni came back, she handed Gromske the knife and sticks. He smiled and said, "Thank you. So-tiik."

I was glad to hear the word Ossi and Huldor had so often used to say *thank you*. Ahni beamed and tucked her tangled hair behind her ears.

Gromske sliced the meat into thin strips. He laced them onto the sticks and gave us each one to hold over the fire. As we waited for them to cook, he passed the basket of dried blueberries and cranberries to us. We nibbled on them as we sat around the fire. Ahni was definitely no longer afraid of Gromske. I decided that the miracle of berries, a squash, and meat sizzling on sticks were more convincing than all the reasons I could give that Gromske was not a ghost.

The cattail roots were ready before anything else, so we ate those first. The roasted meat was next, and last was the squash. "Good meal," Gromske said.

"Better'n just mushy cattail," Ahni nibbled her stick to get every bit of meat off. Then she pushed hair out of her eyes and licked squash from her fingers. She belched twice. "Haven't eaten this good since loggin' place. Tummy say thanks. What other word he say for thanks?"

"So-tiik," I told her as I wondered about the logging camp she mentioned again, sure there was a story she didn't want to tell.

"So-tiik. Thank you." Ahni said to Gromske who offered her the basket of berries again.

Gromske threw Shadow strips of roasted fat and a whole strip of meat. The dog ate them in an instant and then sighing deeply, he curled up by the fire. The squirrels in the woods would be safe the rest of the day. I filled the pot with river water and set it over the fire. A cedar tree grew nearby so I stripped some of the soft green sprays and dropped them in the hot water. Soon the air was filled with its comforting scent. When the tea had cooled, I passed the pot to Gromske who breathed the wafting aroma before taking a small swallow. "Aa-vyh! Good! Cedar drink is good."

He passed the pot to Ahni who greedily gulped several swallows. "This good! Make more often," she said looking at the cedar tree. She took another swallow before passing the pot to me. I did as Gromske had and deeply breathed the fragrance before drinking. We passed the pot from one to the other until it was empty.

The fire died down. I was about to put more wood on it when Gromske held up a hand and said, "Nay. Nay. Come." He signaled us to follow him.

"Not safe. Not going. Still might be a spook who feed us. Get us softened up. Fatted up. Not trusting him." It crossed my mind that Ahni might be right. I reached into my pocket and held the moonstone. It warmed slightly. I looked at it. The blue and yellow swirls gently swelled and ebbed. My thumbs didn't prick or become tingly. I sighed with relief.

"I'm going," I told her. Shadow awoke and began following Gromske. I did, too. Ahni picked up the hammer and trailed behind. A raven followed.

CHAPTER 22

Gromske led us to the sandy river bank where my canoe leaned against a downed tree. He ran his hands along the surface of the canoe, especially the parts that had been restored. He inspected the seams Ossi had so carefully dabbed with tree pitch mixed with ash to make the mended canoe water proof. He nodded as he finished running his hands along the whole keel. "Good canoe."

"Ossi patched my canoe when it was broken." I explained and ran my hands along the patches and seams, too.

Gromske nodded solemnly. "Ossi. Gone to star sky."

Tears came to my eyes once again. I nodded. Gromske held his hands to his face. His shoulders shook. His whole body quaked. Shadow whined softly as if he understood, too. Ahni tapped me on the shoulder, "Why he cry so much?" she asked.

I wiped my tears. "Oriina was his sister. Ossi and my mother were his friends."

We all sat on a log listening to the burble and splash of the river waters as they flowed over rocks and lapped the shore.

Gromske ran his hands over my canoe again then asked for more of my mother's story.

I shook my head. "I don't know much other than my mother and father each thought the other had died during a tremendous storm. But my mother had lived after she was flung to a far shore of Lake Kawishami where my twin Selene was born. Years later, when Selene came to the inn, she told me about the man who'd forced our mother to weave lengths of beautiful cloth. In return he'd brought

97

her bowls of cold gruel, wormy cereals, and bare bones to eat. He'd abused and beaten her when she was no longer able to weave. She died of her injuries."

It was a terrible story. Gromske kept touching the canoe as I told him what I knew about Ossi. He, too, had been on his separation journey. When he returned, he found no one alive at the burned and devastated village. Ossi had waited for Gromske to return, but he hadn't, so he only stayed long enough to build cairns over the burned bodies.

Gromske shook his head. "So much sadness. Everyone was gone when I finally returned. The stories of Ossi, Oriina, and Etta Carina are heart- breaking. Along with our mothers, fathers, grandparents, they are gone. Gone to the star sky. Now, it's just us—you and me—left of the Ice People. I am glad you have come. So glad."

I nodded and felt something as soft as a feather brush my cheek as my tears fell. They fell for my mother. For Ossi and Huldor. For the people I'd met in portals of the dead. They fell for Father, too, even though I didn't know if he still lived or had died.

CHAPTER 23

That afternoon, after Gromske inspected the cave Ahni and I'd dug deeper under the massive root of the fallen tree, he led us to his dwelling place. According to Ossi, twenty years had passed since marauders set fires to burn the village. Young trees grew all around. Dried grasses covered the whole area erasing all signs of ashes and scorched earth. Even with winter coming on, there was beauty in the place where Gromske lived. The deep blue sky arched overhead. Stately trees grew on the tall hills beyond the old village. Cairns rose from the ground—memorials where Ossi had heaped stones to mark the lives and deaths of his, my, and Gromske's people.

Gromske opened the deer skin flap of the shelter he'd built for himself on the ruins of the village. He beckoned us to enter. I did eagerly. Ahni followed me reluctantly whispering, "Good spirits help me, strike down man if he try an' eat my liver."

His home was a small round building. Saplings bent into a dome shape framed it. Birch bark and deer skins enclosed the structure. A circular hole in the ground had been hollowed making a firepit. At the top of the dome was an opening for smoke. Gromske had hung bundles of dried plants from the ridgepoles. I smelled mint and chamomile, as well as other heady aromas. Baskets were heaped with chaga, chanterelle mushrooms, and roots of some kind.

Gromske's bed was a knee-high frame piled with furs. The bed looked warm and cozy. Much better than the root cave Ahni and I slept in. A few old tools and a pot that must have survived the long-ago fire hung from a branch above it.

Mounds of furs from foxes, wolves, beavers, rabbits, bears, deer, and many other animals—even rabbits and squirrels—were on the other side. Ahni ran her hands along the soft, smooth furs. Her eyes widened with wonder.

I didn't like all the animal skins, but Gromske needed them for clothing and blankets, so I tried not to think of how many animals he'd killed. I pointed all around me and said, "Your home is nice and warm."

Gromske replied, "Ya. It is so. Thank you. *So-tiik.*"

Outside again, he showed us his bathhouse. It, too, was round with a sapling dome. A tree stump formed a seat. Stones surrounded the fire pit. A blackened iron, three-legged frame spanned the fire pit. A kettle hung from it. Gromske said, "The kettle heats water for bath."

He'd thought of everything. He had a house, a food storage building, and a place to wash. He'd built it all on his own with the things he gathered that hadn't been destroyed, and whatever he could glean from the land and woods. I felt a thump in my chest as I thought about how he must have felt when he returned to his home, found everything destroyed and everyone dead.

I wanted to know his story. Ossi had waited two months for Gromske to come back from his separation journey, but he hadn't returned.

"Ya," he said when I asked. "When I saw the cairns, I knew Ossi had returned from his journey, found everything destroyed, and left when I didn't return. I stayed just a short while, then left, too." Gromske wiped a bit of spittle from his chin, then continued. "I wandered alone until winter brought brutally cold winds. Luckily, I came upon a logging camp. They were in need of more loggers because two had died when a tree fell on them. I stayed the whole winter logging. I learned their language—this language—and had a good place to stay. The food was plentiful, but plain. Two more winters I logged, even though I felt a great sadness every day and a pull to come back here. So great was the urge that I knew I needed to return here to my village even though it had been burned and destroyed. I still needed to live here. Be here. To be with the spirits of my family. And to be here hoping Ossi or someone else would return."

Gromske wiped his eyes when he finished his story. I looked at the cairns and understood his longing to be where he'd grown up with his family surrounding him. I wondered why I didn't feel the same way when I thought of the log hovel I'd shared with my father.

Ahni started tugging on my arm, breaking into my thoughts. The sky was darkening, so I finally said to Gromske, "We have to go now. So-tiik."

Gromske nodded saying, "Wait." He turned toward his own domed sleeping place.

"Why's he going?" Ahni asked.

"I don't know, but he wants us to wait."

Gromske soon came back carrying two lush black bear furs. He wrapped one around each of us.

"So warm! So-tiik," I said grateful for the thick fur.

"So-tiik," Ahni said as she pulled the fur closer around herself. "Maybe he not so bad. Maybe not bad spirit after all," she added as we headed back to our own little root cave.

CHAPTER 24

I awoke during the night as if a voice called me. *Walk among us.* Was it the spirit voice of my people? People I'd never known? Grandmas and grandpas? Aunts and uncles? Cousins? I was where they'd lived. *Come. Walk among us.*

Silently, I arose careful not to wake Ahni. I wrapped myself in the bear pelt Gromske had given me and crawled into the night. Shadow whined and followed. In the star-lit night, as I walked toward the stone cairns, a familiar feeling came over me. I felt queasy. The ground beneath me shivered, then quaked. I heard the river waters ripple and slap the shore. My vision turned hazy. Disoriented, I held onto the stones of a cairn. I saw hazy glimmers. I had entered a portal.

I heard voices of my people. Their voices mingled in the mists of night. Voices of people who died long ago—before I was born of the comet. I heard melancholy laments. Laments of sorrow and pain, moans and weeping. So many voices were still trapped in the flames of the past.

At each cairn I felt a presence beyond my own. At one, my knees quivered, and I trembled in the presence of shrouded mists. The mists seemed to reach out to me, so I whispered, "I am Luna. Daughter of Etta Carina. I was born when the comet flew overhead."

Two shimmering spirits appeared. The whispered voice called them Grandmam and Grandpap. Grandmam was wrapped in a wolf pelt. She stirred something in a wooden bowl with a carved spoon. Grandpap wore a fringed deerskin wrap. He sharpened a knife on a stone.

"I am Luna. Daughter of Etta Carina," I said again. The mists swirled closer, enveloping me.

"Mother gave birth to twins," I said. "We are daughters of the comet. Me and Selene."

The mists warmed me. I heard whispers, "Etta Carina? Does she still walk the earth?"

I felt a heavy sorrow swell in my chest as I said, "Etta died. She died too young." Then I told of how my mother—their daughter—had been captured on the day of the destruction. I told of my father trading his horse for her; how a storm separated them on the day I was born. Each thought the other had died. I also told of my mother living long enough to give birth to Selene, but later she'd died at the hands of an evil man.

The mists wavered and keened a song of sorrow, tears and pain. I hugged myself and let my tears fall. A calming serenity came over me. I whispered again. "I am Luna. Daughter of Etta Carina." Melancholy still filled the air, but I no longer heard voices of pain and suffering.

The haze and mists floated higher. "Grandmam? Grandpap?" I asked. A miasma enveloped me. Warm. Comforting. I felt my feet lift from the earth until I was suspended in a surrounding light. I heard words. Whispered words. Words Ossi and Huldor had said one to another. *Sak-arat-luk ovra.* Dearest one—love greater than gold. Softness brushed my cheeks. The mists whispered again. *Sak-arat-luk ovra.* Tears filled my eyes. I was uplifted, heartened by the words of endearment. The smoky shadows hovered a while then wafted away. A lump formed in my throat. Tears fell as I watched the misty shadows fade into the still night. The ground beneath me no longer shivered and quaked. My vision cleared. No more mists and shadows remained. I was no longer queasy. The portal closed. I was alone.

Shadow sat at the edge of the forest. Did he hear what I heard? Did he see what I saw?

In the dimness of the night, I walked from cairn to cairn—each a marker, a tomb, a memorial. At the one my Grandmam and Grandpap had come to me, I stopped. My heart pounded. My knees quivered and trembled, but there were no more shadowy figures shrouded in the mists wafting over the cairns.

I awoke to the sound of the wind. It whipped the mat Ahni and I had woven to cover the opening of our huddle. Had I actually risen from my bed to the beckoning of the voices to visit the stone-cold tombs of my people? Had I dreamed about walking among the souls of the dead? I shivered. Dream? Reality? Shadow nudged my elbow with his wet nose. What was he telling me? That he'd been with me on my night walk into the portal? Or had my trembling wakened him?

Every day, even as the snows deepened, Ahni and I made our way to Gromske's hut where he set his fire and roasted food for us. We sat cross-legged savoring fish, venison stews, and roots. He taught Ahni how to make wild rice cakes. First, they cooked the kernels until they were soft, then after mixing in chopped hazel nuts and cranberries, they mashed it all together. After patting the mush into little cakes, Gromske sizzled fat in his pan, and Ahni put the cakes in to fry. The nutty cakes were delicious. While they worked together, Ahni and Gromske talked and laughed together a lot. At times, they laughed as though laughter was the only language they needed.

I watched as Gromske placed his hand on Ahni's, showing her how to hold the knife to chop carrots or rutabagas. He taught her how to cut along the back bone of a fish and then slide the knife to remove all the bones. She no longer called him Ghost Man or shrank behind me to be safe from him. At times, I felt jealousy creep into me. I had learned a lot from Father, but he hadn't been as gentle and caring as Gromske was with Ahni. At other times, I was glad that she was with a kind man, and I remembered how Ossi had taken care of me when I had crashed my canoe by his home high on a rocky ledge.

Each day I walked among the cairns. I stopped at the one that had become special to me. The floating hazes comforted me. At the cairns, I felt calm and heard within myself melodies of gladness as a feather-soft touch brushed my cheek. When I left, I felt empty and miserable thinking of my people—the Ice People— all dead except for me and Gromske.

One blustery winter day, the sun didn't so much as peek from behind the clouds for a second. Snows fell heavily. Winds whipped up a fury I'd never known before. Ahni and I huddled together in our root cave, shivering despite the furs we wrapped tightly around ourselves. The wind tore our roof mat away. It tumbled in the turbulence and was soon out of our sight.

"What we do now?" Ahni asked.

"Huddle closer and hope the snow doesn't bury us." I was already trembling. Shadow burrowed his way under the furs with us. The rabbit made her way deeper under the roots.

"Look!" Ahni pointed.

Gusting winds picked up my canoe and spun it in the air. "Oh, no!" I shouted. If the canoe crashed into a rock or tree, I would never be able to get it mended again. I jumped out of my fur robe and chased after it as it twisted and whirled in the wind. That same wind pulled the breath out of me and whipped my hair across my face. I gasped as I chased. The bone-chilling wind blew right through my thin clothes. Ice crystals formed on my eyelashes and in my nose.

The canoe tumbled toward me. I grabbed for it. At the same moment, it spun and hit me full on. I fell face first into the drifting snow. I lay there. Stunned. Out of breath. Freezing.

Wanting to crawl to shelter, I raised my head in time to see the canoe roll and slide jamming itself between trees. Snow from branches dropped onto my chest. I struggled to breathe. My lungs screamed for air. Two hands grasped me by the shoulders and helped me stand.

CHAPTER 25

Gromske held onto me in the buffeting wind while we stumbled to the shelter. "Take everything," he said as the wind almost knocked us over. Ahni handed me one of the bear skins, our food sack, my pack, and then she wrapped the other bear skin around herself and the rabbit. Gromske hoisted my tool sack onto his own back, kept one arm around me while I held Ahni on my other side. Shadow followed closely behind in our tracks as we made our way to Gromske's *itok*, the word he used for his domed shelter.

The five of us, including Shadow and the rabbit, huddled in the *itok* as the storm raged for three days. We kept a small fire going day and night. We ate sparingly so we didn't have to brave the winds going to the food storage shed. Crowded together, Ahni and I asked Gromske to teach us words in the Ice People's language. Soon we were challenging each other to remember the most words. Each evening, we knew it was time to roll into our furs for sleeping when Gromske softly sang a song in his language.

The melody was familiar to me. Even some of the words. Ossi had sung the same song when he told his story. The song was an invitation to the sun, the moon, and all the stars to sing. For the clouds, waters, the earth, and the forests to sing. For all to be well throughout the night.

Aurinko laulaa.
Kuu ja tahdet laulavat.
Pilvet ja vedet laulavat.

Maa laula.
Metsat laulavat.
Kaikki on hyvin koko yon.

We spent the rest of the winter living in Gromske's *itok* because snow had filled our root cave and the woven mat covering the opening had blown wherever the wind carried it.

Every time the moon was full or a sliver of the new moon shone, Gromske built a fire in the bath dome and carried buckets of water from the river to heat on the stones. Each time Ahni and I bathed, I noticed the pouch she wore around her neck. I asked, "Why don't you take the pouch off so it won't get wet."

"Never take off."

"But why not. You can put it back on as soon as you're done."

"No. Never. Mine. Good people gave present to me. I be strong when I wear it."

"Who gave it to you?"

"Good big people. Other big people not good."

"What's the gift in it?"

"No more talk about my pouch. Miss those good people much. Much!"

We were silent as we bathed, untangled and washed each other's hair. We scrubbed each other's backs. She'd told me before that she didn't trust big people. Again, I wondered why she never talked about her mam. What had happened to her?

"Why we wash so often?" Ahni asked as we dressed. "I not even itty-bit dirty."

I didn't have a good answer for her. When I lived with Father, we didn't wash all winter. After the lake warmed in the summer, we'd shed our winter layers of clothes and jumped in for a swim and our first bath of the year.

Even though Ahni didn't like washing, she got used to the baths. She liked the time we spent together in the warmth. I combed my fingers through her hair and held it near the glowing fire to dry before braiding and wrapping the braids into a crown. Then she did the same to my hair.

When we returned to the *itok*, rosy-cheeked and clean, Gromske would be stirring cedar sprays in hot water, steeping them for tea. He'd then head to the bath dome for his own wash.

One day, Gromske encouraged Ahni to tell a story. To tell why she was so alone in the world. At first, she just said, "Not talk. Not much to tell."

Remembering that she'd liked her Grammy, I urged her to tell how she and her Grammy read together.

"Grammy teach me read little words from a book with stories about a princess. Gram tell me to pretend I a princess as we read." She stopped to sip her cedar tea.

"Go on," I encouraged.

"I liked good story about Princess spending days in icy, frosty palace place. That a big fancy house with towers and windows. Soft beds. Big tables piled with food."

Gromske smiled and nodded as he added another chunk of wood to our fire.

"Did the story say what she did during the day in ice palace?"

"Book old. Found in junk pile. Pages missing. So don't know, but Grammy tell me make up what I think happen. Princess never have fun. Alone all the time. Except for mean man who teach her to pickety pockets and steal lots of things. Then mean man bring her somewhere deep in woods where she workin' hard. Scrubbin' floors. Big people nice to her at first, but when they find out princess born durin' 'clipse time, they blame her for all bad things happenin.'"

"Does the princess in your story ever get away? Ever have a happy ending?" I asked.

"Bad people make princess leave an' go to woody forest alone lookin' for home. But she get lost and meet a wolf woman. Finally find Grammy. She tell princess about good warm place to go if she have to run from mean man. Place with bubblin' mud pots. But I not have Princess go there. I make up good endin.' I decide she hide from cruel people, fly up an' up 'til she find nice warm palace in the star sky with Pegasus. There she learn story about David an' Goliath an' how little people be smart an' take down big bad people. Then forever an' ever, she watch over all little children make sure they sleep safe at night. An' have lots an' lots a food."

In her words, I heard parts of Ahni's own story. Her own childhood made her yearn for little children, herself included, to be safe. The mean man must have been her Pap, but again, there was no Mam. Would she ever tell?

When the snows quit falling and icicles formed on tree branches, I knew spring was on its way. At night the snow crusted over, so in the mornings we could walk on top, going wherever we wanted. Gromske had a pair of skis he'd made long ago.

Ahni and I took turns learning how to glide down hills without falling. A raven waited on a tree branch and flew from tree to tree as we skied.

When the river ice opened and the ground softened, Gromske began to cut saplings. "What these for?" asked Ahni.

"An *itok*. For you," Gromske answered.

"Our own *itok*!" Ahni put the rabbit down and ran to a flat area a little distance from Gromske's *itok*. "Put it here!" she said. "Then we still be close to each other."

We helped Gromske hold the saplings in place while he bound them together with supple alder roots. When the frame was finished, he showed us how to cut and weave birch bark in and out of the saplings to make the circular wall. Ahni and I wove the bark as high as we could reach. He finished the upper layers for us. While he heated and stirred pitch from fir trees, he told us how to make three small wooden paddles that we used to spread the pitch along the seams.

"What we do this for?" Ahni asked.

"Keep rain out," he said.

As we spread the pitch on our new *itok* I thought of how lucky I was to have found Gromske and the village where my mother had lived. I felt I was where I belonged. That thought made me think of the comet-borns held prisoners by Harmonia. They weren't where they belonged, nor were they with a kind person. They needed to be freed. I became apprehensive at the thought of Harmonia. I hoped she'd forgotten all about me.

Thoughts of saving the children of the comet imprisoned in the stockade, gnawed at me every day. Now that the river was open, it would be easier to travel to the sanctuary. But what would I do next? How could I get to the stockade without anyone seeing? And capturing me? Maybe Gromske would help, and maybe Tumla would help once we got there. Maybe. Maybe. Maybe. My thoughts jumbled. If I was going to save the comet-borns from being sold, it would have to be soon. Just thinking about what was ahead, I nearly froze stiff at the thought of danger. What if Harmonia caught me, and I was imprisoned and sold, too?

The day after we finished making our *itok* and the frames for beds, Gromske said, "River water are high, but not dangerous. In your canoe, we all can go to a big village where two rivers flow together. With money from furs we sell, we can buy supplies we need."

Even though I was anxious about the comet-borns, I readily agreed to the trip to the village. I had my own pouch of coins. Maybe I would find something I could use for the rescue. Ahni wasn't as excited.

"What if constable man be there lookin' for me? Wantin' to drag me back to Orphan House?"

"We won't let that happen. No one can take you away from us. Unless—unless you get caught *borrowing* things that don't belong to you."

"I not borrow anythin', an' I promise no picky pockets. I only pretend have lame leg so people give me coins to get out of their way. That all right?"

"Don't even do that! Or I might send you to Orphan House myself," I teased.

"You do that? If you do, I gone. Then who wash your back an' help braid your hair?"

"You're right. I wouldn't do that, but you have to be good."

The next day, we loaded Gromske's furs into the canoe. "We go tomorrow," he said. "Bath time tonight."

"Bath time! Not full moon yet! Pretty soon my skin fall off—will fall off from too much washin'!" Ahni crossed her arms across her chest and frowned.

I pointed to the smudges of soot on her face and arms from when she'd helped set the morning cooking fire. "Easy enough to clean without a bath," she said as she spit on the hem of her dress and rubbed her face and arms.

As she did that, I looked at her ragged dress. Climbing a tree to peek into a bird's nest, she had ripped one sleeve almost completely off. Stains and smaller tears were everywhere. After our bath, I'd have her try on a dress Huldor made for me. If it was much too big, I'd spend some of my coins to get another for her.

I looked at my own dress. When I'd put the pale green dress on for the first time, it had been the beautiful color of a Luna moth. Now it was faded and stained beyond ever coming clean again. Maybe I would buy a new dress in the village. I stroked the one I wore. It held so many memories. I didn't want to part with it.

CHAPTER 26

We paddled for two days. What a sight we must have been. Gromske in the back paddling.

Furs heaped in the middle. Ahni and I squeezed into the little space in front. Ahni—holding her pole—pretended to paddle along with Gromske. Me—squished even more as she wiggled and poled along. Shadow would not be left behind so at the last moment, he'd jumped to the top of the furs. His ears perked. Alert and woofing at every bird that flew overhead, even the raven.

The first night, we slept under some trees. When we reached the village the second evening, we slept on the bank a distance away. A light rain started to fall so Ahni, Shadow and I huddled under the canoe. Gromske found a hollow that he curled in covered by one of the furs.

The next morning, we awoke to the clamor of a whole village of people stirring. Horses neighed and stomped their feet probably demanding oats. We ate the wild rice cakes we brought with us. I began to plan how to spend a few coins from my pouch. A honey treat for all of us would be nice. Besides, I wanted something to help free the fenced-in comet children, but I didn't know what I'd need.

The village was bigger—much bigger—than the hamlet where the Harvest Moon Festival that I'd gone with Father was held. Ahni clasped my hand as we tagged along behind Gromske.

"Don't lose me," Ahni said as we walked along a cobbled path.

"If we get separated, head for the river and the canoe," I said. "If I get lost, I'll do the same."

"Everything so big. How I find river?"

"Look," I pointed. "See how all the buildings are laid out in rows on sloping hills? If we get separated, just go downward away from the hills. That's where the river will be. Then walk along the bank until you find the canoe."

"Sounds easy, but don't lose me! I no like lotsa people an' strange places."

I knew how she felt. More than one person bumped into me, hurrying to pass. Even Shadow never left my side. We reached the center of the village. It was full of wagons and carts loaded with squawking chickens, smoked fish, crocks of pickled pig's feet, woven rugs, cheeses, and lots of other things. Gromske told me to ask where he could set his furs. No one seemed to care, so Ahni and I helped Gromske bring the furs to a vacant corner. We settled there as people began stroking the furs and asking prices. Depending on how big the fur was, Gromske would tell how many copper or silver coins he wanted for it. Usually, the buyer would suggest something less, and the haggling started.

The pile of furs dwindled. By the time the sun was high in the sky, Gromske had sold all the largest ones. Only a few rabbit, mink, and weasel were left. I was just beginning to feel pangs of hunger when a woman carrying a huge basket on her head came by.

"Bread. Fresh from the oven this morning. Rye bread. Stone-ground wheat bread. Ground the wheat myself. Oat bread. Muffins. Buy your bread here!"

Ahni jumped up. "I hungry! Want bread!"

The woman set her basket down. "Let's see here. What kind do you want and how many?"

The loaves were so big; we'd only need one, but Gromske said to me and Ahni, "Choose what you want." We did, and he picked one for himself, too. Gromske handed the woman the coins she'd asked for.

"Thank you," she said smiling. "That will lighten my load."

"Come back later if you have any left," Gromske said.

"Why?" I asked after she'd gone.

"I haven't had good bread for years. No way to make it. We'll take whatever she has left over to eat on our way home." He brought his loaf to his nose and sniffed. "Ahh, delicious. Like my mother and grandmother made. She's a good baker woman."

Gromske handed Ahni a few coins. "Go find a cheese cart. Bargain for big chunk to eat with bread."

Soon Ahni came back smiling, happy to have done such an important task. "Just five coppers for these two cheeses," she said. "An' I no borrow nothin' while there!"

"Good job," I said with my mouth full, chewing on bread and cheese at the same time.

When the sun lowered in the sky, Gromske handed me some coins and said, "This is a good time to buy things we don't have. Sellers don't want to take loads home, so you'll get good prices."

"What do you want me to buy?"

"Whatever is good. If you buy bacon or ham hocks, smell and look carefully. No maggots."

With those few instructions, I headed to check all the wagons and carts. I had just quibbled for a big chunk of smoked bacon when a commotion further down the lane drew my attention.

A fancy man, dressed in a striped suit with a red scarf around his neck, spoke into a tube-shaped thing that carried his voice loud and clear. "Step right up. Ladies. Gentlemen. Even boys and girls. Come and see for yourself this rare opportunity. We have right before us today a most beautiful young lady." He stopped then, prodded the young lady whose head was bowed so low her hair hung over her face, and whispered to her, "Stand straight!"

People crowded in from all directions blocking my view. I could barely see the beautiful young lady or the fancy man as he continued, "Ladies and gentlemen. Boys and girls. You see before you a most rare and unique sight that you'll be talking about for years."

I stood on my toes and stretched my neck trying to see what or who he was talking about.

"Better yet, open your pouches, and be ready to bid, because you are about to have the singular chance to bid on a child born under the passing of THE COMET. Yes! THE BLAZING COMET that flew the skies just fifteen years ago. Today you have this once in a lifetime opportunity to buy this valuable girl for your own good fortune. She is of the age when her blessed gift is blooming and ready to make you rich!"

My heart thumped. Harmonia! Harmonia from the Sanctuary for the Children Born of the Comet. Where was she? I stood on tip-toes to see better. Who was about to be sold? I needed to see. I inched my way closer to the Fancy Man and the girl he was selling. I was shoved, elbowed, and pushed back by the crowd of eager bidders, but I persisted and managed to force myself a little way forward.

"Let's start the bidding! Ladies and gentlemen, do not lose this opportunity to purchase your own fortune maker. Just think of the rare, mystical, magical, supernatural, unique, priceless talents and skills she may possess."

Someone pulled my hair and pushed me back. Others shouldered me away.

"Let's hear those bids!"

"Two coppers!"

"Five!"

"Three silvers!"

I was not deterred. I needed to see. On my hands and knees, I crawled forward. All I could see were the man's feet. One was thick and bent. I'd seen the man at the sanctuary!

"Eight silvers!"

Nine! Ten! Twenty!

I inched my way to the front and looked up to see the girl who'd told me she was Liida. Her bright dark eyes filled with tears that streaked her cheeks. She wore the same brown shirt with the yellow and orange comet blazed on the front that the children fenced in the sanctuary wore. A leash held her to a pole. A rag wrapped around her mouth made it impossible for her to talk. I imagined she would have something to say about all this, if she wasn't gagged. When I was in the stockade for the Festival of the Night Sky Dancers, Liida had told me to get away. To climb the stockade if I had to. I remembered clearly what she'd said. *It's the only way to save me and yourself. Run!*

I thought of my mother and Huldor who had been sold this way because they were of the age to bear children when the comet was overhead. I had to save Liida. Still crouched on the ground, I opened my pouch that held the coins from Huldor's inn, and without another thought, I called out, "One gold coin!"

CHAPTER 27

What a stir I caused! Everyone turned to see who bid a gold coin. The other bidders muttered, not able to match my bid. As I stood and brushed grit off my hands, I saw Harmonia standing to one side, smiling because of such a high bid. Her eyes scanned the crowd, searching for the bidder. I ducked behind a portly man.

Finally, the fancy man with the talking tube said, "We have a bid for one gold coin. A good investment for a lifetime of monetary returns, but this girl born of the Comet is still worth much more. Who bids two gold coins?" The crowd muttered, but no one offered a better price.

"Who bids one gold and twenty silvers?"

Silence.

"Come on folks, this is a rare opportunity. Open your pouches! Think of a future full of riches. Who bids one gold and ten silvers?"

Silence.

"One gold and five? One gold, four? Three? Two? One gold and one silver?"

I held my breath.

"Going once for one gold."

I crossed my fingers.

"Going twice for one gold."

I peeked at Liida from around the portly man. She looked frightened.

"Sold! For one gold coin! A bargain!"

As fast as I could, I handed my gold piece to the man, untied Liida, grabbed her hand, and turned to get as far from Harmonia as I possibly could. Before

Liida and I could make our way through the throng of people, I heard cursing and the words, "Stop that thief!" Then a hand clutched my shoulder. "You! What do you think you're doing?" Harmonia snarled.

Liida tore the rag from her mouth and whispered, "Don't stop. We gotta get out of here."

I yanked myself out of Harmonia's grasp. Liida and I jostled our way through the crowd. Harmonia caught up and grabbed me by the hair. Liida shoved her away, freeing me. Together, we elbowed and ducked our way through the crowd. We stumbled and ran.

I heard Harmonia shriek, "Come back here. You can't get away. I'll find you. You'll never be free! You worm bag!" Then she shouted some bad curse words and ended with, "I'll chase you to the ends of this earth if I have to."

Liida and I ran, shoving and rudely forcing our way through the people who still mingled. I held onto Liida's hand and said, "This way!" We dodged people, zigzagged through carts, got chased by angry geese, but finally made our way to the river and hid among the trees.

Out of breath, we rested, but listened and watched for Harmonia. "Why is she so angry?" I asked. "I won your freedom fairly with a coin no one else could match."

"It's not me. It's you. You can't imagine how crazy wild she was when she found out that you'd escaped the sanctuary. Neoma, Ayla, and Elio were supposed to keep an eye on you. They had excuse after excuse for how you got away, and they blamed everyone except Harmonia herself. Neoma even said you made yourself invisible. Elio said you put a paralyzing spell on him when he tried to stop you, and Ayla said you grew wings and flew out of her grasp. Harmonia actually held trials, trying to figure out who helped you. She held people's fingers to flames, trying to get them to admit they helped you. Because of that, there are several very disgruntled villagers."

"But she didn't know I was born under the comet so I was nothing of value to her."

"After the triplets said you could make yourself invisible, fly, and cast paralyzing spells, she was even more sure than ever that you were a prized comet-born. Besides, it didn't matter to her if you were comet-born or not. You got away from her and foiled her plan whatever it was. She went crazy wanting to get her hands on you."

I worried about Harmonia finding us, so I pulled Liida further into the woods. I also worried that Gromske and Ahni would wonder why I hadn't returned, but we'd agreed if we got separated, we'd meet at the canoe, so maybe they wouldn't worry too much. Cautiously, Liida and I made our way closer to the canoe and stayed hidden watching for Harmonia and jumping at every little sound.

The sun was nearly set when Shadow came running. He jumped on me, licked my face and whined. "He's asking where you've been and why you didn't take him." Liida said as he began giving her a good sniffing.

Gromske and Ahni followed soon after. They both smiled when they saw I was safe, but looked puzzled when they saw Liida. Ahni pointed and asked, "Who she?"

I told the story of how I bid a gold coin to free her. Then I handed Gromske the bacon along with the coins I hadn't spent.

"Is she going with us?" he asked nodding to Liida.

"Yes, if she wants to," I said. "She's free to do what she chooses."

"I have no place to go. Until I know what I want to do, can I stay with you?"

Ahni interrupted by saying, "You stay with us in our new *itok*. Plenty room." Then she added, "We sold 'most all the furs. The baker woman came by again. We bought her last two loaves." Ahni held up seven fingers. "Baker woman—she say every this many days, they have market, so we go for more bread an' sell more furs. I think she likes him." She pointed to Gromske. "An' he likes her. Lots an' lots! They smile at each other much, much, much!"

Gromske pulled his hat lower to hide his face. Even so, I could see he blushed because of what Ahni said.

In the morning, we ate bread and cheese before setting off for home. Without the huge pile of furs, there was room for all four of us and Shadow in the canoe. We had two full days of hard paddling against the current ahead of us.

At one of our stops, on a stretch of sand on the river bank, Gromske pulled out a loaf of bread. "Wild rice and cranberries," he said as he divided it among us.

While we ate, I told how I first met Liida and how Harmonia kept the children born of the comet in a stockade.

Liida said she and many others missed their families and were unhappy about not being able to get away. They hated the idea that Harmonia could sell them, especially because she promised the buyers that they'd get rich from the comet-born's gifts. Liida said she'd been brought to the auction block because Harmonia said she'd been causing "disharmony" among the kids in the stockade. "I'll never be able to thank you enough for buying my freedom."

Gromske nodded. He looked at Liida. He looked at me. "Are you comet-born, too?

I nodded.

Liida said, "I knew it. I knew you were one of us as soon as I saw you."

"What about the others?" I asked. "Are they still in the stockade or have they all been sold?"

"Still there," she said, "but terribly unhappy and feeling hopeless. We hardly get anything to eat any more. And as a punishment we have to work the fields even when if it's freezing cold, raining or snowing. Guards always watch us to make sure we don't run away."

"We need to get everyone out," I said.

"It'll be really dangerous. Double dangerous now that you've saved me. You don't know how cruel Harmonia can be. Everyone is afraid of her, and she has spies everywhere. Even so, I agree they need to be saved, but I'm afraid to go back. You should be, too."

"Tumla was good to me. He helped me get away. Made me good boots and gave me food. Maybe he'll help us."

"Maybe, but Harmonia was really hard on him. Tied him to a post and whipped him because she suspected he'd helped you. Made you good boots instead of flimsy shoes. He wouldn't admit it even when he almost fainted with pain."

"Oh! No! I hope he's all right."

"He was still bruised and hurting when I saw him last, but he kept making shoes and boots. You'll need a really good plan before you try to save the others. Failure would just mean more punishments and pain for everyone."

We arrived home late on the second day. It seemed strange to be thinking of Gromske's home as my home. The log and tin hut by Lake Kawishami had been my home with Father. Huldor's inn had been home with her and Ossi. Now Gromske's. I wondered. *How many more homes would I have?*

The first morning we were back, Gromske put the three of us to work. We pulled weeds and turned the soil near his garden spot while he did the hard work of digging to add several rows for more plantings. In no time, Ahni was covered with dust and dripping with perspiration. "Why all this hard work? An' why he make garden big an' bigger?"

"Count," I said. "The garden used to be just for him. Now there are four of us. Remember how we ran out of carrots, beets, and rutabagas during the winter? We only have dried meat, berries, and grains to eat now. We might even run out of those. Then we'll have to dig for roots and hunt for mushrooms until the berries ripen. The cattails won't be in season until the leaves turn colors. We'll have to fish. Maybe even roast the rabbit."

"Noooo! Never eat Bunny! I help work, but me thinks borrowin' much easier," Ahni said with an impish smile.

That evening, Gromske sat by the fire putting the final finishes on a new canoe paddle. "Much easier with two paddling whenever we go to the village," he explained as we ate more of the baker woman's wild rice and cranberry bread with cheese and wild leeks.

"Do you like her?" I asked.

"Who?"

"The baker woman."

"Friendly and makes good bread," Gromske nodded.

I thought of Huldor and Ossi and how their eyes always brightened when they saw each other. "But do you really like her? Wouldn't you like a woman friend and not just be with us?" I pointed to Ahni, Liida, and myself.

In the flickering flames, I couldn't tell if he reddened or not. He tore off another bit of bread, chewed it slowly, then he looked at the small pile of furs he still had in his *itok*. "We plant garden. Then go again. Sell the rest of furs. Buy things we need, but no more comet-born girls," Gromske scratched his beard as he smiled.

Later, I told him I wanted to free everyone who was still held in the stockade held by Harmonia. "We might have to make the garden bigger and make more *itoks*."

Gromske said, "Lots of work, but it'll be worth it to save them. I'll go with you."

I turned to Liida. "Getting everyone out of the stockade might be the easiest part of saving them. After they escape, how are they going to find their homes after all these years? How many will want to stay here with us? If lots do, how are we going to feed them all?"

"Even getting them out won't be easy. I don't think we should even try. I don't ever want to go back there. I'd rather grub in the garden all day."

Disappointed, I said, "You're free now. Don't you want to free the others?"

"Most of them probably don't even want to leave. Many were taken as very young children and have no idea where their homes are. They don't even remember their parents. They've gotten used to the stockade and each other. Why would they want to leave?"

"Maybe they all wouldn't want to, but what about those who do? Those who don't want to be sold?"

"Some are angry because their parents took money from Harmonia. They might not want to go back either."

Ahni piped up, "I know a place. Big enough for many people. Warm all winter. Bubbling mud pots always ready to cook chicken or two." Her shoulders slumped. "No garden. No store house with lots of food. Close to Orphan House. Maybe not such a good idea."

"Well, let's not worry about any of that now. Let's figure out how to get to the stockade without being seen so we can get everyone out and away. Even that seems impossible without a lot of help. Gromske will help, but it would be even better if you came, too."

Liida groaned and said, "I'm not going back. You can't imagine what Harmonia would do to me if she caught me. And you, too. And she's gotten some of the kids to spy for her–to let her know who's discontented enough to escape."

"You can read thoughts. What is Harmonia thinking? Can you figure out if at least some want to escape?"

"Huh! I don't know if I can really read any thoughts. Sometimes I don't even know my own."

"But at the festival of the Night Sky Dancers you said I had to run so I could save myself and you."

"That was no thought reading. I just said anything that came to mind. Did you hear what the others called me? Crazy girl! They were right. I was just a crazy girl pretending I could read thoughts so I could be like everyone else and have a gift from the comet, too."

"You mean . . . ?

"I mean I have no gift. Don't now and probably won't ever. You spent your gold piece for nothing. And you? What's your gift from the comet?"

"I can see and talk to dead people. I've entered portals to be with them. In my dreams, and on the wind, I sometimes hear or see what I think might be warnings. Other times I think my gift is not a gift at all, but a bunch of disastrous happenings that follow me."

Liida shrugged. "Oh, you can enter other realms, see and talk to the spirits! You can do that even when you're in the sleep world? Harmonia told us it's called Cosmic Travel. Harmonia! She was anything but harmonious. She harped about harmony and cosmic balance, but there was no cosmic balance in her village. She'd love you and your Cosmic Travel. Maybe, instead of selling you, she'd keep you. Forever and ever. How'd you like that?"

"I wouldn't," I admitted. "But what can I do to help free the others?"

"I don't know. Everyone who had gifts was just beginning to learn how to use them. Harmonia made us practice so we'd get better. Everyone did, but most hid their gift from her so they wouldn't get sold. I think she wanted to sell me, not only because I caused trouble, but because she knew I was faking mine."

Liida stared into the fire for a while before going on. "Look, there are some kids who can move objects just by using their minds and visualizing it. Antti is getting good at it. Maya can use her mind to raise things off the ground. Their gifts are called telekinesis and levitation."

I tried to image lifting and moving things just by willing it. It seemed impossible, but some might think entering portals of the dead was just as impossible, and I'd done that. "Could they lift other kids over the stockade?" I asked.

"Maybe. It might be the only way to get them out. Lukas makes fire with his fingertips. His gift is *pyro* something or another. He might be able to make a distraction while others escape. Aada can really read people's thoughts. It would be lucky for you if she was reading ours now. She thinks if she tries really hard, she can even send her own thoughts into the heads of others. When she does, they think it's their own thought."

The next morning, I wandered around the cairns, touching each one. Gentle breezes wafted. Mists floated over the stones. The spirits I thought of as my grandparents quivered. I reached out, wanting to touch them. Just then, Liida came running down the path. "Aada is reading my thoughts!" The mists vanished. I felt lost. Anger surged within me. Why did Liida have to interrupt?

"What was it?" I asked impatiently, still feeling anger.

"She asked who bought me, where I was, and if I was all right."

I didn't know if Liida was pretending, or if she'd really received Aada's thoughts.

"Send her something back." I said still feeling irritated.

"I've been trying, but don't know if it's working. I hope she's getting mine because she'll know who wants to escape and can help make a plan."

Liida sat under a tree for a long time holding her head and thinking the thoughts she wanted Aada to intercept. As for myself, I kept thinking the same thoughts, too, but it seemed like a farfetched idea that Liida and Aada could communicate at such a distance. I wasn't confident anything would come of it. And if Liida had pretended before, maybe she was pretending she'd gotten a message from Aada now.

Around our evening fire, Liida and I talked about saving the other comet-borns. Gromske said, "You know, I will help you do what you have to do."

Liida nodded. "You'll need a good plan."

We made a plan. Gromske and I would canoe to the sanctuary. We hoped some of the comet-borns could use their gifts to help with the escape. It wasn't much and it depended on many unknowns, but it was all we had. We settled on going when the moon was but a sliver so we could hide the escape in the darkness of night.

Before we left to free the comet-borns, Gromske wanted to make one more trip to the village where he'd sell the rest of his furs and buy grains and other foods we'd need when there were more people to feed.

"He really REALLY wants to see the baker woman again," Ahni teased.

"I do need to buy many things," Gromske answered with a small smile, "but I won't buy another girl like Luna did. Anyway, enough people are coming to stay. No need to buy any more."

"Buy lots of bread," I said. "And cheese if they have any."

"Yes, yes," Gromske said.

I gave him my pouch of coins. "We're going to need a lot. Maybe you could buy a goat for milk."

"Yeah! Two goats," Ahni said. "I love goats. Never could borrow one. Too noisy."

Gromske asked Liida, "Do you want a goat, too? Should I buy three?" He shook his head as he thought about it. "Three goats in the canoe. They'd eat all the bread and cheese on our way back."

"No goat for me," Liida laughed.

In the end, Ahni decided to go with Gromske to the village. Liida and I stayed behind. We planned to fish, scout for mushrooms, pick fiddle head ferns, and leeks. We were going to need a lot of food.

When Ahni and Gromske returned, Liida and I were on the river bank fishing. What a sight! An over-loaded canoe, paddled by two weary people, and two bleating goats standing on top of some bulging sacks. Even the raven that usually roosted across the river bobbed its head like it was laughing.

Seeing Gromske was an even bigger surprise. He no longer wore his fur and skin clothes. "Village clothes!" Ahni said. "He bought 'em from rag dealer, but they not rags. Real shirt. Real pants! No more half-wild forest animal an' half-man."

Not only that, but he'd stopped at a barber for a shave and haircut. "Guess what else?" Ahni tugged on my hand jumping up and down.

"What else?" I couldn't imagine. I was still in shock seeing the change in Gromske.

"He bought me a dress, too. It be blue. It's in the canoe."

I wanted to tell her that she was rhyming, but didn't want to interrupt.

She whispered to me, "I like him better as woodsy animal man, but baker woman likes him as village man." Like I had, like Ahni had, Gromske had now been transformed, too.

The goats had leaped out onto the shore before the canoe was even pulled all the way to the river bank. Ahni ran right after them trying to grab onto the ropes tied around their necks. They, probably overjoyed to be free of the canoe, pranced, frolicked, and sprang away from all her attempts. I laughed. Ahni laughed even as she made a fruitless dive after one of them and landed face first in a mud puddle. I couldn't help but remember when I'd first seen her, half-naked, chasing a chicken, and sliding on the slippery ground of the bubbling and spewing mud pots.

Gromske, too, stopped unloading the canoe to watch and laugh at Ahni rubbing mud off her face and clothes while the goats hopped and scampered in every direction.

"She could catch them if she quit chasing," Liida said.

When Ahni finally gave up trying to capture the goats, they settled to munch on spring grasses. We carried all the supplies to Gromske's *itok*. Liida poked up the embers in the fire pit, and added more wood while I stirred a bit of flour and bacon in with dandelion greens and flowers. Ahni washed mud off herself in the river, and Gromske handed each of us a loaf of bread.

"How's the baker woman?" I asked with a smile.

Before Gromske could answer, Ahni said, "Wooo-weee! All smiles—both of 'em when they see each other. Me thinks she give bread for not so many coins. Eyes sparklin', twinklin'. Smiles big. Big! BIG! He give her nice mink fur. For no coins. Just more smiles."

Gromske pretended not to hear everything Ahni said, but I noticed he reddened a bit and got busy passing out cheese. "No more talking. Let's eat."

Liida had been right. The goats were used to people, so while we were eating, they wandered in and nosed around everything. Gromske untied the ropes from their necks and said, "They'll need shelter or else they'll be sleeping with us. I better get busy building one."

Ahni's eye lit up. "Wow-ee! Bunny an' me want goat sleepin' with us."

The next day, after helping Gromske make a goat shelter, we started building another *itok*. "How many do you think will come here after we free them all?" I asked Liida. "How many *itoks* are we going to need?"

"I don't know," she answered, as we wove bark in and out of the saplings to enclose the dome. "Maybe only seven or eight will risk escaping. I don't think Sage and Livvi will want to leave, but they can help by using their night and distance vision to spy on Harmonia and others who might try to stop the escape. Lukas, Greta, Aivo, Antti, and Maya will want to escape for sure. Maya and Antti can levitate and move the escapees over the stockade. I don't know who else is brave enough to escape. Besides, the stockade is the only home they can remember."

I figured out how many days it had taken me to travel from the sanctuary to Gromske's. Six. I had followed the river's current. We'd have to paddle against it so I added a day or two. I looked to the moon. It was half way through its waning phase. We had to start the journey soon to get to the sanctuary during the dark of the moon.

Ahni happily agreed to stay with Liida to care for Shadow, the rabbit and the goats. She named the goats Bernie and Patches and was training them to come when she whistled. They already ate out of her hands and followed her everywhere.

"They don't want me to go anywhere without them," she said combing their hair with a spruce bough. "Besides, I've had enough of big bad people lockin' up nice people like me in Orphan Houses, or nice people like Liida in stockades."

Gromske and I set off in the canoe. A raven followed us day by day as we wended our way toward the sanctuary. To pass time, we told each other more about our earlier lives.

Gromske told about good times growing up with the Ice People and finally about leaving on his separation journey. "After I returned to the village and found it burned and everyone gone, I grieved for a long time. I hoped Ossi would return so we could rebuild our village. He never did come, but I stayed with my memories. It was a lonely life. I was glad when you and Ahni came. Now it looks like, there will be more. Maybe it'll become a village again."

Gromske encouraged me to correct him if he didn't pronounce words right or put sentences together the way they should be.

"You already talk good," I praised Gromske.

He frowned. "Not good enough."

I remembered Huldor had been easy to understand even if she just said things like *"Ye be needin' somethin' to eat."* Gromske had a good motivation to learn—the baker woman—so even as he paddled, he asked me questions and I helped him learn more.

One day, Gromske pointed to the raven as it crossed the river ahead of us. "That raven follows us. It has even been roosting in the trees by our *itoks.*"

"I've seen it, but haven't paid attention to it. Just another raven," I said.

"I think not. Maybe it's your spirit raven."

I told Gromske what Ossi had told me about his spirit animal—an owl. It had even fought the pillagers who'd attacked him while he was on his separation journey. It probably saved Ossi's life when it clawed at the eyes of the raiders, blinding some, so they'd fled.

"My spirit animal was a ptarmigan," said Gromske. "It couldn't fight for me. Thankfully when I fell from a ledge and broke my leg, it brought me seeds, berries, leaves, and insects to eat. I didn't starve. Soon I could use my leg again."

"Your broken leg—is that why you didn't return to the village when the three full moons of your separation were over?"

"Ya. At first, I yowled in pain. Yowled like wild cat caught in a trap. I tore strips off my shirt and wrapped stiff branches around my leg to brace it while it healed. I couldn't walk any distance for a long time. The ptarmigan fed me—saved my life."

"If the raven is my spirit animal, how would I know for sure?"

"If it is, you are as fortunate as Ossi was to have the owl. Our ancestors believed that ravens are messengers between the living and the dead. They connect us with the spirit world."

That sparked my imagination. I thought back to all the times I'd seen a raven roosting on branches near me. Was it the same one? Had the raven helped me enter portals of the dead?

"What else do you know about ravens? They seem like such mysterious birds."

"They are. Watch yours closely. Try to understand its messages."

I watched the raven. It flew ahead. Perched. Then flew ahead again. I wished I knew if it was trying to bring me a message. It stayed with us the whole time we paddled toward the sanctuary. My moonstone warmed in my pocket. I was sure I was doing the right thing, but it was the stone telling me, not the raven.

"We're close," I told Gromske. I recognized the way the river bent around an outcropping of stone.

Two days later we hid the canoe and spent the day scouting the woods, skirting the village, finding the best path to the backside of the stockade. We watched the skies, too. The sun shone. No storm in sight, but we cut branches to shelter us from rain if it did come. Then Gromske and I waited for darkness of night.

CHAPTER 29

I closed my eyes and thought about what I needed to do. I hoped Aada was tapping into my thoughts, but didn't really believe she could. I planned to skirt the village shops and houses by going through the woods to get to the backside of the stockade. It was up to those who wanted to escape to get up and over the stockade and into the woods. I'd wait for them there.

Then messages started to flood my head. One message told that several cometborns were ready and waiting to be lifted out. I was to hoot like an owl to let them know when I got there.

I itched with anxiety and hoped the message was real. Gromske stayed with the canoe when I set out to meet the escapees. The night was warm and clear. A sliver of moon shone, but I easily ducked from tree to tree. Twigs snapped under my feet. A small animal scampered across my path. I hoped I didn't encounter a wolf or a bear. Watchful, I didn't see any of Harmonia's watchers lurking in the woods and hoped no one in the village knew what was about to happen.

By the time I got to the back side of the stockade, the sky clouded and the wind picked up. Just as I began to hoot like an owl, the sky rumbled. I whoo-whoo-ed a second time. Lightning zigzagged across the sky. Could anyone hear my whoo-whoos? I tried again. I couldn't see over the stockade. It was so high I didn't believe Antti and Maya could levitate anyone that high and send them over the wall. Nevertheless, I whoo-whoo-ed and watched intently for someone to come flying over.

I waited wringing my hands. My heart pounded with excitement and fear. I heard some twigs snap behind me. I froze hoping it wasn't Harmonia. My hands clenched into fists. I was ready to fight if needed. I finally peered around the tree I was hiding behind. A fox scooted into the woods. Thunder rolled. I shivered.

I hooted again. Nothing happened. Not even thunder and lightning.

I wished I knew what the comet-borns were doing behind the stockade walls.

Thunder rolled. Lightning cracked. Just as a light rain started, I heard a big plop. Running into the woods toward me was a yellow and orange glowing globe with a white swooshing tail.

Someone had escaped!

"Over here!" My heart raced. The plan was working.

"I'm Aada," The girl gasped for breath. "More are ready to come over the wall, too."

"Quick!" I said pulling Aada behind a big tree. I still only half-believed what was really happening. "Spread some dirt to cover the comet on your shirt. It's glowing in the dark. Harmonia will spot the glow and know where you are."

As Aada smeared dirt to cover the glowing comet, she said, "It was really scary flying over the wall! I wish Sage was coming. She can see things in the distance, even right through walls, and could warn us if Harmonia or anyone we didn't want was on their way. Sage saw you coming before you even hooted."

Plop. Plop. Two more glowing comets dropped over the stockade wall and ran to us. "It's Lukas and Aivo," Aada said. "I can hardly believe it. The escape is working! Maya and Antti are levitating us over!" We pulled Lukas and Aivo deeper into the woods and helped them rub dirt on their shirts to cover the shining comets.

"This is Aivo," Aada pointed to a tall and slender boy. "He's a shape shifter."

Aivo greeted me with a nod of his head. "If Harmonia and her crew try to stop us, I'll turn into something they don't want to mess with—like a fierce bear. That'll scare them off." "But I hope I don't have to. I'm not too good at shifting back to myself."

"Just let me know when you want a fire," Lukas offered.

"Not yet. Fire would give us away for sure," Aada said.

Lukas explained, "I can light my fingertips. Fire comes in handy sometimes."

"Oh! No! I think we're in for big trouble," Aada said as thunder rolled, and the rain changed from a drizzle to a soaking downpour. "And not just the rain. Sage just sent me a message. She sees a lot of people gathering in the village. They have things like nets, slings, ropes. They're coming for us! How did they know we were escaping?"

"Someone must have snitched!"

"I bet it was Hermi. I think he can control someone else's thoughts. He's been bragging about it. Worse yet, he practiced on me," Lukas said. "Once he sent me the thought that a swarm of mosquitoes was attacking me. It was so real. They buzzed. I swatted. They buzzed some more. I kept on swatting. Hermi just laughed as I tried to get away. I thought about setting his hair on fire as pay back, but I didn't."

"Or how about Silas?" Aivo said. "He says the rest of us are crazier than bats. That none of us have any special gifts—that the comet thing is just a hoax. Have you noticed how he is always nice to Harmonia? Picks flowers for her? And tattles on others?"

"Well, we can't worry about who told. Good thing we know they're onto us, but we have to hurry up and get far from here."

Plop! Greta landed. "They didn't tell me the landing would be face first!" She laughed as she wiped mud from her face onto her sleeve.

Plop! Plop! Noah was over the wall. He spread mud on his shirt as he said, "Antti and Maya will be next. Maya has been lifting us while Antti actually moves us over the wall. They're getting tired, and they need to get themselves over soon because Harmonia and her cronies are coming already. It's going to be tricky!"

"I can divert the attention of the villagers and maybe slow them down," Lukas almost had to scream to be heard over the heavy downpour. "Wait for the thunder and lightning. That's when I'll do my thing."

"Hurry!" Aada said. "Harmonia is gathering her followers to capture us! Who knows what kind of punishment she has ready? Lukas, throw some fire now!"

"I hope Antti and Maya get here before the next thunder roar," said Lukas, "because that's when I need to start the fires, then we have to get out of here fast!"

I added, "We have to run to the river where Gromske is waiting for us in a canoe.

Aada said, "That's a long way—mostly across open fields. It's going to be dangerous because they could capture us in the field. I'll lead with you, Luna, looking for the safest way."

Plop! Maya was over. Right away, she stood at the wall and concentrated on lifting Antti. We waited. Thunder rolled. Lukas got ready. When a flash of light split the sky and snaked to the earth, Lukas lit his hands, then flung flames to the village center.

In the distance we heard screams. "Sage says some hats and clothes are on fire! A bench is burning, so are some bushes. Flames are even shooting up from a roof top. Everyone is screaming and running around. Oh, no! The rain quenched the flames as soon as they got going. Lukas! Throw more fire! We need to get out of here! Fast!"

"Wait! Antti isn't out yet!"

Maya concentrated on lifting Antii. Nothing happened. She left the shelter of the woods and stood next to the stockade. The rest of us waited, hoping Antti would be over the wall soon.

"Aada, can you contact Antti to see what's holding him up?"

"I've been trying, but either he can't answer or the rain is blocking our thoughts."

"He should be over and out by now! Maya! Help Antti!"

"I'm trying!"

Thunder rolled. An ear-splitting crack of lightning followed. Then silence.

"A-A-IE-EEEE!" Antti flew over the stockade. Arms flaying. Feet kicking. "A-A-EEE?" He landed flat on his face, not on a soft spot, but on a hard rocky area. I ran in the blinding rain to see if he needed help. Noah knelt beside him.

"He's not breathing!" Noah pressed on Antti's chest and began chanting.

Earth bind bones.
Wind bring breath.
Fire spark heart life.
Wind. Fire. Bring breath and heartbeat.
Earth. Twine roots. Bind bones.
Wind. Bring life breath.
Fire. Bring spark to beating heart.
Earth. Wind. Fire. Bring Antti back.

I knelt with Noah and repeated his words, calling for healing and strength. Maya and Aada crept close and hummed as we chanted. Lukas tossed flames into the winds that carried them to the village square.

"It's no use," I heard Lukas mutter. "The rain douses the fire before it even gets started."

"Hurry! They're coming!" Greta cried through sheets of pouring rain.

Antti moaned and tried standing. "Not yet," Noah told him. "Don't move yet."

Noah called as thunder roared, "Everyone! Here! Fast! We need to help Antti." Greta and Aivo ran to us. Noah chanted healing words, lay his ear to Antti's heart and pressed his chest. The rest of us held hands and surrounded them. We all joined Maya and Aada's humming. Soft and soothing. Hushed and gentle. Our humming swelled. Intensified. Urgent. We swayed together.

Noah entreated. He yelled into the storm, "Earth, wind, fire!"

Thunder rolled. Lightning split open the sky, and still we hummed.

A surge. An ebb. Rise and fall. Over and again. Our humming, our swaying, Noah's chanting, the falling rain, the trees bending to the winds—all, I hoped, would heal Antti.

In the distance, above a soft ebb in our humming we heard the clamor, the shouting, the rushing of a horde from the village square. The sounds shocked us from our reverie. I called above the gushing rains, "Now! We have to go now!"

"Maya! Help me with Antti," Lukas cried.

Maya raised Antti from the ground. Aivo and Noah stood him on his feet, one on either side. Antti's knees buckled. "Hold him steady. Off the ground if you have to, but be gentle. He has more than one broken bone. A leg for sure." Noah kept moving his hands from Antti's head to his feet as he went back to quietly chanting.

Aivo hoisted Antti to his shoulders. We ran. Noah chanted. We hummed as we stumbled and ran through rain-sodden grasses. *Hmmm-mmaaiii-yyyaaa-mmmaaiii-laaaa-hmmmm.* Thunder rumbled and bellowed. Rain soaked our clothes, washing the mud that was supposed to hide the luminescent comets on the escapees' shirts. The shining orbs drew Harmonia and village folk directly to us.

Aivo called for Lukas to take his place carrying Antti. In a blink of the eye, Aivo yelled out, "Brother Bear! Come to me! Be one with me!"

A huge bear emerged from the darkness and loped alongside Aivo. Before I had a chance to be frightened, the two became one. I blinked. Had I just seen Aivo and the bear join together? I wiped rain from my eyes. The bear ran with us, looking over his shoulder at the mob brandishing torches, yelling insults, and running in our direction.

I stumbled! Stood! Ran! When I stumbled again, Aivo the bear was there protecting me and nudging me to my feet.

CHAPTER 30

The shouts from behind us grew closer.

"Stop! You'll never get away!"

"The river will swallow you!"

"Come back before it's too late!"

Out of breath, we finally reached the river. Gromske helped Greta and Aada into the canoe. "I'll get them to other side and come back for more."

As Gromske paddled away, Noah called out, "They're almost here! We can't wait for the canoe."

I plowed into the swift waters to cross. The current knocked me off my feet. My soaked clothes and boots pulled me under. I struggled to the surface, gulped for air, but got a mouthful of water instead. Noah thrashed next to me. Holding onto each other and gasping for air, we kicked our way to the far shore.

Maya skipped across not even getting wet as she called out, "Look, if you come one at a time, I can lift you just enough so you can walk above the water." On the other side of the river, we saw a giant net whirl through the rain. It landed ensnaring Lukas and Antti.

Safe on the far side of the river, I shivered and counted. Two were in the canoe with Gromske. Noah, Maya, and I stood on shore. Five had made it across. Three had not. We knew Lukas and Antti had been netted. We worried what would happen to them. Aivo, too. Aivo who'd joined himself with Brother Bear. Where was he?

It was not raining on our side of the river, yet a pouring rain still cascaded down on the river and on the sanctuary side. The river rushed and swirled with high waters. The sky rumbled and lightning cracked the dark open for an instant.

"This isn't right. Someone is making the rain," said Maya.

"I didn't even know that one of us could be a rainmaker? Who is it?"

"The rainmaker must be working with Harmonia!"

"Traitor!"

When lightning flashed again, a mob of yelling town folks surged to the river bank. They carried nets and waved bludgeons. "You'll never get away. You'll drown in this torrent. Come back, and we won't hurt the others."

"What should we do?" I asked. "We can't leave Antti and Lukas behind. And what about Aivo? They might kill the bear not knowing who it is."

Harmonia surged to the front of the crowd. "You'll all drown! Or starve! You'll be outcasts and forever running from me if you escape. Come back now and no harm will come to you." Her sodden hair draped over her face. She tried swishing it out of her eyes, but the rain beat it back. Lightning blazed in the sky. She looked completely stricken by the rain. Her voice faded into the thunder as she yelled, "Get back here. It is my command! Now!"

Maya said, "I'm not going to just stand here listening to her." With that, she started lifting people on the other side off their feet and dropping them back down.

Their threats turned to "Ouch!"

"Stop that!"

"My ankle!"

"That hurts!"

"Lift them higher!" I encouraged. "Look, Harmonia has ducked behind the others. If you can find her, lift her really high. Drop her hard! There she is—cowering in the back!"

"I can't see her. When I find her, I'll give her a good lift."

"On your left." Noah pointed. "See the gate watchman? Beside him is the barber. Harmonia is trying to hide behind him."

"It might be tricky, but I'll give it my best."

We watched Maya clasp both hands together. She wove all but her pointer fingers together. Holding her pointers together, she aimed at what little she could see of Harmonia. We all held our breath. At first nothing happened, but then, "AIY-EEE! HELLLLLL-P ME-E-E!"

Harmonia rose into the torrential rain. A gust of wind blew her sideways. Maya pointed higher and higher. She raised her arms as high as she could. Harmonia was above the tree tops screaming, "HELLLLLP!"

Suddenly, Maya dropped her hands. Harmonia crashed to the ground! The townsfolk forgot about us and surrounded Harmonia. We heard her moan and sob over the wind and rain. "My ankle! My leg!" The town folks swarmed around her and yelled cuss words at us.

"Time for us to get as far as we can before they figure out how to cross the river," said Maya, "and before the rainmaker moves the rain to this side of the river."

Greta and Aada crawled into the canoe with Gromske. Pushing it into the current, he said, "We'll meet you down the river where it's safer."

The rest of us started running even though we were wet, tired, and cold to the bone. I was anxious about Antti, Lukas, and Aivo, hoping they'd get away, too.

Noah must have been thinking the same because he said, "I hope Harmonia treats Antti gently. His leg is giving him enough pain. As for Aivo, he practiced shape shifting, but he always had trouble shifting back. Remember the first time he turned himself into a bear? He couldn't turn back for five days! We used to suggest that he practice by shifting into a smaller animal, but he said his body wouldn't fit with a rabbit or a fox. It had to be big like a bear."

"I remember," Maya gasped, almost out of breath. "We hid him whenever Harmonia came to the sanctuary so she wouldn't find out what he could do. We even told her that he was sick when he didn't go to classes those days."

I had a pain in my side and was breathing heavily. I stumbled and panted, "We need to slow down. I can't keep running this fast. I need a short rest."

Across the river, the rain still swamped the shoreline. Several people bobbed in the river, but made no progress in crossing it. We couldn't see what else was happening through the curtain of the steady downpour. In the distance, we no longer heard any shouting and yelling. More importantly, we hoped Harmonia was too injured from her fall to lead the crowd after us.

As we rested, Maya, Noah, and I came up with a plan. We agreed that we'd worked too hard for us to get caught now. "Luna, you should go first," Noah said. "You know the way. Maya and I will follow."

Maya spoke up, "I'll trail a bit behind you, Noah. If anyone gets dangerously close, I'll lift them up and drop them like I did to Harmonia."

The next day, the sun barely peeped above the horizon when we dragged our-selves into a little clearing where Gromske waited for us. We started a fire the old-fashioned way—without Lukas. Aada and I waded in the shallows digging for clams. Greta and Gromske scouted the woods for mushrooms, buds, any-thing edible. After eating, we found shelter in the trees and slept for a couple of hours.

Gromske woke us when the sun was half-way to the highest point in the sky. Noah and Maya got into the canoe with Gromske. Aada, Greta, and I walked. Greta's gift wasn't one that would help her detect anyone coming for us. She could only recall all her past lives in detail so she walked in the middle. Aada could try to penetrate the thoughts of anyone who might be following so she trailed a bit behind us.

I wove in and out of trees keeping the river in sight. The next day, we found Gromske waiting for us again. Greta and Aada got into the canoe as Maya and Noah got out to walk with me. I told Gromske he didn't have to wait for us any-more. We were far enough away from the sanctuary that we didn't think anyone was following, but we'd be on the look-out.

Noah said, "I hope the rainmaker doesn't know how to stop the rain. What a mess that will make! And it'll keep Harmonia and the others busy a long time. The gardens will be ruined. There's bound to be leaky roofs to fix and mud slides to clear away."

Gromske wasn't so sure he should leave us on our own. "Think about Ahni," I said. "She's probably already worrying about us."

"You're right," Gromske said as he scratched his chin. "I'll head back now, but you be careful. We'll start making another *itok*," he said dipping his paddle and taking the first strokes away from shore.

Poor Gromske. His life had been peaceful before he took me and Ahni in. And now, several others were heading toward his *itok*, too.

We walked three more days keeping a slow but steady pace. We picked ber-ries, dug for roots, and found fresh fiddle head ferns, dandelion greens, winter greens, and spicy leeks to eat. At dusk on the fourth day, Maya sat on the river bank listening and looking for anyone who might be following.

Noah fretted. "I should have stayed back to help free Lukas and Antti from the net. I could have healed Antti's broken bone so he could walk on his own. Even if they get free from the net, how is Antti going to walk? It's not possible."

Noah moaned and held his head in his hands. All together, we sat hushed nibbling on white clover flowers, too tired to talk anymore. In our silence, we each blamed ourselves for leaving Lukas and Antti behind.

After a while I lay down and put my ear to the ground. I broke our silence. "I don't hear footsteps on this side of the river. And listen to the birds. They've been singing like this for a long time. If someone were coming, they'd stop and flit around in the trees. I think we're safe for now."

We slept the whole night, determined that for the next few days we'd walk long and fast until we got to Gromske's camp. We awoke to a dense fog.

"Rats!" Maya said frowning. "The fog'll dampen sounds so we won't know if we're being followed."

Walking fast was not what we did that day. The fog did not lift. Maya stumbled and hurt her ankle. Noah found a downed tree branch that we made into a walking stick for her. The leaves and berries we needed were harder to find in the fog. I tumbled into the river when I bent over to drink. A sharp rock tore a jagged gash in my arm. Noah stopped the bleeding, and I tore a piece of the hem from my skirt to bind it. Stumbles, cuts, twisted ankles, and fog. We made very little progress that day. Even through the fog, I felt comforted when I saw the raven following.

"Maybe we should just rest and wait for the fog to lift," Maya said holding her ankle.

No one argued. We all had sore feet and backs from slipping on mossy banks and stepping over and around large stones and fallen trees. We were lolling around, chewing on tender river birch leaves, when Noah said, "Look over there. Someone's coming. I can barely make out the forms in this fog, but it's more than one or two. We need to hide!"

"How close are they?" I asked.

"I don't know, but they're on the other side of the river. Could be Harmonia and others." I strained my eyes trying to see what he saw through the fog. When I saw what looked like people coming our way on the other side of the river, I hissed, "Hide!"

CHAPTER 31

We scampered behind rocks and trees. I crouched behind a bush hoping its leaves hid me well. My arm throbbed. I pressed on it, but the bleeding started again. A mosquito buzzed close to my face. I swatted at it.

"Hush! They're closer." Maya tore branches from a cedar tree and balanced them on top of her head, camouflaging herself as she peered out from her hiding place behind a large boulder.

We waited in silence—silence except for the mosquito that relentlessly whined and landed on my nose. Its tiny legs tickled. I wiggled my nose. It flew to my brow, then to my ear. I shook my head. It buzzed, circled my face, and landed on my hand. I dared not swat as it sank its thin needle into me.

I thought back to when I'd been a young child. Father and I had often sat outside at our cooking fire. On one warm spring night, he let a mosquito land on his arm. As he told me that mosquitoes had not one needle, but six, he let the mosquito sink its needles into his arm and slowly fill with blood. He said its wings made the whining sound. Then he pointed at the abdomen, thorax, head with the eyes and antennae, and six fragile legs. I imagined all that now as I closed my eyes and tried not to give in to my urge to smash the mosquito right there on my arm. How could such a tiny and fragile creature be so irritating when it whined and buzzed?

"The fog has lifted a little. They're closer now. Everyone, stay where you are and hope they'll pass by without noticing us." Maya whispered. She held cedar boughs in front of her face as she stole a quick look over the rock.

143

"I wish I could make myself invisible," Noah whispered.

I held my breath and watched the mosquito fill with my blood. Father made them seem like fascinating little creatures. I didn't see anything fascinating about the one on my hand.

"It's two people carrying a third on a stretcher."

Noah whispered, "Is it Lukas carrying Antti?"

"It could be. Someone else, too, but it doesn't look like Aivo."

"The fog's lifting! Maybe we can get a good look at who it is."

We waited. Silently hoping.

The fog lifted. The sun shone. Its rays sparkled and danced on the river waters. On the far bank, Lukas set down the makeshift carrier they'd made for Antti. Two saplings poked through the sleeves of two shirts. Antti lay precariously on the uncomfortable bed made from the shirts. We climbed from our hiding places, waving and cheering them.

It was Tumla helping Lukas lug the carrier. He called out a greeting as he helped set Antti down. We bombarded them with questions. "Did Harmonia get hurt when Maya dropped her? What did she do after catching you in the net? Who was helping her? Tumla, how is it you're here? Was it still raining when you left? Have you seen Aivo or the bear? How did you get away?"

A swarm of mosquitoes buzzed around them. Tumla waved his arms like a windmill. Lukas laughed as he swatted at his own arms and face. "Enough questions. Let's keep moving to get away from these blood thirsty creatures. We need to move. Now!"

I remembered my own mosquito. His—no, *her* belly was round with blood. Only female mosquitoes drink blood. I squashed her, leaving a red smear on my hand.

Antti sat up, winced, and swatted at the horde of hungry mosquitoes. "Tonight, we'll tell you everything. Thanks to Jupiter and all the moons above that Tumla is helping us."

I smiled as I dipped my bloody hand into the river. There was Tumla without the silver disc hiding his face. Of course, he had helped. He had helped me escape, too.

The waters were still high, and the current swift, so I called to them, "Gromske's *itok* is on that side, so you're better off staying there. We're the ones who have to look for a safe place to cross."

Later, when we stopped for a rest, Lukas sent fire to us from across the river. The flames landed perfectly on the stack of birch bark and twigs Maya and I had gathered. Then Noah tried healing Maya's ankle and stopping my arm from bleeding. I untied the binding and watched as the bleeding slowly stopped and the gash started to mend itself. Like magic, I thought. Then I wandered into the woods, found an open glade full of strawberries. I picked the berries along with dandelion greens and some wild ginger. Happy that the sun was now shining and to have the others across the river from us, we sprawled on the grass to eat.

While we sat along the banks on either side of the river, Lukas started telling their story. "The rain never quit pouring down. Entangled in the netting, Antti and I tried everything to get out. We'd almost succeeded when Isaac the barrel maker thumped us each on the head. He threatened a harder whack if we didn't stop struggling. Isaac and the barber gathered the edges of the net to make a big sack and dragged us all the way to one of the stone keeps."

I knew what he was talking about. Harmonia had locked me into one of the keeps, too.

Lukas added, "We were, and still are, full of bumps and bruises. Antti was in constant pain when they dragged us. Even though we were wet, cold, muddy, and hungry, there was no way I could set fire to anything in the keep. There was nothing burnable but the ragged blankets we wrapped around ourselves."

"Then Harmonia, the baker, the barber, and the barrel maker. . . ."

Noah interrupted by laughing. "Sounds like a tongue twister. Baker, barber, barrel maker!"

We all laughed. It felt good to be together with the sun shining. We were warm, dry, and fed. And free of Harmonia and fears of being sold. Noah said it again, "The baker, barber, and barrel maker."

We joined in. We sang it again and again. "The baker, barber, and barrel maker."

We laughed so much our cheeks began to hurt. We'd been nervous and on edge for so long, we relaxed and sang it again.

"Tell us what happened when Harmonia, the baker, barber, and barrel maker did whatever it was that you were going to tell us," Maya urged.

"Well, our stomachs howled with hunger, and we shivered so much our teeth chattered, and we were trying to break through the door when we heard someone unbar it. Then, Harmonia, the baker, the barber, and the barrel maker came in carrying a pot of tea and corn bread with honey."

"Let me guess," I said remembering what happened to me. "When you drank the tea, you became sleepy."

"No," said Lukas. "As soon as I touched the pot of tea Harmonia had carried, my hands trembled, and I became suspicious that it'd been tainted. We poured it out as soon as Harmonia, the baker, the barber, and the barrel maker left and barred the door again."

"We ate the corn bread and honey. They were good—not tainted at all," Antti added.

"We huddled, making a plan to pretend to be sleeping when they came again. We'd overcome them and escape. It seemed simple, but Antti had a broken leg, so the only thing he could do would be to swing the tea pot at someone hoping to stun him."

Lukas added, "I wished Noah had been there to mend Antti's leg, but he wasn't, so I just had to keep him comfortable. Then Tumla unbarred the door, crept in, and helped us escape. Thank goodness because I couldn't have carried Antti all this way myself."

Tumla said, "I'm glad I could help. Ever since I helped Luna escape, I've wanted to do more. But now, we need to keep moving in case Harmonia and others are following. By the way, where are we going?"

"We're still about four or five days away, depending how fast we can go," I said. "We're headed for Gromske's place. Greta and Aada went with him in the canoe to make more *itoks* for all of you."

"What's an *itok*?" Antti raised himself up on one elbow.

"It's a domed shelter made of saplings covered with bark and skins."

Lukas said, "Good. Now we'd better get moving before the mosquitoes eat us alive or worse yet, the baker, the barber, and the...."

"Enough! Let's not start that again!"

We all laughed and set out walking once more.

CHAPTER 32

Three days later we came to a bend in the river where the banks had been eaten away and the waters spread wide and shallow. We crossed there so we all could be on the same side to help carry Antti.

That night, Tumla told us, "The triplets can't be trusted. Neoma and Ayla help Harmonia all the time. I think Elio does, too. They're afraid because Harmonia threatens to sell them even though they're not comet-born."

"I figured that out when I was there. Neoma and Ayla were supposed to keep an eye on me at the festival, but thankfully, they were having such a good time drinking ale they forgot about me."

Antti added, "I'm still amazed at Rosa's courage. We figured out that she's the rainmaker. She did what Harmonia told her—made rain to hamper our escape—but she made it rain on the village, too. When Harmonia told her to stop, she said she was trying, but it didn't work. The rain and thunder kept on."

Antti laughed, "Hermonia just might find out that now the comet-borns are learning and getting better using their gifts, they can use them against her!"

"You should have seen and heard how angry Harmonia was!" Tumla added. "She blustered and stormed even though she had a broken ankle and sore ribs from the fall. She drowned out the thunder with her rantings!" I was glad to see Tumla no longer wore the silver disc to hide his face. Better yet, no one seemed to care about all his lumps and scars.

"Rosa said she didn't know how to stop the storm, but I think she purposely didn't so we could get away," Antti said.

"You should have seen the mess the village was in with the river overflowing its banks. Mud everywhere!" Tumla shook his head, then added, "I don't know how they're going to clean everything up. The dining hall was even flooded."

"Rosa's the rainmaker?" Maya asked. "She never let on. Mostly, she just cowered in a corner and cried for her mom and dad. Isn't Harold her brother? He always came to comfort her when he could get to the stockade."

"Story is," Noah said, "Rosa put up such a screaming tantrum when her parents sold her that Harmonia insisted Harold go along to calm her."

We traveled together, taking turns carrying Antti, and telling stories until the day I saw a majestic pine with a huge gash along one side where no branches grew. It was the tree Ahni said lightning had struck and wounded. She had said it was shorter to walk to Gromske's rather than follow the river which bent away before turning back. Tired of walking, tired of foraging for food, and tired of carrying Antti, we were happy to be so close to Gromske's.

I heard Shadow yipping like crazy before I even saw him. A weight dropped from my shoulders as I almost crumbled to the ground. "We're almost there!" I gave a big sigh of relief just as Shadow bounded out of the underbrush. I slumped to my knees and let him jump on me and lick my face as he wiggled and wagged his tail. I wrapped my arms around him and carried him in my arms.

It wasn't long before Gromske, Ahni, Liida, Greta, and Aada followed Shadow. Ahni ran to me, "You gone so long! Never leave me so long again."

I set Shadow down and gave Ahni a big hug. "Have you had fun with Greta, Aada, and Liida?"

"You know what they do? Greta tells strange stories she say she lived in past lives an' Aada reads my mind. I no like that! It good when they help in garden an' build *itoks*. Not so good when Aada tells what I thinkin'."

"What about Liida?" I asked.

"Oh, her. She jist sit around thinkin' or somethin'. She not much fun."

"Do you want to see something fun?" Maya asked.

"Just no be diggin' through my thoughts," Ahni crossed her arms and scowled.

Maya used her gift of levitation to lift a goat off ground. It *maa-ed*. And *maa-ed* some more until she gently put it back on its feet. Ahni grinned and yelped with delight. "That fun. Lift somethin' else."

A moment later, Ahni wished she hadn't said that as Maya levitated her into the air. "Put me down! Lift goat. Not me!"

Gromske smiled—just a little smile, but I wondered how he was feeling about all the shenanigans coming into his life. As though he knew my thoughts, he scratched his head. I think he questioned it all, too.

CHAPTER 33

"Bear!" Ahni yelled pointing.

Aivo lumbered along behind us. "No problem," I told her as she clung to me.

"No problem. You gone gooney or what? There a bear an' he probably hungry 'nough to eat every last itty bitty bit a me!"

"C'mon. I'll introduce you to the bear. His name is Aivo. One of these days, he'll figure out how to shed the bear part and become his real self."

"You name bear? You wackier than I thought. An' what's this 'real self' he changes back into?"

"Aivo, come here. Meet Ahni." I beckoned to him.

"Oh, no! Don't want no meetin' with hungry bear." Ahni ran to Gromske, grabbed on, and hid behind him. "Protect me! Luna crazy an' outta her head!"

We were all still laughing as Aivo romped up to Ahni and held out his paw.

Unbelieving, but curious, Ahni let go of Gromske, shook Aivo's paw, and then spent the rest of the day walking side by side with him, even patting his fur from time to time. When the goats saw the bear, they spooked. They madly leaped and ran in circles. They hurdled the garden fence, sprang into the air for no reason at all, zigzagging all over the place. It wasn't until they'd completely worn themselves out and realized the bear wasn't chasing them, wasn't even paying attention to them, that they settled down.

It was the opposite with Shadow. Shadow was true to his name and tagged along as Aivo the bear wandered through the camp. "Splain this shapeshiftin' thing to me," Ahni said as she watched Shadow follow the bear from *itok* to *itok*.

Greta and Aada took turns telling her how Aivo was born during the passing of the comet in the sky. That was how he was given the gift of being able to invoke an animal and become one with it. Once Aivo figured out the right words to tell the bear to leave him, he would become Aivo the human again.

"C'mon, bear. Shake Aivo outta you." Ahni demanded as she looked for seams or rips she could pull open to find Aivo.

"Burp," she said. "Burp big. Let Aivo out!"

"All good ideas," Lukas told Ahni, but they won't work. I think Aivo just needs to find the right words to undo his invocation of the bear to be one with him."

Just then Noah came back into the camp. "I've found the perfect spot for healing Antti's broken leg. I'll need some help getting him down by the river."

We all traipsed along so we could see what Noah was going to do. He'd dug a depression along the shore. He pointed to a bend in the river. "I found lots of clay over there. You can help by digging in the water and bringing handfuls over here. Clay is what I need from the earth to bind bones."

Gromske and Tumla sat on a mossy log and watched as we all tossed our boots and shoes aside and started digging in the shallow water. We pulled globs of gray stuff and patted it into sloppy masses. We heaped it into the depression as Lukas scooped handfuls of water in and mixed it into a muddy slurry. When it was deep enough, Lukas and Noah carried Antti and laid him in the pool of mushy sloppiness.

Earth, bind bones.
Earth, give strength.
Earth, make whole.
Earth, mend breaks.
Earth, bind bones.

Maya started to hum. We joined her as Noah chanted and spread clay and mud over Antti's leg. Our humming swelled and receded. Over and over again. Aivo the bear sat nearby scratching his ears and watching Noah. The air crackled with electricity. The river hummed and rippled with us. Leaves rustled in the breeze.

Hummmmm
Baiiiii
Aiiiii

Maiiiii
Lahhhhh
Hummmmm

Chanting, humming, crackling, rippling, rustling. Over and over again. Finally, Noah stopped chanting. His silence was only broken by the whirling river and fluttering leaves.

Noah held a hand out to Antti. We watched—holding our breath. Antti stood, putting all his weight on the leg that hadn't been broken. Slowly, he lowered the other one to the ground. Tentatively, cautiously, gingerly. He put a little weight on it. Then more. He took one step. Two. Three. A grin broke across his face. Noah laughed in relief.

"You did it! You mended Antti's leg!" We all jumped with joy.

"I didn't do it alone. You all helped, and earth bound the break. My first broken bone—fixed! Now I know what to do!" Noah held his face with his muddy hands as he beamed with happiness.

"Now," Antti said as he gingerly walked over to Aivo the bear, "If we could just figure out the words to release Aivo from Brother Bear."

"What words he say to get himself into bear body?" Ahni asked. "Maybe just have to say them backwards, now."

I remembered the words so I told everyone, "He said, 'Brother Bear, Come to me. Be one with me.'"

As one, Antti, Maya, Liida, Aada, and I all chanted, "Me with one be. Me to come. Bear Brother."

Nothing happened. We tried again. Nothing. Aivo was still the bear, scratching his ear with a hind paw.

CHAPTER 34

A crescent moon floated above us as we sat outside circling a fire while eating fresh fish with mushrooms and berries. I looked around. Not counting Gromske, Ahni, and myself, there were nine more people. Gromske's *itok* was behind us. Ahni, Liida, and I would still sleep in one. Maya, Greta, and Aada moved into the one we'd made before we left for the sanctuary. The boys moved into the two that had just been built and started building another one. Tumla moved in with Gromske. Soon there would be six *itoks* surrounding the fire circle. It was beginning to look like a little village.

I sighed. I was glad I'd been able to save so many comet-borns from Harmonia. I wasn't glad there was so much noise with everyone talking and making plans. Evenings had always been quiet as Gromske, Ahni and I watched the stars overhead. Now there was laughter, talking, and the scrambling for the last berries to pop into their mouths making it impossible to hear the gentle sounds around us. I missed hearing birds twitter as they settled for the night. As hard as I listened, I couldn't hear the soft hoo-hoos of owls or the snapping of branches as deer came to drink at the river's edge in the twilight. I watched the raven that I now thought of as *my* raven, move to a higher branch. I silently wished for quiet and the sounds of nature as dusk drew its curtains to darken the sky.

I'd always wondered what it would be like to have a friend. A friend to walk with at festivals. A friend to talk to. To giggle with. Pick berries with. Maybe I could become friends with one of the girls. We were all of the same age and all born under the blazing comet. I watched as Aada pulled Liida's hair back and wrapped a vine around it. Greta laughed as she plucked dandelions and wove them into a crown that she put on Liida's head.

"I'm so glad you're here," Liida told Maya, Greta, and Aada as they all sat closer to the fire. They'd lived together for a long time so knew each other well. They all laughed when one of the goats grabbed the dandelion crown off Liida's head and started munching on it.

"Show that goat who's boss!" Aada said to Maya. Maya stood, wove her fingers together, and without touching it, lifted the frisky goat off its feet. It dropped the dandelions as it dangled about a foot in the air.

"Baa-aaa!"

Ahni danced around the goat. "Lift it higher! Naughty goat!"

"Enough silliness for now," Maya said as she gently lowered the goat to the ground. It ran off as fast as it could, leaving the half-eaten dandelion crown on the ground.

I should have been laughing and enjoying what the other comet-borns were doing, but I wasn't. I tried laughing when the goat swayed in the air, but the sound strangled in my throat. They spent the rest of the evening having fun practicing and showing off their gifts from the comet. I couldn't join in. My gift wasn't fun like theirs. I felt so uncomfortable that I wasn't sure I even wanted to be part of their playfulness. I felt tongue-tied and didn't know what to say to anyone so I finally got up and walked to the cairns.

"Grandma? Grandpa?" I asked, hoping to see the mist and hazes waft and swirl around the stacked stones. Mist diffused a soft light, but none took shape. Tears came unbidden. I'd traveled far to be with my people. I'd wished and hoped to find a village of the Ice People, but all I'd found were cold stone cairns marking their graves.

What was I to do now? I had wanted to save the comet-borns. I'd succeeded, and I was glad they wouldn't be sold and used to enrich others. Now what? Would we be all together for the rest of the summer? Through the falling leaf time? The winter? And beyond? What did I want? I listened to all the chatter and laughing. I'd never been with others my age. I didn't even know how to talk to them. I wasn't sure that would ever change.

I imagined my twin sister Selene who was traveling with Lady Magda pretending to tell fortunes. She was also comet-born. Would she ever find the gift given her or would it be lost when she pretended to be someone she wasn't? Magda was teaching her to imitate a fortune teller. Father would have called them frauds and phonies even though he was the same when he put on his robe and turban and pretended to be the fortune teller, the All-Seeing Eye.

And then there was Liida who wasn't sure if she could really read thoughts or not. What was a gift of the comet? Something real? Imagined? Magical? What about Noah who'd just mended a broken leg? Or Aivo who was still a bear? I was more confused than ever. I wasn't even sure my gift was real. Maybe everyone could enter portals of the dead as I had, or maybe I'd just dreamed it all.

Laughter interrupted my thoughts. I clenched my fists. I wanted to be by myself, to think. To ask Grandma and Grandpa what I should do. I felt the cold earth beneath me and shivered. The haze lifted and swirled away. The gentle light of evening faded.

I sat there for a long time listening for quiet breezes, listening for night songs, but the chatter and laughter overran my ears and thoughts. Maybe if I returned, I would find something to chatter and laugh about, too, so I headed back to the evening fire.

"And then Harmonia's henchmen dragged us in the net. Antti was in horrible pain."

Tumla picked up the story from there. "You can't imagine how angry I got when I saw Antti and Lukas snared, then dragged toward our village in the pouring rain. Antti cried out in pain. I knew I had to help. My pleas to Jupiter were answered when the drenching rain came down so hard everyone had to run for cover. That's when I decided I'd free Antti and Lukas no matter the danger to myself."

He stopped for a moment to wipe his brow. "I kept imploring all the moons of Jupiter. Well, after I unlocked Lukas and Antti from the keep, I made the decision right then and there that I'd escape, too, and travel with them. Lukas needed help carrying Antti. Besides, I was done with Harmonia ordering me around and selling the comet-borns."

The next evening, Gromske visited the cairns with me. He stopped at every one and spoke to the spirits whose bodies lay beneath the stones. Spirits of people who'd been part of his everyday life. They'd fished, hunted, eaten, and told stories together. Soft mists followed us, warmed us. I wanted to feel one with my people, my ancients, as Gromske called them. I wanted to enter the portal to my grand-parents again, but the earth beneath me didn't shudder.

Disappointed, I asked, "Where did our people come from? Or were the Ice People always here?" Harmonia had claimed to be from the Pleaides. Father said Mother had also, but Gromske, Ossi, and she actually were from the burned-out village where we stood at that moment. "Did the Ice People come from another planet or even a different galaxy?"

"When we return to the fire circle, I'll tell our story," Gromske held his hand on the stones marking his family. My heart felt heavy. My grandparents didn't appear to me anymore, but I looked forward to hearing Gromske's story about our people.

Later, as we all sat around our evening fire, Gromske tapped a small drum. A soft hollow thrum, thrum, reverberated into the night air as he tapped. He began, "Luna wants to know where her people came from, so I will tell the story." He cleared his throat, put the drum down and started. "Long ago. Five or six gen-erations ago. I don't remember. Etta Carina. . . ." He stopped and looked at me. "Your mother would have remembered. She was a better listener and had a bet-ter memory. She, my sister Oriina, Ossi and I sat around a campfire, just like we all do now, while our grandparents told the story of our people."

Lukas put more wood on the fire and lit curls of birch bark by sending flames from his fingertips.

"Our long-ago people didn't always live here. They were from an ice-covered land far from here. One day, the very earth they stood on shook and trembled. Steam rose from a nearby mountain. The quaking and steam lasted for days. Frightened, our ancestors huddled, arguing about what to do until an old woman named Agga, who was known for her wisdom, stood on the talking stool and said, 'We have angered the mountain gods. They huff and puff. Soon, the quak-ing and steaming will turn to rumbling, growling, and roaring. Rocks, dust, and a scorching river of bile will cover the land. The mountain will erupt smother-ing the life out of us and destroying all. We must leave before that happens. It is our punishment for not following the good ways. We will either perish here, or be doomed to wander for generations without a land of our own to call home. Let us leave this place now. We'll go before the destruction and annihilation of us all fulfills the prophecy and appeases the mountain gods.'"

I shivered at the image of the destruction as Gromske continued the story of his and my people.

"Those long-ago people who lived in a world of ice, bundled what they could as the mountain rumbled and spewed steam and ash. They packed their dried fish. They wrapped babies and young ones onto their backs. They carried the old and lame on make-shift chairs and beds. They set out wearing long skis strapped to their feet. They skied over crusty snow. They sank into soft snow. They skied in the shadows of towering ice bluffs. They kept clear of huge gaps in the ice where deep blue abysses beckoned the unwary. They pushed on as the mountain rumbled behind them. They headed into the unknown facing the great star of the north, letting it guide them away from the stormy gods."

More shivers ran up my back. I imagined every step my ancestors took away from their home. I saw the angry mountain. I felt the quaking of the earth. I envisioned them carrying the burden of their fears. I knew how they felt as they fled from their home and ventured into the unknown. It was what I'd done after Father sold me to the farmer and abandoned me. I, too, had fled into the unknown, looking for my mother's people. For safety and family.

Shadow whined, so I pulled him onto my lap. Ahni was fast asleep leaning against Gromske as he gently thumbed the drum and continued the story of the ancients.

"When they tired, they rested and slept. When they hungered, they ate. The rumbling softened in the distance. They looked back to where their home had been. Clouds of frosty ash-gray smoke rose from the mountain. 'Further. We must go further.' Old Agga demanded as she pulled her furs closer around her bony body.

"They watched fire burst toward the skies and flaming bile spew over their lands. They watched as the whole side of the mountain tumbled into the sea. Finally, after three full moons, the great star of the north was no longer in front guiding them, but now shone behind them."

"How is that possible?" Greta asked.

"Didn't you pay attention in Harmonia's classes? Don't you remember when she brought a ball and told us it was the very planet we lived on?" Lukas asked. "We all laughed and she got really mad. Made us all go out into the cold without our coats."

Lukas picked up the ball he and Liida had made of mosses bound together by twine that they'd played catch with earlier in the day. "Here," he tossed it to Noah. "You can explain better than I can."

Noah pointed to the top. "The top of our earth," he said. "It's called the North Pole. If you're here," he said pointing to a spot on the side of the ball, "and walk toward the North Pole, you'll always have the north star—Polaris—in front of you. When you reach the pole and continue going, you'd be walking south and Polaris will be behind you." While he talked, he walked his fingers up to the top of the ball, and then down.

"Oh, I understand now," Greta said.

I was glad she'd asked. Now, I knew, too.

"The people still walked on ice-covered lands and avoided great expanses of open water. Everything looked white. Some became blinded by the whiteness all around. White snow and white frost for as far as they could see. Animals were even white. The bear. The fox. The hare. The owl."

Lukas put more wood on the fires. Sparks flew to the sky.

Gromske continued, "Finally, they'd traveled so far, they no longer walked on ice and snow, but on soft mosses. They walked until they came to a land where dwarfed and spindly trees took root. Bushes of berries grew in abundance, and the sun shone longer each day."

Night had fallen. Ahni drooled a bit as she slept leaning against Gromske, and Shadow snored softly in my lap.

"They walked still further until they came to here. Here, where a river runs nearby. Here, where deer, bear, fox, hare, otters, fish, and so many other animals and birds live. Here, where the birch, cedar, willow, and pine are straight and tall. If the land was good for so many birds and animals, it would be good for people, too. The air, waters, open fields, and forests were full of food. They would have a good life here. No mountain rumbled and threatened to spew molten lava. They'd left the angry mountain gods behind."

Gromske's story filled me with awe and pride. My ancestors found this land filled with everything they needed for a good life. I wanted to know more so I asked, "Did any of our ancestors branch off from the others? Go in another direction? Maybe start a village somewhere else?"

"That is a question I have often wondered about, but never found the answer to."

The idea that there were Ice People somewhere else intrigued me and made me more curious. "Ossi didn't know who the marauders were who destroyed this village. Do you think it was possible that those who destroyed this village were actually Ice People, too?"

Gromske looked at me for a long time before answering. "I hope not. The marauders could have been a roving band of no-gooders from anywhere. I hope they weren't Ice People. If they were, I hope we never meet them again."

CHAPTER 35

The next morning, I was startled to see a stranger sitting by the morning fire. I was about to ask his name and where he'd come from when Liida said, "Oh! Ho! Aivo, you finally figured out how to shed the bear! How did you do it?"

Aivo, the shapeshifter, was tall, slender, with broad shoulders. I'd only seen him before in the dark on a rainy night. I liked him immediately. When he smiled, his eyes sparkled. "Thank you for risking everything to save us, Luna." He gave a small bow, and I liked him even more.

Of course, Aivo was the center of attention as we built up the morning fire. "You eat grubs an' worms an' stuff?" Ahni asked holding her belly and making a face. "I saw you scratch your ear with your back paw. You still do that?"

I laughed at Ahni's questions, but was glad she was asking them. I'd wondered the same things—not the part about scratching his ear, but what he'd eaten as a bear.

"Are you going to shift into a bear again, any time soon?"

Aivo's eyes crinkled as he smiled and said, "Not any time soon, but I definitely need to practice until I get the hang of this whole shapeshifting thing."

After we ate, Gromske announced he'd be going to the village—to get bread and cheese. "Does anyone want to go with me? Four can fit in the canoe."

Tumla, Lukas and Antti wanted to go. Liida and Aada told Tumla to look for a map so they could find out how to get home to their parents. After they paddled away, we divided into work groups. Liida and Greta tended to the gardens.

Ahni and I headed to the woods and sunny glades to search for berries and mushrooms. Aivo and Aada gathered fire wood.

In the late afternoon, we sat on the shore weaving fishing nets and devising forked branches for fishing in shallow water. I was deep in thought remembering the pelicans that Father and I had watched as they flapped their wings to drive fish into shallow water where they scooped them up in their huge bills. I wondered if we could find a way to do something like that.

Aada and Liida were on the rocky bank near me. I listened as they talked about returning home to find their parents. They'd been taken by Harmonia when they were nine or ten years old. Harmonia and two men had come to their homes. They'd been told that children born of the comet were special. She promised to bring the children to a wonderful school where they would eat delicious meals three times a day. They would live in a secluded village in the great outdoors, learn trades, get an education, and return home when they were ready. Their parents had been very poor, struggling to feed many children so were eager to let their comet-born children go to such a perfect place with so many promises.

They had homes to go back to. I was glad for them. I wondered who else wanted to leave. I thought of the moss-covered log and tin hut Father and I had lived in. It had been my home. When I'd fled, I'd left the door wide open and told the woodland creatures that it was theirs. They could weave webs, bring in twigs to make nests, or use my corn shuck bed to make their own home. It would no longer be mine.

Ahni had lived among the bubbling mud pots after she'd fled her cruel father. Now she settled into our *itok* and followed Gromske around just as Shadow and the raven followed me. Would she ever want to go elsewhere? A gentle breeze ruffled the leaves of a river birch. I thought of Huldor's inn. I had felt the song of the wind in my heart while there with her and Ossi. They had become my family and gave me a good place to live, but then the inn burned. It occurred to me that even though I'd found this place where my mother and her family had lived, I didn't feel it was my home.

My heart sank. I'd lost so much. Wanting to be alone, I walked to the cairns hoping to see my grandparents emerge from the mists. The cairns were cold as I walked among them. No mists wavered before my eyes. No gentle hummings came to my ears. At the cairn where I'd found the spirit of my grandparents, only a chill greeted me. Why? Had the boisterous comet-borns chased them away, or had they been waiting for their village to come alive again with laughter and story-telling around the evening camp fires so they could be free to leave? I didn't know.

I did know I missed the warmth and comfort of the mists so much that I felt numb. My knees weakened. My heart was heavy. I wanted to collapse and cry out in despair.

CHAPTER 36

Ahni spent hours on the river bank pretending to fish, but I was sure it was because she missed Gromske so much she watched for him to return. I missed him, too. The comet-borns laughed as they played a game of tag. I thought I should join them, but they hadn't invited me, so I just sat and watched the river waters slide by. I thought about how excited Gromske had seemed as he'd readied the canoe to go to the village. Ahni would have said, "Wowsee. He eager to see the baker woman again." More laughter rang out as the goats hopped around like they wanted to play tag, too. The quiet was gone. I missed it.

"Gromske and the others won't be back for six or even seven days," I'd told Ahni the day they left.

"Why so long?" she asked.

"You know it takes two days to get there and more than two to come back against the current. And then they need a day or two in between to rest and to buy the things they need."

"An' smile at baker woman. He do lottsa that. An' buying arm loads of her bread."

"Do you like her?" I asked.

"Maybe a little. When she give me lump a sugar. Or little berry tart. But Gromske almost forget I be there when he be lookin' an' smilin' at her. I worry. Good people sometimes turn bad."

"I think you're a little jealous of the attention he gives her."

Ahni's shoulders slumped when she said, "Bad things happen when man smile at woman an' she smile back."

I remembered all the good things that happened when Ossi and Huldor smiled at each other, but I suspected there was a different story behind what Ahni said. Maybe it was about her mam, so I asked, "What do you mean?"

Ahni crossed her arms and gave me her old Lamb-i-kins scowl. I didn't dare laugh. Little by little, she was becoming *civilized* as Father would have said, but I was glad she still had some of her old spunk. She'd had to be tough and bold to survive on her own. I hoped she'd never need to be on her own again. Or that I never would be on my own again, either.

Still with her arms crossed, Ahni scowled and said, "No talk about bad people."

When Gromske finally pulled the canoe onto the shore, Ahni greeted him. "What took you so long? You been gone eight days. Eight days!" She held up eight fingers. "You shoulda been back yesterday or day before."

Gromske picked her up and swung her in a circle until she forgot her grumpiness and laughed with delight.

Tumla was not with them. "Where is he?" Aada asked.

"He had some good luck. Miss Ruth told him the only boot maker in the village was very old, had stiff hands, and could hardly make boots or take care of himself anymore. He went to see the boot maker and made a deal with him. He's going to live there, take care of the man—Thomas—and help cobble boots. Thomas said if it all worked out well, when he died, his shop would be Tumla's."

"Who's this Mizzruth you be talkin' about?" Ahni asked, tugging on Gromske's arm.

Gromske's eye twinkled. "Miss Ruth is the baker woman. Wait until you taste the rye and molasses breads she sent along. And she sent something special for you, Ahni."

I watched Ahni as she fought to cloud her face while, at the same time, a smile was trying to burst forth. She was deciding if she should be angry that the baker woman now had a name or if she should be happy she'd sent something special.

Antti handed a map to Liida. Lukas pointed to it and patted his own chest saying, "I'm the one who got the map, but Antii was afraid I'd set it on fire, so he took it from me."

"Actually," Antti said, "Tumla is the one who got the map for us. The Widow Smythe lives next door to the boot maker. She has two curly-haired young ones.

Can't tell 'em apart except one's a boy and the other's a girl. Well, Widow Smythe has lots of maps. Her husband, long dead, was a surveyor, so, in exchange for making a pair of boots for her son Walfred, she gave Tumla a map."

"Wowee! You talk a lot," Ahni said to Antti. She was wiggling and shuffling her feet, waiting for Gromske to give her that *something special* from Mizzruth.

"I can talk some more, and move you way over there, if you want," Antti teased, patting Ahni on the head.

"Noooooo! It time to eat bread. Molasses an' rye. I hope bread good. And time to find out what Mizzruth sent me."

Gromske handed Ahni a wrapped bundle. She ripped it open, licked the top of the roll and said, "Mmmmmm. Good. What is it?"

"Sugar and cinnamon," Gromske said. "Cinnamon is really hard to get, so you must be very special."

"Yummmmm." She licked her fingers and took a bite. "I so glad when Mizzruth thinks I'm special. I like her, but hope she never turn mean."

Gromske handed me a sugar and cinnamon roll. "Miss Ruth thinks you're special, too."

I tore my sweet cinnamon roll and gave half to Liida. We ate it slowly, savoring each mouthful. After eating, Liida spread the map on the ground, and we gathered around. I found the river I'd paddled for so many days. It had a name—Big Fork River. I traced it with my finger to the huge lake marked Kawishami where I'd lived in a moss-covered log and tin hut with Father.

Aada jumped and clapped when she discovered her village wasn't far away. "Look, I can go this way. It's longer, but it passes through several settlements so I can rest and get food." She pointed to the route.

"If I had a canoe," Aada added, "I could paddle to the village down the way, and then take a tributary called Cedar Swamp Creek. It goes right by my farm. It's at least a week away by water, but if I have to take the walking route, it'll be more."

Gromske scratched his head and said, "Maybe we can build you a small raft. It'll work well on this river, but maybe not so well on a creek named Cedar Swamp."

"That'd be better than nothing," Aada said. "I'll be thankful to even get halfway on the river."

Liida was near tears. Her voice broke as she added, "I don't even know what direction to look. I can't find my village on the map. Muskeg. I can't even find Balsam Lake or Deer River. They'd lead to Muskeg. Tell me if you see any of those."

CHAPTER 37

I stood among the cairns. No mists swirled. No voices came to me. I found no comfort in trying to imagine my grandparents and their life in the village before it'd burned. It'd been days since they'd enveloped me in their warm haze. No softness brushed my cheeks. Tears filled my eyes.

The comet-borns were busy. Aada was getting ready to leave the next day. The raft Gromske and Aivo were building for her was almost done.

Lukas and Antti sat on the river bank. They planned to travel from festival to festival. Lukas practiced setting his fingers on fire while Antti "magically" moved objects around. Together they were sure they'd draw big crowds. "Our pockets will jingle with coins." They laughed looking forward to new adventures. "We'll return before the winter snows come," they promised. "We won't be here to tend the gardens so we'll use our coins to buy sacks of beans, dried corn, and jugs of molasses to help out here."

"While you're at festivals," I told them, "Look for two fortune tellers, my twin sister Selene and Lady Magda."

"We can do that. If Selene looks like you, we'll find them for sure."

Everything changed as fast as a whirlwind, but not all was happiness. Liida tore up the map when she couldn't find Muskeg. She wanted to go home, but didn't know where to go.

Lukas and Antti invited her to travel with them. They said she could surprise people by reading their thoughts. Or she could pretend to tell fortunes. My heart

171

flipped when she agreed. Would she tell real fortunes or make them up like Father, Selene, and Magda did?

At first, I was glad Aivo, Greta, Maya, and Noah said they'd stay. Then I noticed that they often gathered with their heads close together, whispering. They never invited me. I wondered what they were planning. I didn't feel a part of anything they did.

Finally, Aivo told me. "We want to free the rest of the comet-borns. We're not sure if they'll want to come here or not, but if they do, we'll have more people to tend the gardens and make them bigger. Even though it's too late to plant anything, we'll fish, hunt, and do our best to have enough food for everyone all winter. And don't worry, we're going to build—not *itoks*—but real houses. With hard work, this will soon be a real village with houses and gardens."

I felt torn. What about me? Their plans didn't seem to include me. They were so busy figuring out what they were going to do, they hardly paid me any attention. Ahni followed Gromske everywhere. She even took big steps to follow exactly in his footsteps. She constantly begged to go to the village so she could thank Mizzruth for the sugar and cinnamon roll. And maybe get some more. I was among so many, yet I was alone.

What should I do? Stay to build log houses? Garden? Hunt? Fish? Help free the rest of the comet-borns? Settle where the Ice People had settled? I walked to the cairns. I desperately wanted answers. I squeezed my eyes shut, willing a portal to open. I wanted the ground to shake; my vision to blur. I wanted all the things to happen when portals opened. I wished and wished. I opened my eyes. No portal opened. What good was my gift if I couldn't call to the dead when I wanted? When I needed to?

I couldn't use my gift to make a living. Not even to entertain. No one would pay to see me enter a portal at a festival. I couldn't lift and move logs to build houses. I couldn't read thoughts or make potions. I couldn't do anything good or useful.

I was slumped and feeling bad for myself when my raven fluttered by and perched on a branch overhead. If the raven was my spirit animal, it should connect me with my ancestors. But they no longer came to me in the cairns. How could I connect with them and find answers to my questions? I wanted help to decide what I should do. Maya and Greta had gone berry picking. They didn't invite me. Shadow followed Aivo and Noah as they cut trees for the logs they'd need for *real* houses. They didn't think the *itoks* were good enough.

Dismayed, I walked to the river's edge and sat in my canoe. My raven followed, then perched on a low branch of the willow that bent over the river. I watched as it preened its feathers. The river burbled and gently splashed against the rocks. What should I do? Stay? Leave? The bird preened some more. Angry that it gave me no answers, I threw a rock at it. It hopped to a higher branch.

Laughter arose from the freed comet-borns. Alone and feeling dejected, I shaded my eyes from the sun reflecting off the river waters. A gentle breeze rippled the waters. My canoe rocked gently, its bow on the sandy shore and the stern in the water. I ran my fingers over the ribs of the canoe. It had brought me so far since the day the farmer had lunged at me, and I'd pushed him away with the paddle. I'd been so angry. My mouth filled with bile. The sourness is what I felt now. My whole journey in the canoe had been to find home—somewhere I could find the happy song of the wind in my heart. I had found that with Ossi and Huldor, but the cruel fire had taken it all away. I swallowed hard trying to clear the bile and anger. More laughter rang out from by the garden. Two little goats pranced by. I felt worse than I ever had. I threw another rock at the raven. It gronked and flew away. Some spirit animal!

The next day when Liida was leaving with Lukas and Antti, she turned to me and said, "Thank you for saving me. I'm free now. No more Harmonia! Maybe I'll even find a home for myself at one of the festivals." She stopped and looked at me intently before saying, "Now that you've saved me, you still need to find your own way and do what you're best at." She paused, then added, "You can only do that if you stay away from the crow."

What did she mean? She was warning me. I needed to find my own way? What was I best doing? I couldn't think of anything. And I should stay away from the crow? Images of the dream I'd had when Harmonia locked me in the stone keep flooded back to me. A river. A farmer. A bee filling my ears with honey. And a crow insistently pecking and rasping, *"Caw! Caw! What's your name? Caw! Caw! What's your name?"* Goosebumps stood out on my arms. My blood rushed, pounding in my ears. A crow I had to beware of? Harmonia! How could she still be a danger to me?

Gromske and Ahni helped Aada load her raft with a sack of food and sleeping mat. As she began poling herself down the river, Noah, Aivo, Greta, Maya, and I waved farewell to her from the bank for as long as we could see her. I almost envied her floating down the river as I had often done in my canoe. The one difference, she knew where she was going. Home.

I wanted a home, too, but where? And with whom? Tears of profound pain brought a thorough numbness to me. Gromske took my hand and led me to a log. We sat in silence as I dried my tears on the hem of my dress.

"Why the tears?" he asked.

"So many changes," I began. "I'm glad I helped free some comet-borns, but now they're all busy with their plans. You've found friends in the village. I'm not sure where I belong and what I should do. I can't do anything helpful."

"I can't make your decisions for you. You're old enough now to decide those things for yourself. I will always help you however I can, but the choices will be yours." Gromske paused and reached to hold my hand. "I want to tell you something I've wanted to tell you since the first day you came here."

"Your mother," he started in a soft voice, "Etta Carina sang as beautifully as any bird. She had the best memory and told wonderful stories. She wove as skillfully as any spider. Even with her lame leg, she could swim like an otter. She made the best fried cakes. I never told her, but I loved her. I even loved how she teased me when she hit the mark on a target that I'd missed. Her eyes sparkled. Her smile was a little crooked so one cheek dimpled. I hoped she liked me, even though I was clumsy and made too much noise to be a good hunter."

Gromske's voice cracked. He took hold of my other hand, too, and said, "I want you to know that I hoped to ask your mother to stand with me in the uniting ceremony, at the same time Ossi and my sister did."

My tears swelled. My mother was alive once again in Gromske's eyes and voice. She had been loved and wanted. He'd loved her, not like Father had, because she was of the age to birth a child when the comet passed overhead, but for herself. He'd loved her for how she made him feel when he saw her smile and her eyes sparkle. I stroked the dress I wore. It was her dress. I remembered how it had smelled of cedar and basil and chamomile when I'd first put it on. The color had been the beautiful green of a Luna moth. Now the dress, after many washings, had faded to the gentle sheen of the moon's soft glow.

CHAPTER 38

In the following days, we worked hard hoeing and weeding the gardens in the coolness of the mornings. We rested when the sun was high in the sky, and fished when it lowered behind the trees. Around our evening fires—besides swatting mosquitoes—Noah, Aivo, and Maya refined their plans to return to the Sanctuary to free those left behind.

"It'll be more difficult this time," I said. "Aada's not here to transfer thoughts to someone in the sanctuary so they'll be ready. Maya can still levitate and move everyone over the fence and stockade, but it will be harder without Antti helping. And what about those who don't want to leave?"

"We'll figure something out. Besides, last time, when Liida and Aada were transferring thoughts, someone must have intercepted them and told Harmonia so she knew you were coming. We don't want that happening again. Surprise will be on our side."

I did not want to take part in the rescue. Liida's warning about the crow scared me about Harmonia. I wanted to stay far away from her. I didn't want to be sold! Even now when I was in the woods and fields looking for roots and berries, every snap of a twig, every darkening of a shadow, every chill of the breeze set me to ducking down, hiding, and looking around. Were gifts of healing, shape shifting, recalling one's past lives, and levitation going to help the remaining children escape? Children? They were no longer children. Like me, they were fifteen. If Father was right when he notched the log wall of our hut to mark the years since Mother had died, we'd all turn sixteen sometime during the coming leaf fall. All

175

of us comet-borns would be old enough to make our own lives and decisions as Gromske had said.

I fretted again. The thought frightened me. Old enough to make my own decisions? Be on my own? What would I do? I didn't have a useful gift. How would I survive on my own?

When Noah, Aivo, and Maya headed for the sanctuary, Gromske, Ahni, and I paddled to the village of Big Fork. Greta stayed behind to care for the rabbit, goats, and gardens.

"What supplies do we need?" I asked Gromske as we drifted down the river.

"No supplies this time," Gromske said. "Just a visiting trip. Time for us all to get to know each other better."

"We goin' to see Mizzruth so I thank her for cinnamon an' sugar bun." Ahni cuddled Shadow on her lap in the middle of the canoe. She could barely sit still looking forward to eating more sweet buns.

A "just a visiting trip" was fine with me. I was eager to see Tumla. The boots he'd made for me were beginning to cramp my toes. I jingled the coins from Huldor's larder I still had tied in a pouch around my waist. The coins meant freedom. I could buy what I needed, even pay for my new boots this time.

Gromske sang and smiled as he paddled. He didn't even notice a butterfly landing on his hat. He wore what Ahni called "his village clothes." He had scraped off his beard that morning when he washed. I knew who he was looking forward to seeing and getting to know better.

At the village, I looked for Tumla right away. A big sign over a shop read: *Thomas' Bootery. Soles fixed. New made.*

"What do you think of the sign?" he asked, coming outside to meet me.

"Who's Thomas?" I asked.

"Thomas is the old cobbler, but now everyone in the village is calling me *Thomas the New Cobbler.*" He laughed a bit. "Thomas or Tumla. Makes no difference to me. I'm glad I'm here. The townspeople are glad I'm here, too, because old Thomas can hardly see anymore. No one even minds my lumpy bumpy face when they come to get fit for new shoes."

"Of course not," I told him. "You never scared me either. I think Harmonia just made you think you were ugly so you would stay and be her shoemaker."

Tumla picked up a piece of soft tan leather. "I've learned a lot since I've been here. There's a big world beyond these forests and lakes. Bigger than where the huge bison herds roam. After bison hunting, I never had the freedom to explore other lands or to find a new life outside Harmonia's walls. This is a huge country we live in."

I didn't know, and I couldn't even imagine the wide-open prairies Tumla described when he told of bison hunting. My whole world since leaving Lake Kawishami had been following the river flowing past the Big Fork village.

Tumla measured my feet. Then he stretched and shaped the leather. "I'll take you to Widow Smythe's later. She has lots of maps. One shows the whole of this country. You can find a place called California way to the west. Some folks are talking about joining wagon trains to go there. They've heard about gold flowing in streams. You just dip a pan in the water and pick the gold out of the sand. Imagine that! That'd be safer than getting mixed up in a bison herd."

Tumla ran a knife around the edge cutting off extra leather. Fascinated, I watched my new boots take shape and wondered if it was true about gold flowing in the streams of California. That seemed far-fetched. So, I asked, "Are you thinking of going to pan for gold?"

"Oh, no. I prefer to stay in this village. Here, I can watch Widow Smythe's youngsters grow; make good shoes; and become part of this village. Best of all, there is no Harmonia."

CHAPTER 39

The next morning, Miss Ruth and Widow Smythe took Ahni and me to see the school house. "If you stay here in the village, you can go to school."

The idea shocked me. I had never thought of going to school. Father had taught me everything I knew about reading and writing. I had read the first two McGuffy readers from cover to cover and bits of the others. In the woods, he taught me about the tiniest plants to the tallest trees. While we sat on the shore of the lake, he talked about the fish, clams, and other good things the waters provided. At night, we had looked to the skies. Father pointed to and named all the constellations we could see. I memorized them all. Cassiopeia was easy to find it because it looked like a big W. Ursa Major and Minor looked like dippers. My favorite was the Pleiades, the star cluster Father said my mother had come from to be his wife. That, of course, was one of his wildly imaginative stories. I could read and write and do my sums. I didn't think I needed any more book learning.

As we approached the school, Miss Ruth proudly said, "We painted it red because we want our children to have a nice school." I looked at the color and thought maybe my canoe had once been that new and bright.

A bell hung from a tall pole. Widow Smythe said, "The teacher pulls the rope and rings the bell as a fifteen-minute warning in the morning. At that time, I have to hustle my two children to gulp down the last of their breakfast, gather their books, and run to school before the second bell rings. That means it's time to go into their classroom."

Inside the school house, wooden planks that Widow Smythe called desks, and benches to sit on filled the room. A wood burning stove stood in the middle. Books on shelves covered a whole wall. Maps were tacked up and covered another whole wall. The third wall had drawings of animals and birds that looked like they'd been made by children. A round ball hung from the ceiling. "Globe," said Widow Smythe pointing. "We're so lucky to have it."

I went to the globe and remembered the story Gromske told of how our ancestors had left their homes when the angry mountain gods spewed hot rivers of flames that destroyed their village. I asked Widow Smythe where we lived now. She pointed to a spot and said, "Right about here."

As she continued talking, I walked my fingers to the top of the globe and then studied the other side. My ancestors, the Ice People, had lived somewhere on that side. I ran my fingers along the names of countries and wished I knew where.

"My husband, bless his soul," Widow Smythe explained, "was a surveyor and helped make maps. The dear man bought this globe for the school when he once traveled all the way to a place called Chicago."

Faded and much-used books marked each place for someone to sit. I ran my fingers over the boards that made up the desks. There were low ones and high ones. Widow Smythe explained. "All the children meet in this one room. The little ones sit in front where the low benches are. The biggest sit in the back. The older students help teach the younger ones how to read and do sums. The teacher works hard to keep up with everyone. Go ahead. Sit. Try out a desk."

I sat and looked around thinking how lucky the children were to have a school with shelves filled with books. Widow Smythe pointed to something that looked like it had fallen apart and some mischievous children had put back together. "That's a piano. It's seen better days," she laughed.

The school smelled of chalk dust and unwashed children, yet I thought how it would be a good place to learn when the weather was bad. I hoped that in good weather, the children would walk in the woods, smell the cedars and pines, open rotting logs to see how many creatures lived and made their homes in the dead trees. That's what Father and I had done in good weather,

Ahni found a bench just her size in the middle of the room. She hugged a book to her chest and said, "This be so much fun. Books to read. No one yellin' at me to do somethin' pro-duck-tive."

After leaving the school, Ahni and I spent the day wandering the village. Besides the bakery and bootery, there was a saloon with loud music that could be heard from three doors away. We walked past a rooming house, a stable where horses neighed, and a fish market with many cats lined up outside. We'd just passed an herbalist's shop and were about to go down another street when Gromske caught up with us and said that Miss Ruth had lunch ready for us.

Gromske set a table outdoors. Widow Smythe, Tumla, and Thomas the old bootmaker came, too. Miss Ruth set a canning jar filled with wild flowers in the middle. Smiling, she said, "Gromske picked these this morning." Her eyes softened as she looked at him. He looked down, smiling, and I saw a bit of red creep up into his cheeks. My heart gave a flip. They liked each other! Ahni was right. I wondered if he planned to stay in the village. No wonder Miss Ruth and Widow Smythe had showed me and Ahni the school house. They must be hoping we'd all stay.

That afternoon I returned to the school. Miss Pearl, the teacher, was there picking up an armload of books. I told her my name.

"Welcome. I'm glad to meet you. Miss Ruth told me about you and I hope you'll stay to be a student here at the school."

"I will be staying only a day or two, but if you don't mind, I'd like to look at your maps some more. I've never seen a globe before either."

"Come. Are you looking for anything in particular?"

"Yes, if you could point out where we are, and the river that runs by, I'd like that a lot."

Miss Pearl looked at several maps before stopping at one. "Here you go. This one shows our area, and this one shows the whole country and its territories. We're about here. You'll notice our river joins with smaller rivers, then flows into this bigger river. That river flows in every direction joining with other rivers and creeks until they flow to what the French explorers called *Fond du Lac* or Head of the Lake. See this great big lake here? The French called it *Lac Supérieur*. I love geography. I wish I could say the same about my students. I'm glad you seem fascinated."

As Miss Pearl talked, I ran my finger to Lake Kawishami and then forward to where she'd said we were now. The river forked into two. I traced one branch into the wilderness, to places unknown.

Miss Pearl smiled at me, "Oh, I do hope you stay and become one of my students."

I was fascinated by the maps. The map didn't show forests or towns or people fishing in the rivers, but I tried to imagine what lay beyond the village, along the water ways. Dangers? Adventures? Kind people like Tumla, Gromske, Ossi, and Huldor, or people to beware of like Harmonia and Lady Magda?

Miss Pearl broke into my imaginings. "I need to leave now, but you can come back tomorrow. Or any time you want."

"Thank you," I said. My mind felt like a twig twitching and waking me to many possibilities.

CHAPTER 40

Our "just a visiting trip" stretched two more days. I was tired of not having anything to do except look at maps in the school and listen to Ahni's stories about how much fun she and her friends had jumping rope and taking turns on the swing Tumla had made for them on a tree branch. Gromske was unloading a cart of logs when I asked him when we'd be leaving. Rolling up his sleeves to his elbows and wiping sweat from his brow, he arched his back and stretched.

"Not today," he answered. "Not tomorrow. Or even the next day."

"Why not today or tomorrow?" I thought of Greta who was looking after the goats and bunny as well as tending to the garden all by herself.

"Come. I have a surprise for you."

Together, we went to the edge of the river. There, leaning against a tree, was a canoe. A very red canoe. "Is that my canoe?" My canoe had once been all red before it had crashed and been beaten against many rocks, fixed and fixed again; its seams blackened with sealer and the whole bow replaced. I blinked. "My canoe? It's beautiful! It's as red as the school house!"

"Yes, your canoe. We painted it with left over paint from the school. But don't touch yet. It needs to dry another day or two before it goes into the water."

I did want to touch it and run my hands along the smooth sides, but I just stood back and admired how beautiful it was. I couldn't quit smiling. "Thank you! It's perfect."

"Don't thank me. It was Miss Ruth's idea. I took her for a short paddle last night, and she said it needed to be painted. Tumla helped, too."

My breath almost stopped as I looked in awe at the canoe, but then a shadowy thought stirred in me. Gromske talked about Miss Ruth, Widow Smythe, and Tumla all in the same breath as if they all belonged together. A twitch a jealousy flickered in me. Then a twitch of suspicion. We couldn't leave until the canoe dried, but I felt there was more than a painted canoe keeping us from leaving.

"What were you unloading all those logs for?" My voice quivered a bit. I wanted to know, and at the same time, I didn't want to know.

Gromske's cheeks flushed a bit, but he looked straight at me. "I was going to tell you tonight, but now that you've asked—the village carpenter and I are building another room onto Miss Ruth's house. She's hoping you and Ahni will stay with her—and me. The two of you'd have a room of your own."

"Stay here in the village? You and Ahni and me? With Miss Ruth?" My whole body heated. My stomach felt funny. I looked at my canoe. It was built for traveling rivers and lakes, not staying in villages. "What about Greta and the goats and the garden—your *itok*, the cairns, and the place where our families lived before the marauders?"

Gromske took me by the hand and sat us both down on the sandy bank of the river. "Maybe it's time for me to leave all that behind. To quit grieving. To quit thinking what could have been and make a new life. It'll all work out. When Noah, Aivo, and Maya return from saving more comet-borns, the *itoks* will be full again. Greta has been good with the goats and cooking. There'll be plenty of good workers to keep the gardens, fish, and hunt. I'll go back whenever they need help, but that probably won't be often. You're all old enough to make your own lives. You could choose to live here in Big Fork, or return to the cairns with the other comet-borns."

My thoughts muddled. He said I was old enough to have my own life. The truth was, he needed his own life, too. The realization hit me hard. I depended on Gromske for so much. I couldn't look at him. I pinched my lips together until they hurt. I persisted—not wanting to hear or believe what he'd said. "When are we going back? To the *itoks*? To our garden and the cairns. Where our ancestors had lived?"

Four days later, we shoved the canoe back into the river. We—only Gromske, Shadow, and I—Ahni insisted on staying with Miss Ruth. She wanted more time to giggle and play with Athena, a girl her own age. I felt happy for her, but I also felt a great emptiness in my chest. She no longer needed me. Once, she hadn't wanted me to ever leave her, but now she was leaving me. I tried to be happy for her. She would have a home with Miss Ruth and Gromske, friends to play with, and a teacher to show her books and maps. What did I need? I wasn't sure.

The previous evening, Ahni hadn't even paid a bit of attention to me even though she knew I was leaving in the morning. She and Athena played guessing games, braided each other's hair and then played hide-and-seek. Best of all, Miss Ruth was eager to have her stay. I was the one left alone.

I tried not to laugh as Ahni told me what Miss Ruth expected of her. She held up a finger each time she counted off one of the rules. "Wash breakfast dishes. Help make bread. Listen to teacher. Be home before dark when playing with friends, an' ask afore borrowin' anything." The Lamb-i-kins of old was fading away day by day and transforming into a new person.

As Gromske and I climbed into the canoe, Ahni stood on the bank smiling and waving to us. Tears filled my eyes as I looked back. Miss Ruth had an arm around Ahni's shoulder. Tumla, Widow Smythe, her son and daughter stood together calling out, "Come back soon."

Greta was fishing from the bank when we landed the canoe. The rabbit and the goats chewed grasses nearby. "You got here just in time," she called out. "I just pulled in another big one."

Greta cleaned the fish. Gromske stoked the cooking fire while I went to the garden to pull a few carrots. I liked how normal it all felt so I picked a handful of purslane, the cursed, but delicious weed that invaded gardens. I popped some into my mouth. It tasted slightly salty, so I picked more remembering how much I'd hated when Purslane had been my name.

"When do you think Noah, Aivo, and Maya will be back with the others?" Greta asked as we sucked the last bits of flesh from fish bones.

"They should be at the sanctuary by now, or at least close to it." All the way home, I had thought about Ahni and her new friends. I planned to make friends with Greta. She and I didn't have any gifts that we could use to get rich. We could just be who we were. No lifting people. No making fire with our fingers. No healing bones.

Just as I was planning a game I could play with Greta as a way to start making friends with her, she said, "I hope Grace and Hattie escape this time."

"What are their gifts?"

"They have good ones. Hattie can read the lines in our hands. Sometimes, to be funny, she makes up things. Once she told Noah he would meet a beautiful princess, but that her hair would turn into hissing serpents at night. Poor Noah had nightmares three nights in a row. Grace finds roots and leaves she uses to make love potions. If we made her angry for any reason, she threated to make us fall in love with worms, beetles, or worse yet, with Harmonia!"

It was the most Greta had ever talked to me. I had a glimmer of hope that she and I could be friends. I would like that, but the glimmer died when she said, "Grace and Hattie are my best friends."

To cover my disappointment, I kicked a small stone into the fire and asked, "What's it like to remember all your previous lives?"

"Nothing special," she said. "In fact, it's boring compared to what everyone else can do like Lukas making fire at his fingertips, and Antti moving things around. Those gifts would be fun. Even Hattie and Grace can have fun with theirs, too. No one really wants to know about my past lives."

"I do. I know nothing about my past lives if I had any. Tell me yours."

"You really want to know?"

I nodded vigorously. I liked Greta. I still wanted her to be my friend even though she hoped for Hattie and Grace to escape. I wanted to be happy like Ahni. Gromske put another log on the fire. Sparks flew into the air as he said, "Sounds like those would be good stories."

Shadow lay at my feet. The goats finished grazing and bedded down under some trees. "Well," Greta looked to the sky above. Her eyes glossed over as she started, "One of my lives took place almost a thousand years ago in a place called Moc'Tan. It was a place of beauty. Long coasts of soft white sand stretched between inland jungles and the sparkling blue seas. When I was about twelve and changing from a child to an adult, my parents brought me to the high priest so he could perform the purification ceremony to mark my passage. Along with all my aunts, uncles, and cousins, we journeyed to the tallest of the surrounding hills."

Mosquitos swarmed and buzzed us. Gromske got up and cut some cedar boughs. He handed one to each of us and laid the rest on the fire.

Greta swished mosquitoes away and then started again. "The priest led a parade of white robed followers to greet us and lead us into a glade that was surrounded by fruit trees of every kind. My mother asked why we were treated like royalty from another empire. He said it was because I had been born in the year of the great comet. My parents beat their chests and moaned. For my people, to be born of the comet was not a good omen. Special skills were not bestowed. In the lore of our ancestors, it meant my life would be short—perhaps only half of the 52-year cycle engraved on our calendar that most aspired to live to."

"So, the comet didn't give mystical gifts to those people?" I asked thinking of Aivo and the others who might be trying to save the rest of the comet-borns at that moment.

"Not to the Moc'Tan people." She waved her cedar branch to chase away a mosquito. "Only our gods and priests had magic—not ordinary people."

"What was the purification ceremony like?" I had never heard of such a thing.

"At the ocean, seven priestesses waited for us. They removed my clothing and dunked me into the briny waters. They held me under until I thought I would burst not being able to breathe. Then they helped me out, draped me in a soft white gown with real gold threads woven into the hem and all along the sleeves. I felt very special as they brushed my hair, braided it into seven plaits, wrapped them around my head and stuck in seven long tail feathers from the most sacred bird—two green, two blue, and the three longest were yellow."

I tried to imagine the beauty of the robe and feathers as I said, "You must have looked lovely."

"Then the priest led us to a clearing where a great feast was laid out. My mouth watered to see trays of roast quail, luscious fruit, and sea creatures still in their shells."

My mouth watered, too. I could never have even imagined such a feast.

"After we ate, a chorus of singers enchanted us as well as drummers, pluckers of stringed instruments, and flautists. When we'd eaten our fill, the high priest announced that the most important part of the ceremony would take place at the top of the most sacred hill.

"Father whispered it was an honor that the priest was taking me to the top of the hill to rename me and tell of my destiny. I was excited and eager to learn my new name, and what the future held for me."

At this point, Greta rested a moment while she looked at the moon. "It was a night like this. Moon rays shone through the jungle trees, and all was calm. Even the ocean waves swelled in a gentle harmony. A few birds sang their evening songs, and a spider monkey settled quietly on a branch. The priest signaled me to follow as he started up the long steep stone-way built into the hill. My parents started to come, but he waved them off. I looked back. My mother smiled and held her hands to her chest. She was as excited as I was to learn my destiny."

I almost forgot to breathe. I was impatient for Greta to tell the rest of her story. She switched away mosquitoes and then began again.

"Seven more priestesses waited at the top. One played a delicate tune on a flute. One held a huge platter of bananas, pineapples, and papayas. Another held a shawl—more beautiful than the robe they'd dressed me in after my purification in the ocean. In the center of the purple shawl was the blazing gold orb of the comet and its silver swish of a tail. On one half, gold threads swirled into suns; on the other half, silver threads spun into moons. A raised platform was cushioned with layers of downy feathers. A priestess held my hand as I stepped onto the platform. The view of the blue ocean and the verdant jungle took my breath away. I stood tall as the priest waved a feather and proclaimed my new name to be *BriggaXla*. I beamed as I repeated *BriggaXla*. Xla added to any name was as near to deification as one could get in human life. Overjoyed, I waved to my parents. I called out *BriggaXla* hoping they could hear."

I forgot about the mosquitoes buzzing as I held my hands to my heart. I was enraptured, waiting to hear the rest—what Greta's destiny had been in that life.

"The priest then waved the feather again and spoke in the language of our ancients that I didn't understand. '*BriggaXla. TumKuKul.*' The priestesses laid me on the soft feathers and gently closed my eyes. Did they want me to spend the night? '*BriggaXla. TumKuKul.*' I settled into the comfort of the feathers. '*BriggaXla. TumKuKul.*' I peeked just enough to see the priest wave the feather over me again. '*BriggaXla. TumKuKul.*' When flute music stopped, I peeked again. The priest held a shiny dagger aimed at my heart."

"Oh, no! Did the priest stab you?"

"He must have. After feeling a sharp pain and hearing my own scream, I have no recall of what happened next. I wish with all my might that I had some other gift. I hate remembering my past lives. I hate being born again and again—each time under the cursed comet."

Greta's voice caught. She held her face in her hands. Murmuring she said, "I have now lived fifteen, almost sixteen years, as Greta. I've been imprisoned and then freed. I like living here. I like fishing, caring for the goats and the gardens, but I don't have a good gift. I hope when I die this time, it will be the end of all my lives."

My heart turned icy cold thinking of the sorrows she had to relive over and over again through her memories. I thought of my own sad experiences—entering portals of the dead and watching them crumble and waft away with the breezes. Those brought me great sadness, but what Greta suffered seemed far more disconcerting and painful.

Greta looked forlorn. I could understand why she didn't want to have memories of her past lives. Gromske and I both went to her side and put our arms around her as she sobbed.

CHAPTER 41

A few days later, Gromske got ready to leave for the village again. After he'd settled a bundle on his back, I walked with him to the river's shore and handed him the canoe paddle. I would not be going with him, but would stay to help Greta with the goats and garden.

"When you come back, maybe you could bring a laying hen or two. It would be nice to have eggs. There will be many more of us when everyone returns from the sanctuary."

"I will bring as many chickens as I can bargain for," he answered, then handed the canoe paddle back to me.

"Why?" I asked. "You can travel faster in the canoe."

"It's your canoe. I don't know when I'll be back, but it'll be before the leaves fall for certain. Miss Ruth told me about a village of native peoples not far from Big Fork. They're skilled canoe makers. I'll offer skins, fur, fish, and even my labor for a canoe of my own."

Gromske talked and planned as though Big Fork was already his new home. I felt a lump grow in my throat. A twinge of jealousy. He'd found the baker woman and other good people to live with. I was glad he would no longer be alone, but I'd miss him and his gentle ways.

"Tell Ahni I'll come visit someday soon, but not until the others return. I need to help Greta with the animals and garden." I secretly hoped that she and I would become friends as we worked together.

Gromske whistled as he whittled a tree branch for a walking stick. He was happy even though he was leaving the cairns of his ancestors. He had a new life waiting for him. I'd left two homes behind already. Could I do it again? As I watched and listened, I felt hollow and alone. The home of my ancestors would not be the same without Gromske.

That night as the moon floated silently above, Greta looked to the dark skies. Her eyes became glossy as she told the story of one of her previous lives on an island surrounded by perilous ocean waters that frequently sank fishing boats. She'd been collecting sea shells along the shore with her mother when a large wave had engulfed and carried them to the depths. When she finished, we sat silently for a long time, listening to the sounds of the night before Greta started another story of a past life.

"My people feared a huge creature named Meh-Té-Yaché who was rumored to live in an ice castle on one of high peaks nearby. Snow covered the mountains the whole year. Whenever the torn corpse of a person or animal was found on a narrow path, it was almost unrecognizable, so no one ever willingly went in search of the creature. All who had encountered it never lived to tell, so we didn't know for sure what it looked like. From its tracks, we knew it walked on two feet. From the length of its stride, it had to be twice as tall as any person. Even its tracks held a vomit producing stench that warned my people to flee."

My stomach revolted as Greta told of the formidable creature. "Were you born of the comet in that life, too?"

"I was, but the mountain people didn't consider it unusual. Stars, comet, and meteors were frequently visible flying across the sky from their high mountain home. You probably want to know how that lifetime ended for me."

I did, but hadn't been sure I should ask.

"One day I was collecting twigs, lichen, and mosses for our cooking fires. I had wandered quite far from camp when I slid on some loose stones. I screamed as I dropped off the trail and slipped down a steep face of rock. My descent ended when one of my legs caught between two boulders. While I wriggled, trying to free my leg, I smelled a most repulsive odor wafting on the wind warning that Meh-Té-Yaché was nearby. I entreated the most sacred of mountain gods, KonoSakuya, to save me. The stench became stronger. Acidic surges burned my nose, my throat, my eyes. I heard thudding footsteps behind me. My last words were *KonoSakuya, please help!*"

"Did you see the monster?"

"Thankfully, I only remember hearing and smelling." Greta shook her head. "I'd pleaded, but KonoSakuya hadn't come to save me."

Greta and I listened to our fire crackle and thought about her story. Greta broke the silence by saying, "Tell me about your life before you came here."

"I'll tell you what my father told me about my mother. Then I'll tell you the real story." I passed her the basket full of berries we'd picked that afternoon and started my story.

"One night when Father was a young professor of plant physiognomy, he sat at his campfire deep in the woods where he'd spent the day searching for rare plants. As he looked up into the dark sky, he saw a star streak from the Pleiades constellation. Within an instant it plummeted smack-dab into the middle of his fire.

"At the moment of impact, the star exploded and a beautiful woman rose from the embers. Flames swirled about the glimmering presence. Her hair swirled like wispy smoke around her head and radiant face.

"When she raised a hand, the wind stopped blowing; the leaves on the trees did not rustle, and all the forest creatures stood still. The river even stopped rippling. The night owl did not *whoo*. The fox did not chase the hare. The bear dared not scratch a tickle on his nose.

"In the great hush, the moon glided from one side of the sky to the other. When it paled as morning light crept above the horizon, the being flickered once, twice, three times. And, according to Father, she became Alcyone, a star from the Pleiades, his wife—my mother."

"What a fantastic story!" Greta clapped her hands. "It is so much better than anything I have to tell."

"That was one of Father's invented stories," I said. "My mother was born right here in this very place. He also told me about when I was born. He had been paddling my mother across a huge lake to get here for my birth. A great fog covered the whole lake and a strong wind blew and twirled the canoe—my red canoe. He said that at the moment I was born, my mother died and her body had been swirled out of the canoe never to be found. When the fog lifted, he and I, a newborn, lay together on the sands of Lake Kawishami by the hut we lived in until he sold me to the farmer."

"So, you never had a mother, and your father sold you?"

"It is so."

"It was my mother who sold me to Harmonia. You escaped the farmer and helped me escape from Harmonia. Your life has been full of escapes."

"That could be. I even had to escape from Ahni once after she'd tied me to a tree."

"Sweet Ahni? That's hard to believe."

"She was different then—just a dirty, ragged little homeless girl who called herself *Lamb-i-kins*, but there's more to my story," I said. "It's not something made up, but what really happened. I have the gift of entering portals of the dead. When I entered my mother's, she wove the real story for me.

"In the midst of winter, my canoe spun on crusty snow to a glade where soft green mosses instead of snow covered the ground. The surrounding hillside bloomed with trilliums and violets. A glimmer of lights floated and hovered all around me.

"When the eerie lights dimmed, I saw a woman—my mother—with long dark hair sitting at a wooden loom. As she bent to her weaving, I heard a gentle whoosh of the shuttle, the thud of the beater bar, and the creak of the treadle. I shook my head to clear the sounds and the vision. She raised her arms welcoming me as she wove a story. I stepped close to see the weaving.

"The first image was of her as a youngster toddling and holding her mother's hand at a river's edge. In the second, tumbling waters and surging ice swept them away. The next woven images showed my mother limping, using a crutch. In others she played and grew. Finally, she wove horrible flames of red and orange burning a village.

"In the freshly woven cloth, I saw the comet—a fiery ball with a long trail of light following—passing in the darkened sky. As the treadle lifted a web of threads, and the shuttle passed through, and the beater bar pressed them into cloth, a red canoe appeared spinning in the glow of the passing comet. The whooshing, creaking, and thudding of the loom continued, but I distinctly heard my mother cry out 'Curse the pain! Curse the pain!' The very words Father had mistaken for *Purslane* when he named me for the weed. That's when I was born in the red canoe."

Greta and I swatted mosquitoes at the same time. I was ready to escape into our *itok* to get away from their whining and stinging, but Greta asked more about the weaving I saw my mother making while I was in her portal.

"The weaving then showed my mother lying on soft mosses writhing in pain. An otter rubbed its cheek against hers, and a fox brushed her forehead with its tail. With a moan, a gasp, and a final struggle, she gave birth. She took the newborn—my twin sister—into her arms. With the hem of her dress, she wiped the baby dry, then held it to her breast. When she slept holding the baby close, the animals slept at her side except for the bear who stood at the edge of the woods watching and guarding her."

I felt the pain of my story all over again. To Greta, I said, "Father never knew that his wife—my mother—lived on for many years. He never knew I had a twin born that day. I never knew about my twin for many years either."

CHAPTER 42

Greta and I told stories late into the night. I told stories Ossie had told me about my people. The next morning while remembering the stories, I walked among the cairns. No matter how long I stood; no matter how long I listened; the voices of my ancestors no longer came to me. I felt like a stranger standing amidst the cairns in the place where my ancestors had hunted, fished, cooked around fires, rocked their babies, sung, and danced.

Greta broke into my musings when she called from the garden, "Come see how the corn is growing."

I headed toward the garden. I'd barely taken two steps when I flew off my feet and up into the air. Whoosh! "Help!" I called.

Greta ran and grabbed onto my feet trying to pull me back to the ground. "I can't hold you!" she screamed.

I rose higher and slipped out of her grip. "What's happening?" I yelled.

"I don't know. Maybe Noah, Aivo, and Maya are on their way back with some of the other comet-borns. Maya is probably doing her levitation trick."

Up so high, I hardly heard the end of what Greta called out. Hoping it was other comet-borns playing a prank, I yelled, "Whoever you are, and whatever you're doing, put me down!" Soon, I was flying past the garden and the surrounding woods. I looked down. It was a mistake. My stomach surged as I spun and flew further from Greta who waved her arms and screamed something that was lost in the winds. I hoped to catch sight of the other comet-borns pointing and laughing, so they'd know their stunt worked, and they'd bring me down.

None of that happened. I flew over tree tops following the river toward the sanctuary. Birds fluttered out of my way. The raven followed me. Ahead I saw a speck coming toward me. Closer, I noticed wings. Closer yet, no wings, but arms flapping in the wind. Someone was flying right toward me! Part of the stunt? I didn't have time to think or even be hopeful that once the other person and I met in the air, we'd be set on the ground and have a good laugh. I was sure Maya and the comet-borns were pulling a prank.

Swoosh! The wind swung me around. I flip-flopped in the air. Dizzy from the turbulence, I righted myself just as the other person in flight was right next to me. Harold! His face twisted in terror, but he yelled one word as we zoomed past each other. "Harmo-o-o-n-i-a!"

Harmonia? Then I remembered the words she'd said to me after I'd bought Liida. *"You'll never be free! I'll chase you to the ends of this earth if I have to."*

Harmonia hadn't given up! Harold wasn't a comet-born. What part did he have in all this? I couldn't think of an answer as I tumbled and bumped through a rough patch of air over some tall trees. To my left, I recognized a bend in the river. The wind was bringing me toward the sanctuary and Harmonia. I kicked my feet, paddled, and waved my hands and arms hoping I could turn around and somehow figure out how to descend before I landed in Harmonia's grasp.

CHAPTER 43

Flying in a frightening flight, I saw fallow fields far below me. My flight followed flowing waters and flying falcons. Fear filled my every fiber. I saw flashes of the sanctuary and stockade. They stood out in the landscape below. I was filled with fear.

I awoke face down on cold damp cobble stones. My thoughts and vision were fuzzy. Slowly, my mind cleared and with a chill I remembered flying full of fear of Harmonia and the sanctuary.

My whole body ached as though it had been tossed and battered. Shakily, I arose. In the dark I slid my hands along the stone walls until I came to a wooden door. I was locked in a keep just as I had been when I'd first arrived at the sanctuary almost a year ago. Hungry, thirsty, and cold, I banged on the oaken door. *Bam. Bam. Bam!* My arms and back screamed in pain. Standing on my toes, I looked out a tiny window that was much too high for me to catch a glimpse of anything except tree tops and the black sky. A sliver of moon shone through the glass giving just enough light as I searched the keep for any means of escape. There was none.

I wedged my fingers between every stone checking for loose chinking I could pull out and miraculously remove stone after stone until I could squeeze my way to freedom. I yelled as loudly as my dry tongue and throat would allow. "Help!

Help!" I wished for the ability to walk through stone walls. To see through walls. To be invisible. I wished for anything that would release me from the icy dread I felt. In frustration I kicked at the heavy door. Mistake. Now my foot hurt as much as the rest of my body. I slouched to the small cot and fell onto it. "Help!" I whimpered.

Turbulent dreams swarmed my troubled mind. I swam with a family of otters. I played in the warm sunshine with a mother fox and her kits. A whirring sound frightened the kits into a run. I chased after them and became ensnared in a net. The farmer snickered and guffawed as he drew the net closed, tangling me in its sticky web. My canoe drifted down a river without me. I chased and stumbled after it on the rocky shore. "Stop!" I called to the canoe. It spun along the current always ahead of me—always out of my reach. When it flew over a tumbling cataract, I stumbled over a root and fell into swirling waters.

Flaying my arms, I cried, "Help! Help!"

"Quit fighting. I'm trying to help you." It was a kind voice. Not a voice from my dreams, but one of the real world. Gentle hands stroked my arms. A soft quilt swaddled me. A soothing light shone from a small lantern.

"Where am I?"

"You're at the Sanctuary for Exotics and Children Born of the Comet."

"Oh, no." I groaned. Then I remembered Harold flying past me in the air. Later, I had landed in the midst of an angry crowd. Arms had grappled and wrestled me. During the chaotic struggle to escape my captors, I twisted. They shoved. I strained. They yanked. I jerked, scratched, and thrashed. They wrenched and forced me into the keep. No wonder I was sore and aching.

"Are you able to sit? Swallow some broth?"

I pulled myself upright as the gentle woman handed me a clay bowl that warmed my hands. I raised it to my nose. Warmth and sweet aromas filled my nose. Chamomile, cedar and ginger. I drank greedily not caring if the broth would send me back into a dream-filled sleep or not. I drank until the bowl was empty.

"Did Harmonia send you?" I asked waiting for the room to spin and my eyelids to fall shut.

"Shhh." When the woman looked at the door in the dim light, I noticed her cheeks, neck, and arms were covered with patches of something that looked like soft gray mouse fur. She must be an exotic. "Whisper. Harmonia doesn't know I'm here."

"Then who are you?"

"I'm Clara—known as Clara the Herbalist. For two days now I've watched and wondered why a guard has been at the door of this keep day and night. Two other keeps have guards, too."

I thought about what Clara said. Other keeps had guards. That meant Noah, Aivo, and Maya had been caught, also. Clara tucked the quilt around me and said, "I have to leave before dawn lightens the sky and before the guard wakens. I brought him some special tea I said would warm his bones on a chilly night. He's having a good sleep, but will soon wake up. I have to be gone by then."

"What's going to happen to me and the others?" I asked.

"That I don't know. Harmonia is on a rampage. A wild, crazy rampage. Several of us have been planning to leave here for a long time. We've only stayed to make sure the comet-borns were taken care of. Now, we're ready to go."

I snuggled into the quilt. "Is there any way you can help us all escape?"

"We're trying. It's hard to know who can be trusted around here, and who just pretends to be against Harmonia so they can spy for her. I promise, some of us will get you out of here. Just be patient a while longer." She lifted the quilt from me. "I'm sorry. I have to take this or else Harmonia will know I've been here." She wrapped it around the broth bowl and headed for the door.

"Thank you." I said as I folded my arms around myself to keep warm.

She nodded and was out the door. I heard the bar drop into place locking me in. I wondered if Clara could be trusted or if she was like Neoma and Ayla who pretended to be my friends, but watched me for Harmonia. I had gotten away then, but could I this time?

I trembled in the cold. Sleep only came in fits and starts. How many days? How many nights? I lost track of time as I tried to keep warm. My body begged for food. For something to drink. For sleep. For warmth. But none of that came. Finally, exhaustion drew me into a dream. Ghost Man swirled Ahni high into the air. She giggled with delight begging for him to swing her higher and higher to the very tree tops. Her skirt flared in the breeze. Reds, blues, yellows, and purples. All swirled in dizzying twists and spins. Shadow chased. His tail wagged as he joined in the fun.

The dream faded when I awoke to the sound of the door creaking open. Harmonia, frowning and hobbling, clumped her way toward me. One of her legs and a foot were encased with slats of wood and wrapped with a rough burlap cloth. She leaned on a stout walking stick.

"Are you ready to talk?" she scowled, reached into her pocket, and handed me a chunk of crumbling corn bread.

I was so cold and hungry that I would have torn open a rotted stump and fought a bear for the privilege of eating the grubs inside. I took the bread and bit into it. "Talk about what?"

"No games! Don't lie to me. Tell me about your gift from the comet. I have my ways—painful ways—of getting it out of you, so you might as well tell me."

I'd guessed this was coming. In the cold and isolation, I'd planned my answer. After taking another bite of the crumbly corn bread, I said, "My gift is a poor one. I dream about dead people. It's scary. I wish I had a good gift. One that's worth something."

Harmonia eyed me sharply. "You lied the day you first came here. Your name is Luna, not Purslane. And you're not too young to be comet-born. Bah! Talking to dead people. It would be better if you told fortunes. With the right encouragement, we can fix that. You'll learn. Starting now."

What I'd told Harmonia was true enough. I did dream about dead people, but I didn't tell her about entering portals of the dead.

Harmonia wobbled as she took a step closer to me and raised her walking stick.

Emboldened by Clara's visit and realizing it was my only chance, I grabbed at the stick. Harmonia held onto it tightly. She spun it, knocking me hard on the shoulder. I yowled. Then with her free hand, she yanked my arm almost out of its socket as I tried to get away.

"That's the thanks I get for bringing you food? When I'm done, you'll wish you never had such audacity! This is a place of harmony. You have a few lessons to learn, and they start right now!"

Harmonia swung her stick at me. I ducked. She grabbed for my hair nearly jerking a handful out of my scalp. I shrieked and shoved her as hard as I could. She hit the back wall of the keep and slumped to the floor. I ran for the door, but someone had dropped the bar, locking it from the outside. Harmonia threw her stick at me. It struck me hard high on my temple. Blood gushed. My shoulder screamed with pain and blood rushed down my face, but I was determined not to let her win. I would escape even if I had to fight half the village. Without her stick, Harmonia rolled to me and pulled my foot from under me. On the floor, we grappled with each other. Shoving. Hitting. Elbowing. Kicking. Finally, Harmonia's thrusts and kicks grew weaker, but mine did, too. If I could outlast her, I'd trade her to whomever was guarding the door for my freedom. I breathed deeply and tried to garner any strength I had left.

Panting, almost out of strength, Harmonia shoved a fist into my mouth. I reached to grab her hair, but with a burst of strength, she hit me with her walking stick again. Then she pounded on the floor yelling, "Help me! Bring the net!"

The door burst open. Three men—even in my peril I wondered if they were the baker, the barber, and the barrel maker—rushed in and threw a net over me. I struggled, but I was no match for the three of them. They had me entangled and trapped in no time.

Harmonia drew herself to her knees. "Take her to the stockade and don't bother being gentle. She's caused chaos from the moment she first stepped through our gates. I have some lessons in store for her. We have to make an example of those who disturb our harmony."

The baker, the barber . . . or was it the butcher and the barrel maker? No matter. I was ensnared so tightly that I couldn't so much as stretch out and uncramp my legs. The men did what Harmonia demanded. They hauled me to the stockade. I felt every bump, every stone, every twig poke, prod, and jab. They sometimes swung the bag, kicked at me, and made my ordeal as painful as possible. I screamed. I begged. I was miserable. I hadn't succeeded at saving myself and wondered what had happened to Maya, Noah, and Aivo. Were they as abused and bruised as I was?

When I awoke, cold seeped from the ground chilling my whole body. Several comet-born youngsters stood around me. I looked up and saw the spiked tops of the stockade. Harmonia was thankfully nowhere to be seen. I rose shakily. Every part of my body was sore. Purple bruises showed on my arms. Blood seeped from some of the wounds. I stumbled when I tried to walk.

A girl steadied me. "I'm Hattie. Come and I'll show you where you can lie down." She pointed to a cot. Cold, sore and very hungry, I sank onto it. I wished and hoped that Clara would come again with a warm quilt and bowl of broth. I slept for hours, maybe even days before I felt a soft pat on my shoulder.

"Luna? Are you alright?"

Startled, I opened my eyes. It was Clara. She gave me broth to drink and wrapped me in the soft quilt. I moaned with happiness and hoped I wasn't dreaming. "Quiet. We must be quiet. I've drugged the watchmen, but you never know when they'll wake up."

Clara lifted me to my feet. Two men crept in bringing Noah and Maya, I was overjoyed to see them. Unfortunately, they had wounds like mine—maybe worse.

"Where's Aivo?" I asked.

"He wasn't captured. He managed to change into a bear again just before we were surrounded. The last we saw of him, he was bounding toward the woods as fast as his bulky body would move," Noah said.

In a hushed voice, Clara introduced the two men as Chester the Tanner and Oskar the Carpenter. Chester had a carved wooden leg strapped to what was left of his own leg. He used a walking stick for balance. Oskar had a deep cleft in his upper lip. As quietly as we could, Clara and I climbed over the stockade using the ladder Oskar brought to get over the walls. Chester and Oskar stayed behind to help the rest of the comet-borns escape, too. As soon as we all were over, we scuttled into the woods as quickly and quietly as possible.

While we rested among the dense trees, I asked, "How did you get all this done without Harmonia catching on?"

Chester started the telling, "Clara invited Harmonia to a celebration. She said it was to celebrate the recapture of you and the other comet-borns. Clara is good with herbs, roots, and leaves. She knows how to mix sleeping powders, so she made some and put it into Harmonia's mug of ale. When Harmonia fell asleep, we tied her up good and brought her to a cave in the far hillside. We wrapped her in blankets so she wouldn't freeze. We left a note in the dining hall telling where Harmonia could be found. The note won't be found until morning when everyone goes in for breakfast. We have to act fast. We need to get as far away as we can before her band of followers wake and discover she's missing."

Oskar took over the story. "We've been encouraging all the comet-borns to escape when the time came. That time is now. We have to run to the river and get as far away as possible. Maya and Noah told us about the place you brought them to when they escaped the first time. Can you lead us there again?"

I was overcome with happiness. All the comet-borns who wanted to be free, now were. They were eager to escape from Harmonia. I tried to count how many were going with us, but it was impossible to see in the dark.

"Everyone needs to stick close together," Clara and Oskar said. "Hold hands as we head for the river."

As we ran across the field, my thoughts tumbled. I was excited. I was also concerned. If everyone stayed at the *itoks*, we would have to build many more. And worse, it was too late in the season to plant more gardens. We'd have to do a lot of hunting, fishing, and gathering of roots and berries. I tried to calm myself. I was somewhat relieved that Clara, Oskar, and Chester were escaping, too. With Gromske moving to Big Fork, I was glad they'd be able to help with all that needed to be done. I hoped they'd know about hunting big game and a lot of other things.

CHAPTER 44

We traveled through the dark. When the light of dawn cracked the horizon, we stopped to eat, drink, and massage our sore muscles. Many had sprained ankles from twisting them on roots and stones. Noah helped by healing ankles. He even soothed most of my bruises.

As we rested and the sky lightened, I went from escapee to escapee trying to learn all their names. A girl named Sage stood a distance away and peered into the distance. "I don't see anyone coming," she said. "In fact, it's very quiet in the sanctuary. Without Harmonia giving the order for the ringing of the morning bell, everyone will probably sleep late." Sage was short with a furrowed forehead. I was glad she'd come because she could see into the distance even in the dark. I relaxed a bit when she didn't see anyone coming after us.

Just before we started off walking again, a tall gangly boy named Sylvester knelt on the river bank. He gathered a handful of pebbles, twigs, and leaves.

"What are those for?" I asked.

"I'm going to cast a spell. When and if Harmonia and others follow us, the spell will make them think we headed off into the woods and back toward the sanctuary."

"You can do that?" I was amazed.

"Been working on it ever since the first group escaped. Thought it might come in handy someday." Sylvester's voice was soft and comforting as he told of using his gift from the comet.

We watched as he tossed the stones and twigs toward the woods. As he did so he intoned the words for his spell.

Trees, open path to deep woods
Earth, disguise our footfalls
Pebbles, cover our track
Trees, Earth, Pebbles, lead seekers astray.

We were five days into our walk when Sage announced a canoe was coming from up river.

"It shouldn't be anyone we have to be afraid coming from that direction," I said, "but we need to hide just in case." Remembering the cold, thirst, and hunger of the keep, I felt jittery all the time. Harmonia must be furiously buzzing like a hive of bees.

We ducked behind bushes, rocks, trees, and waited. Rosa whispered, "If it's someone who means us harm, I can conjure up a rip-roaring thunderstorm to give them a good soaking while we sneak away."

I nodded to her and whispered, "Good idea."

Rosa had made the rainstorm for our first escape. I was thankful for the gifts everyone else had because mine couldn't rescue me from a mosquito, or even warn me about a hungry mosquito coming my way.

We were happy when we saw Harold in my canoe. As soon as Noah recognized him, he jumped from behind the bushes and whistled. Harold back paddled and drew the canoe to shore. Noah and Oskar helped hoist it onto the bank.

Harold looked at me and said, "Good seeing you on the ground. Last time you were flying above the trees." We laughed and told everyone what had happened.

"Walter! That was Walter castling you. I bet Harmonia made him do that," Noah said.

"What's castling?" I asked.

Hattie explained. "We don't know what it's really called, but Walter has a chess set and whenever he had the chance, he'd teach us how to play. Whenever his king was in danger, he castled his king with another piece by switching their positions—or something like that. I was never sure if Walter was making up rules to win the game or not."

"And that's what Harmonia had Walter do to you and me," Harold said. "You can't imagine how shocked I was when ZOOM! I was no longer working in the fields but off my feet and flying in the air."

"Oh, yes, I can imagine," I laughed, forgetting for a moment how scared I'd been.

"Remember when he used to switch his empty plate with mine or someone else's that still had food on it?" Hattie grumbled.

"Worse yet, I remember when he zapped a nice rosy apple right out of my hand and replaced it with a wormy one. He's trouble. Good thing he didn't escape with us."

"Hey, you want to know what else? He hasn't been in the stockade for days. Harmonia must be giving him special privileges for his castling trick that brought you into her clutches."

I felt edgier than ever. "Don't worry," Maya said, "We'll all hold onto you so there'll be no more flying through the air to Harmonia."

Rosa sidled up to Harold while he was talking and nudged his elbow. "Remember me?" she asked.

"Of course, Storm Maker Sister. I'm glad you escaped. Now we can find home together."

"You'll have to tell me what it was like flying through the air. I was so mad when you went missing and didn't take me, I was going to start a storm. Good thing I didn't. You might have been downed in a forest somewhere."

"Or struck by lightning. Thanks for not brewing up one of your tempests."

Harold handed me the canoe paddle. "I want to walk with Rosa and the others. You can paddle your way back."

CHAPTER 45

I was a bundle of worries. Not counting myself, eighteen were headed to the village where my ancestors had once lived. There were only five *itoks* including Gromske's. What would he think of so many coming to live where he'd been alone for so long? Our garden would never produce enough to keep us all through the winter. We'd need to gather a lot of cattail roots, berries and mushrooms and do a lot of fishing and hunting. And buy dried foods from the village if we didn't want to starve. I'd had enough of being hungry when I lived with Father. I still had most of the coins I'd taken from Huldor's larder, but wasn't sure they'd buy enough dried beans and bacon to feed all of us. Hopefully Antti and Lukas would keep their promise by returning for the winter and bringing dried foods.

I felt all jumbled with so many concerns. My mind turned to *what ifs*. What if I moved to Big Fork to be with Gromske, Ahni, and Miss Ruth in the village? What if I chose to stay with the comet-borns? What if I didn't fit in with so many my age who talked, laughed, played tricks, and enjoyed each other's company? What if I didn't do either, but traveled on to somewhere else? Or what if I traveled to festivals in the summer, looking for my twin sister? So many *what ifs*, but none appealed to me. A war of uncertainty raged within me.

Each time I bent toward the bow of my canoe, the river's waters swirled. Each time I dipped, pulled, and drew with the paddle, I asked myself *Ancestral home? Big Fork village? Festivals? Ancestral home? Big Fork? Festivals?* I felt as though I was drowning in a swirling whirlpool of indecision with each sweep of the blade.

The tall tree with the scar from lightning was ahead. My raven perched on a low branch. I wished it would give me answers to my questions. I pointed out the tree to Clara who'd joined me in the canoe. "Almost there," I said.

"Good. I've never paddled a canoe before. My arms are sore!"

Clara hadn't complained at all during our journey so I hadn't even considered that her arms might be hurting more than her feet had walking.

Greta ran to the river's edge as Clara and I pulled the canoe to shore. "I'm so glad to see you. I've been trembling-scared ever since you flew up into the air and the wind swooshed you high and away. And then the next thing I knew, Harold plopped right down on the spot where you'd been. I wondered if Aivo was playing a trick. Instead of turning himself into a bear, he'd turned you and Harold into each other!"

Shadow jumped and twirled around me so I picked him up and let him lick my face and ears all he wanted.

I was still laughing as I warned Greta, "Don't give Aivo any ideas about what he might be able to do. He'd think it was a good challenge to try mix us up in each other's bodies. Right now, he's a bear again. Who knows how long it'll be before he figures out how to separate from the bear?" Greta and I laughed again. It felt good to be back.

"And this is Clara. She's an herbalist. Clara saved my life. Harmonia locked me in a keep. I was cold, thirsty, and hungry for I don't know how many days, but Clara brought me warm broth and a blanket. Then she got Chester and Oskar to help free me as well as the comet-borns who wanted to leave. They're following us on foot. Should be here in a few days."

The three of us worked the garden, picked and dried berries in the warm sun of mid-summer. I couldn't relax. More than once I found myself looking to make sure Greta and Clara were still hoeing weeds, kneeling in a berry patch, and not flying off into the skies. Harmonia must be furious because so many had escaped. Did she know about Aivo shape shifting? I hoped she wasn't ordering her hunters to look for him. And she must have figured out by now that Clara, Chester, and Oskar had left her village, too.

Days later, the foot-sore and weary group arrived. Tired as they were, they made a lot of noise moaning, groaning, asking for food and water. Shadow hugged close to my leg, looking at me as though accusing me. His eyes said, "What have you brought upon us?"

The best thing was Aivo. Aivo as Aivo—not as a bear. "I have it figured out now," he said. "I can meld with the bear and separate from him as soon as I want to."

"I saw you join with the bear the last time, but how do you separate?" I was curious.

"First of all, I can't panic if it doesn't work instantly. I have to keep my focus on one thing at a time. I have to imagine and feel the fur leaving me; the paws turning into feet and hands; and I have to envision the bear walking away from me."

"You don't need to reverse the enchanting words you used to call the bear to you?"

"No, not at all. It's all about seeing myself shedding the bear piece by piece. That's actually better than saying special words because if I'm in hiding and want to return to human form, I don't have to give myself away by saying words out loud."

Everyone gathered around our evening fire that night. Aivo sat next to me. There was plenty of room, he could have sat next to anyone. He smiled as he settled on the log we shared. "I hope you don't mind sitting next to a bear," he said.

"Just don't bite." I immediately reddened. Why had I said something so dumb? In reality, I'd never had a boy sit by me, so I had no idea what to say. I looked at my hands and twisted my fingers.

I was thankful when Clara broke the silence and said all the escapees should tell what they wanted to do or where they wanted to go now that they were free. Oskar, Chester, and Clara said they were glad to be far from Harmonia. The two men had been tradesmen in the village. They wanted to be useful setting up new shelters and gardens and helping the comet-borns in any way they could. If Ahni had been there, she would have said Clara and Chester's eyes twinkled when they looked at each other. I noticed, too.

Grace and Hattie told of their plans. When they got to a big town, they would set up a shop together. Grace would make and sell potions, especially love potions. Hattie would read palms. The two were excited as they talked about it. "We'll have a big sign that says *Ye Olde Shoppe of Mysteries Solved: Potions for Sale. Palms Read. Your Future Revealed.*"

As Greta listened to her two friends, she bit her lip, and looked down. Tears filled her eyes. I could tell she felt bad that Grace and Hattie's plans didn't include her. She'd hoped they'd escape so they could renew their friendship. Finally, her shoulders slumped as she said, "I'll never be able to make a living with my gift—remembering all my past lives. I don't even know where my home is so I can't return." Her voice cracked as she added. "I'll just stay here. At least the goats like me, and I like taking care of them. I can do the gardening, too."

Noah, Aivo, and Maya also wanted to stay. Many others, to my great relief, said they planned to find their homes after they'd rested.

After everyone told of their plans, I counted—only about ten or twelve planned on staying. Maybe, after a trip into the village of Big Fork, more would decide to locate there. The comet-borns told of their gifts. I was amazed because I'd never heard of teleportation, telepathy, and extremely acute sensory perceptions. Beatrice told us she could find water using a willow branch. Their gifts were useful, unlike mine and Greta's. They could use their gifts to find their homes or help build new lives for themselves.

Our campfire burned low, and the night birds sang, so everyone started leaving and finding their way to an *itok* for the night. I was calmer knowing most would be moving on. Most of all, I was glad that all the comet-borns who escaped were safe from Harmonia. I felt a bit of pride that I had helped, but worried about Harmonia. Was she still in the cave? Had her foot and leg healed? Or did she still need a walking stick? Would she punish the comet-borns who hadn't escaped? Would she come after me again?

CHAPTER 46

In the morning, I walked the fields and woods surrounding the burned-out village of the Ice People. My mother, my grandparents, Ossi, Huldor, and Gromske had all walked where I walked. I swam in the river where they swam. The moon that shone down on me every night had shone on them, too. I had sought this village and my people hoping for home and family, but the remains of the village with its stone cairns on top of the bones of my people no longer sang out to me; no longer brought me comfort.

That same morning, the freed comet-borns set about exploring. They walked the same trails and swam the same river with no thought of my ancestors. They played tricks on each other. Their laughter rang out as they threw a ball back and forth, and teased each other. I watched as they chased the goats, played tag, climbed trees, hopped from one river stone to the next, and played hide and seek. I wanted to join them, but they paid no attention to me. As they amused themselves and celebrated their freedom, I felt I was the one who didn't belong even though I was on my own ancestral lands.

I missed Gromske. He was at the village of Big Fork. He was planning to make a home with Miss Ruth. He wasn't going to be with me fishing, weeding the garden, or teaching me how to make wild rice cakes. We would no longer be together to tell stories around an evening fire. I missed Ahni. She, too, was with Miss Ruth. In the village, she had friends to play with. Once, she'd told me to never leave her, but now, she'd left me. I felt troubled and alone.

Feeling disillusioned and apart from the comet-borns, I climbed high up a tree at the edge of the woods. My raven alit above me. I heard Sage and Rosa laughing as they chased after a goat that had Sage's shoe in its mouth. I watched Oskar and Chester drive stakes into the ground, marking where they'd build log houses. From my branch, I saw the stakes lined in perfect rows. I shivered. The perfect rows made perfect squares—like the little dwellings in Harmonia's village. I didn't like that. Gromske had built the *itoks* in a semicircle. It was as our ancestors had done.

Off to my right, Noah slashed trees with an axe to show which could be cut down. I winced and imagined the trees bleeding sap from their wounds.

Beatrice held a willow branch and walked the breadth and length of the area. She marked a spot where the branch twisted in her hands, pointing to the earth. "Water," she called out as she stood over the site. "Dig a well here." I thought finding water with a stick was silly. She could have just marked the whole river. That was where Gromske always scooped the water we needed. That was what my ancestors probably did, too.

The busyness and the noise pricked my spine and stood my nape hair on end. Hungry, I swung off the branch and headed to the storage shed to find some berries or jerky. The notched log was up and ready to be climbed. Didn't they know skunks, raccoons, foxes and bears could climb up? The door was even wide open.

I climbed to the top. The storage room was empty! Berry baskets had been cleaned out. The dried fish were gone. No mushrooms. No venison hanging. No nuts. Nothing except for a few stems and leaves on the floor! I swallowed sour bile as I looked into the emptiness. My chest squeezed. Instead of playing games, the comet-borns needed to get busy gathering food or they'd go hungry during the coming winter. With a disgruntled thought, I wondered if they believed one of them could magically make food fly through the air to fill their hungry bellies.

I jumped down and ran to the woods. Tears ran from my eyes as I climbed back up to the high branch seeking refuge. Shadow woofed at me from the ground. I didn't think he liked what was going on either.

Beatrice and Aivo began to dig a well where her willow sticks had bent toward the earth. They laughed together as they leaned on their shovels to rest. I felt a twinge of jealousy. Aivo had sat next to me earlier and now he was having a good time with Beatrice! I tried to block out the sounds when I heard *chop, chop, chop,* and then the falling of a tree as it collapsed to the ground. The *chop, chop, chop* echoed in my ears long after the tree crashed to the earth.

I squelched a scream when I saw Rosa skinning Ahni's rabbit. My stomach twisted as she set it over a fire to roast. Then she stretched the soft furry skin to dry. What would Ahni say? Or do? Most likely, she'd put her hands on her hips, scowl, and roar, *"I roast your liver an' pluck your eyes out. Toss 'em in river for the fishes!"* Or worse. I wished she'd taken the rabbit with her, but Gromske had said they needed to build a hutch first so it wouldn't be getting into the villagers' gardens. Shadow whined as he looked up at me from the ground.

It was bad enough that the food was all gone and the rabbit roasted, but the final disaster almost blew me off my perch. Chester, Oskar, and a couple of boys began tumbling stones off the cairns! I dropped out of the tree screaming, "Noooo! Stop! What are you doing?"

"We're using these rocks to build foundations for our houses. Look how many piles there are. Better yet, we don't have to carry rocks all the way from the river."

"Put them back!" My voice rasped harshly. Tears gushed from my eyes. I grabbed a stone and tried balancing it back in place. It tumbled to the ground. "These *piles of rocks* are cairns. They mark the bones of *my* people! *My grandmothers and grandfathers!*" I hurt so much I couldn't look at anyone as they all stood around me with mouths agape. I picked up a stone and cradled it to my chest. In a voice that sounded as limp as I felt, I said softly, "The cairns are memorials for all who died when marauders destroyed their homes and lives."

I shook uncontrollably, but went on. "They're not something to be torn apart and destroyed just because it's easier than carrying rocks from the river!" I was afraid I would start sobbing, so I turned away. I didn't want to see their faces. Mine twisted with the anger I felt.

"We're sorry. We didn't know." Noah sounded remorseful. Aivo reached out to hold me, but I shook him off. I was going to leave. Still holding the cairn stone, I saw Greta watching. Maybe she'd come with me. She must be as unhappy as I was because Grace and Hattie had decided to leave without her.

"Greta," I called and signaled her to follow me into our *itok*.

I was still holding the cairn stone when Greta lifted the deer skin flap and entered. I calmed myself and said, "Come with me. I'm going to the village to say goodbye to Gromske and Ahni. Then I'm going to leave. You and I could go together in the canoe. We could travel the river looking to find a life for ourselves somewhere else. Our gifts from the comet don't do us any good."

Greta looked stunned. It took her a while to find her voice, but she finally said, "I had wished that I could be with my best friends. That was not to be, but I have discovered what I learned in my previous lives is helping me do things I truly like. And I can do that right here!"

Her words shattered the hope I'd felt. Greta didn't want to go with me. My voice sounded raspy as I said, "What do you want to do? Here? With all the other comet-borns?"

Greta reached to hold my hand. I let her hoping she'd change her mind and come with me. "I like gardening. I like taking care of the goats. Even milking them. I think I did these things in the past because it all comes naturally to me. And I find myself singing little tunes as I gather the goats, dig out weeds or harvest food. Why don't you stay and help me? I'll teach you how."

I plopped onto my bed. Tears came unbidden. Greta sat, too, with her arm around me. My thoughts swirled. Too many changes were taking place—especially the destruction of the cairns and chopping down of trees. Everything was being torn apart. Greta didn't even want to leave with me. I moaned. I felt as shattered as the cairns.

Despite my feelings of anguish and desolation, deep down, I began to realize the cairns would be in the way of building houses that the comet-borns needed. And, the comet-borns would never survive the winter without shelters. Nevertheless, I had trouble shaking my feelings of dread and despair.

I hugged the cairn stone to my chest. I would keep it when I left. For me, it would hold memories of Ossi, Huldor, my mother, and all my ancestors. Embracing it, I felt my anger fade.

I choked out the words, "I know you all need homes. I know this is a good place to build them but. . . ." What I needed to say next made me tremble. In my heart, I knew. "I—I can't stay. I don't want to be like Harmonia finding fault, demanding that everything be my way, and bossing everyone around. You all need to be free. Free to be who you were meant to be."

Greta held me for a long time. "We don't want you to go. We're just trying to build a real village for ourselves. A village without Harmonia. A village of real harmony."

"I understand. I even understand the cairn stones are needed to build houses. I'm glad you're all safe here, but I need to go. To find a place *I* can call home."

Greta reached for my hand. "Luna, without you, all of us would still be suffering Harmonia's rules and nasty moods. We owe you so much. I want you to stay."

I shook my head. "I can't. I need to go."

"Please, just go for a little while, then come back. Whatever you decide, remember, I am thankful for you, and I like being your friend. I wish you well wherever you go."

I wiped my eyes. Slowly, a realization came to me that freeing the comet-borns also meant I owed them a home. I hugged Greta and said, "I'm glad you're safe. Thank you for wishing me well."

I didn't think anyone else would miss me so I left the *itok* and turned toward the river. I was wrong. Aivo caught up to me, slid the pack from my shoulder, and asked, "Why are you leaving? We owe you so much for saving us and bringing us to this place where we can be free."

"I'm glad you're all safe now. Even though I'm leaving, I'm happy for you all." I answered thinking of when I'd left the door open to the hut Father and I had lived in so the forest creatures could find shelter in it. Now I was leaving the door wide open for the comet-borns to build their new homes. Then I thought about Huldor's burned inn. Someday, I hoped, someone would build upon those ashes, too.

"I'm torn. I got angry because the cairns were being destroyed. And yet I know changes have to take place for new dwellings." I looked at Aivo, then added. "This is the land where my ancestors, the Ice People, made their home. Maybe it is for the best that new will be built on the old. Ever since you all arrived, you have brought laughter and happiness to this land. I hope that every once in a while, as you enjoy your freedom, you'll remember those who came before you."

As I said all that, I felt something dark and sad lift from me—a small glimmer and a warmth that it might be true. I actually felt gladness in the thought that the comet-borns had found safety where the Ice People had found safety after fleeing an angry volcano. Laughter was better than sadness. Homes were better than graves.

"I'm sorry to see you leave. I haven't even thanked you properly for saving us at your own peril. We are no longer have to fear Harmonia. We're free. No one is going to sell us. We can make our own lives and futures." He held his hand out. "Are you sure you won't stay?"

I took Aivo's hand in mine and looked into his eyes. I didn't know what to say. Would I miss him? Would I always remember him trying to shed the bear from his being? My chest ached and tears threatened to fall so I let go of his hand and turned to the canoe. I felt a tug in my heart. It was good to know someone was sorry to see me go, but I had to leave.

My raven flew to the bow of my canoe as Aivo gently pushed it into the river's current. Shadow stood with his front paws on a gunwale. Without looking back, I dipped the paddle into the clear waters and headed toward Big Fork.

CHAPTER 47

I left my ancestral home. I still had my canoe—the canoe I was born in. I still had my dog. Shadow had been homeless once. I had been homeless once, too. Maybe I would be again. My raven followed as it had so often on my travels. It preened its feathers as it perched on the bow of the canoe. It would still be with me as I set out on the same river that I'd traveled so long, so often. The canoe, the river, the dog, the raven, and me. We were all together. A turtle slid from its rock into the river. The sound of leaves quivering in the breeze, and the rippling of the waters calmed me.

The current carried us toward Big Fork. It was strong enough that I only paddled to guide the canoe around rocks and dead falls. I decided I would only stay there for a brief visit and then I would continue my journey. To where? I didn't know yet. I just knew I needed to find a home where I could be what was best for me.

Late on our second day, Shadow jumped from the canoe and splashed through shallow water to a sandy shore. I followed him into a sheltered inlet. Shadow ran toward the village barking, then he ran back to me. Back and forth he ran, hurrying me.

Before long, I was met by Gromske and Tumla. "Welcome! Welcome! We're glad you've come!"

Miss Ruth hugged me and said, "I'm happy to see you. Ahni should be here soon. She and some of her friends are playing Hide and Seek. It's a great favorite of theirs." She untied her apron and shook flour dust off as she spoke, then she invited me into her house to sit and have a cup of wild mint tea. While the kettle heated, Miss Ruth showed me around her house. A broom rested against the wall of the entry way. Boots were neatly set upside down on long pegs in a far corner. The biggest area was where Miss Ruth did all her baking and cooking. "We eat our meals at that small table," she said pointing.

Then she led me into a sitting room with chairs and small tables with lamps. On one wall a shelf with books drew my eyes. I wanted to look at the books, but Miss Ruth was already leading me to the back of the house where there were two bedrooms. "This is Ahni's room," she said opening the door to one. I noticed the window sill had a collection of stones and a small basket in the corner by her bed was filled with pine cones. A branch from a tree was nailed across another corner and three nice new dresses hung from it. There were two beds. One was covered with a puffy blue quilt. "Goose down filling. It's so nice and cozy," Miss Ruth said as I fingered the quilt. The other bed was a cot with a patchwork coverlet on it. "For you. For when you visit. Or forever if you decide to stay." Miss Ruth smiled.

Just as we were going outside, Ahni came running and hugged me so hard I almost fell over. Miss Ruth laughed and said, "Ahni, show Luna the garden. Then come in and we'll have the tea I promised her."

In the back yard by the garden was a sod-covered hovel dug into the hillside. Piles of empty sacks were carefully folded into one corner. "We'll fill all those sacks with lots and lots of potatoes, carrots, beets, and beggies for winter eatin' after we pick this year's crops. We'll have much food. We won't have to eat any cattail mush," Ahni smiled as she said that.

After supping on fresh bread, roasted fish, and newly picked potatoes, we rested in the sitting room. Gromske was eager for news about the comet-borns who'd escaped. I tried to draw a picture with my words of all the changes happening: a well being dug, trees felled, delimbed, and hewed into logs for houses. I choked back tears as I told about the toppled cairns and the stones used for foundations for the new houses.

"Might be for the best," he said as he looked up river as though he were trying to envision a new village growing on top of the ashes of the old.

"Yes." My voice was but a whisper. "Yes, it will be for the best."

Lastly, I told him about the empty food storage and that the garden would not yield enough for the first winter if everyone stayed. "Won't be the first time someone hunted for their winter's food." Then he looked at me. The corners of his mouth turned into a smile. "I remember two youngsters having to eat a lot of cattail root mush once."

"I remember," I said with tears coming to my eyes. "Thank you. You saved Ahni and me that winter."

When it was bed time, Ahni pointed to the cot. "Your bed," she said. I crawled under the patchwork quilt cover while she snuggled into her own bed. Then she and I talked long into the night. "I like sleeping and living in a real house. Don't you?" she asked.

"You have it good here," I answered as the moon shone through the little window. "You have a nice room to yourself." It was all so different from what we'd had before, so I told her my memories of us sleeping by the bubbling mud pots when I'd first found her camp so long ago. And how we'd slept under the canoe together and finally in a cave made by the roots of a fallen tree before Gromske took us into his *itok* and then made one for us.

Ahni laughed, "Good memories. I'll remember 'em forever and ever. I liked when we were together. You were always good to me."

She swung her legs from under the covers and sat on the edge of her bed. I sat up, too. "Are you goin' back to the *itoks*? Gromske and Miss Ruth are hopin' you'll stay here with us. I want you to stay, too."

I thought for a long time before answering. "I don't plan to go back to the *itoks*. Not for a while anyway. There are so many changes happening there. Even though it's where my mother lived when she was a girl, it's not where I want to be anymore. Without you and Gromske, it just isn't the same. I still haven't decided what I'm going to do or where I'm going to go. I'll just follow the river and see where it takes me."

Ahni crawled back under her quilt. "I'll decide for you. Stay here with me." She covered her head and pretended to snore. I got under my covers, too, thinking about what would be best for me. It wasn't long before Ahni popped back up and asked, "Is Aivo a bear again? What are the goats doing? Is everyone playing tricks on each other? Lifting them off the ground? And digging around into other people's thoughts? And stuff like that?"

I was glad she was asking about the goats, but I hoped she wouldn't ask about her rabbit, so I changed the subject, "Tell me about school and your friends."

"Bad news about school. Miss Pearl is gettin' married and movin' away. She and her husband want to join a wagon train and go to a place called Callifunia, or somethin' like that. They say lotsa people are going there to find gold and get rich. But I still hope she'll stay. I need her to teach me. I like learnin'. Learning."

We talked more about her friends. My eyes were getting heavy, and Ahni's voice was getting sleepier when she said, "Everything here is good. Feels good not to get chased. No stones are thrown at me, and I'm not called bad names. I no longer worry about the constable man. No more about bad people. Or about Orphan House. Here people like me and take care of me. They'll take good care of you, too."

I fell asleep happy for Ahni. She had a new life. Good things had come to her. It was nice that Ahni wanted me to stay, but this was *her* home. *Her* new life. Not mine. And I was too old for anyone to take care of me. I needed to find my own way, but what could I do?

The next day, Ahni and I walked around the village. It was unlike Harmonia's Sanctuary village. There were as many businesses, maybe even more. The big difference was that there were people out everywhere. They talked and laughed and helped each other. Two of the busiest places were a dry goods store and a butcher shop,

Ahni proudly introduced me to the barber, the cooper, the seamstress and so many others as we walked hand and hand up and down the cobbled lanes. Everyone welcomed me and greeted Ahni with little hugs or pats on the shoulder. I thought about how she had changed from Lamb-i-kins to Ahni who wore a clean dress, combed her hair, spoke so well, and wanted to learn more in school.

When we entered Tumla's bootery, he was cutting some soft sueded leather. He pointed to two stools as he worked. Ahni and I watched as he shaped and stitched the leather.

"What are you making now?" Ahni asked.

"Slippers," he said. "Miss Pearl stopped in a while ago. She wants to give the slippers to her husband when they get married."

"I'm mad at her!" Ahni crossed her arms and scowled like the Lamb-i-kins of old had so many times. "Jest 'cause she wants to get married an' go to place called Callifunia or somethin' like that, we won't have a teacher an' there be no school. She can't do that! I'll have to stay home all day mixin' an' kneadin' dough til my hands about to drop off!"

I tried hard not to laugh at Ahni's sudden change back into Lamb-i-kins—even the way she talked and scowled!

Tumla hid a smile behind his hand and said, "We'll all be having a farewell potluck picnic lunch at the school today. Widow Smythe is making a bucket of her famous fried chicken, so as soon as I finish this first slipper, we'll be heading that way. Until then, it would be nice if you two went next door to visit with Thomas who has made all this possible for me." Tumla gestured to all the tools and stacks of leather in the shop. Then he added, "Thomas has trouble walking, so with your help, we'll walk to the picnic together."

CHAPTER 48

Little by little the school yard filled with people carrying loaves of bread, bowls of stew, platters of roasted meats, steamed vegetables, fruit pies, and buttery cakes. Tumla carried the bucket of fried chicken Widow Smythe had made. Shadow and two other dogs danced along beside him, trying to get a good sniff or taste of what he carried.

I watched as Gromske and some boys carried benches from the school and set them around the yard. Others were setting boards on barrels to make tables. Ahni had scampered away from me to be with her friends. Before she left, she had whispered that they were going to pick wild flowers for a bouquet to give Miss Pearl. They hoped they could make her stay.

I was looking for Miss Ruth to see if there was something I could help carry when two girls about my age came up to me. The taller girl wore her light brown hair in a braid wound around her head. "I'm Rebecca. We already know you're Luna." She pointed at the other girl who held onto her arm. "This is my friend Mary. Miss Ruth told us you might be coming to visit soon." Rebecca smiled as she talked. A dimple showed in each of her cheeks. "We were excited when we heard you'd come yesterday and would be here for the picnic."

Mary welcomed me. She had short dark hair and twisted her skirt in her hand nervously. I noticed her eyes were clouded with a milky-color. I wondered if she could see anything at all. Then she said, "I hope you'll sit with us. Ahni has told us so much about you."

Everything was so new to me. I stammered a bit, but finally got the words out, "Y-yes, I'd like to sit with you. Do you go to school here?"

"We did, but we finished all our levels this past spring. I'm sixteen, and Mary is turning seventeen soon. No more school for us this fall. We'll probably find jobs or find husbands and get married." Rebecca giggled, then she added, "My mother is a seamstress. I already help her stitch sleeves onto shirts or dresses. And make hems. It's really boring doing it all day long, but at least she pays me a few coins that I can spend how I want."

"Well, you're lucky. At least you don't get your hands all yucky while you work," Mary turned to Luna and explained, "My dad is a butcher and ever since I was six or seven, I've had to help him make sausages. It's something I can do even though I can't see very well. Worse yet, when he butchers chickens, I have to reach inside them and pull out the gizzard and all the other intestines. He gets mad if I accidentally tear open the guts because that makes a mess with poop getting all over the good stuff. Can you imagine now that we're done with school, I'll have to work all day long in the butcher shop? I wish there was something else I could do!"

I tried not to squinch up my nose thinking about what she had to do. Rebecca saved me from having to answer. "Well, I hear Simon helps your dad when it's time to butcher hogs. I hear he does it—not because he likes to do it—but because he's sweet on the butcher's daughter! Maybe he'll ask you to marry him. Then you won't have to stuff sausages anymore."

"Where'd you hear that? It's not true. It can't be true. I don't think anyone will want to marry me because of my eyes. I can't mend anything. I make a mess when I try to cook. Mom chases me out of the kitchen and just says, 'Go help your father.'"

Even though I felt a bit sorry for Mary, she didn't seem to feel sorry for herself. She didn't even let her limited vision stop her from what she wanted to do. I was having a good time listening to her and Rebecca talk. Better yet, neither was levitating anything, or talking about someone who could fire up his finger tips or change into a bear. I wondered what they would think when they found out I was born under the blazing comet. Would they think I was strange? Would they even want to be my friend?

Rebecca pointed to a group of boys who'd just finished setting up the tables. "Look over there. That's Simon in the red plaid shirt. The other three are Barton, Toivo, and Johan. They're the only boys in our village our age. Let's wander over, and I'll introduce you to them. Just remember, I'm interested in Johan so don't even think about sitting by him."

The school bell rang as we were walking toward the boys. Mary, who still held onto Rebecca's elbow, said to me, "I guess we're too late. Now we have to wait for Pastor Gruen's blessing of the food."

During the prayer, Rebecca kept her eye on Johan. She whispered, "Let's invite the boys to sit with us."

Right after Pastor Gruen said *"Amen,"* I felt a tap on my shoulder. Turning, I found Miss Pearl smiling at me. "Luna, it's good to see you again. After you're done eating, let's go into the school house together. I'd like to talk to you."

I couldn't imagine why she wanted to talk to me, but I was glad to have a chance to look at the globe and maps again, so I just nodded that I would.

The rush for the food tables was anything but orderly. After filling our plates, Rebecca, Mary, and I found a sunny spot to sit on the ground by a big maple tree. Johan came to sit by Rebecca. The other boys followed. We ate. We talked about everything. We laughed. They wanted to know all about me. I blushed as I told the short version of my story. I'd never had anyone pay so much attention to me. They were all interested when I told about the comet-borns who were now building their own village just two or three days up-stream from Big Fork.

Barton was especially interested when he heard that some had the gifts of levitation and teleportation. "Unbelievable! I could use a couple of them helping me when it comes to lifting and moving logs without even touching them. I'll be helping my dad with logging now that I'm done with school."

Toivo asked, "What's it like to enter a portal of the dead? Can you do it any-time you want?" He seemed disappointed when I said no.

Simon was sitting by Mary when he asked me, "You say they're all about our age? Like you? And live just up river from here?"

I nodded then said, "Yes, the comet flew overhead when we were all born. We're fifteen but will turn sixteen this fall."

"Why don't we go visit them? Maybe help them build their houses. It'd be easy because we wouldn't have to lift anything heavy. Then they could come here to visit. We could have a picnic or something. Then there'd be more than just the few of us. Luna, what do you think? Should we go?" I liked that they included me in their plans and asked for my opinion.

I thought for a minute. If I stayed in Big Fork for a long visit instead of leaving in a day or two, we could all go. I could introduce the two groups to each other.

Getting to know each other and visiting back and forth instead of being isolated would be good for all of them. Then I thought about Aivo and how nice he'd been when I was getting ready to leave. "Of course," I said. "The comet-borns would probably like to know you all, too." As I said that, I remembered Noah and how he'd healed Antti's broken leg. Maybe he could heal Mary's eyes. That would be a good reason for me to stay a while longer than I'd planned.

After eating, Mary held onto my elbow as I led her to the school. Miss Pearl was already there. "Oh, I'm so glad you've gotten to know each other. I'm sure you will become great friends. Luna, you've probably already heard I'm getting married and will be leaving soon. I'm excited, but I'm also sorry to leave. Lots of the youngsters are upset. Their parents, too."

"Ahni is, for sure," I said while looking at the maps on the wall. I studied the two branches that the Big Fork divided into. When I left, I'd follow the bigger one. Or maybe the smaller.

"As I said, I'm sorry to leave here. The students are eager to learn. And they're well-behaved. Well, most of the time." As Miss Pearl said this, she put a handful of wild flowers into a vase. "Look how sweet Ahni and her friends are. They picked these for me and said they hoped I'd stay."

"It's too bad the school will close when you leave. The kids are going to miss you a lot," I said drawing my finger along the map—the direction I'd go when I left.

Miss Pearl laid a hand on my shoulder and looked me in the eyes. "Well, if one can believe what one hears, you'd be the perfect person to take over the job of teaching the little ones their letters and numbers. And more."

I was truly befuddled. Shocked, even. My hand dropped off the map. Me? Teach? I'd never gone to a school. The only teaching I'd had was from Father. He'd been a professor once. He'd even written a book about plants. I still had it tucked away at the bottom of my pack. I shook my head. "I don't know the first thing about teaching."

By now several children and their parents had come into the classroom and surrounded me and Miss Pearl. "Yes, you do know! Ahni told us you've taught her a lot."

"Not only that, Gromske told us you've read all of the first two *McGuffey's Readers*. And that you know your numbers to the hundreds. And can add and subtract in your head. You need to write the numbers down for multiplication and division, but so do most people. Is he right?"

At the moment there were so many people surrounding me murmuring encouragement that I blushed and stammered. "Y-yes. I can, but. . . ."

"And I know from when you visited the school before that you like maps and globes. You could teach geography, too," Miss Pearl said pointing to the maps I stood by.

"I d-don't know. It's too much. I'm not even sixteen and won't be until the Harvest Moon this fall." I was nervous. I'd never had so many people surrounding me, smiling, and encouraging me.

Simon, Johan, Toivo, and Barton made their way through the crowd and stood close to me, too. Rebecca slipped in to stand by Johan. All the boys, and Rebecca and Mary, joined in saying, "Please stay! Be the teacher. The little ones need to learn. You can do it."

I was confused. My thoughts were muddled. The idea of being a teacher or anything else had never occurred to me. I had always thought there was nothing I could do because my gift of entering portals of the dead wasn't at all useful. Now the possibility of teaching swirled in my head. I looked at the maps, the baskets of chalk, the desks, and shelves of books. I could almost imagine myself reading to a group of youngsters.

Gromske raised his voice from the back of the crowd. "Luna, we all think you're just who we need for a teacher. But, we know this is sudden and you might need time to think about it. Let's all go back to eat the cakes and pies for dessert before the flies get into them. You and Miss Pearl can come back later. She'll show you the books. Answer your questions. Then you can make you decision. If we were to take a vote, we'd all want you to stay."

The reasons for me to stay in Big Fork were piling up. I'd have a bedroom with Ahni. Mary and Rebecca wanted to be my friends. When the groups from the two villages got together, I could still see Aivo and Greta from time to time. Maybe Noah could heal Mary's eyes. The two groups could definitely visit back and forth, but I still wasn't sure about the teaching part.

I enjoyed a piece of rhubarb pie. Mary chose a slice of frosted cake. Then she and I helped clear the tables before we went back to the school. While Miss Pearl showed me the primer books the little ones learned to read from, Mary sat at the little battered piano that stood in one corner.

"A spinet piano," Miss Pearl explained. "The blacksmith's family brought it with them all the way from the East Coast. It fell off their wagon in the mountains, but they picked up all the pieces and put it back together when they got here. It looks rough, but it works."

We listened as Mary played a cheerful melody. "She is not only a genius on the piano, but she sings beautifully!" Miss Pearl nodded toward Mary. "She's the only one in this whole village who knows how to play. All she needs is to hear someone hum the tune of a hymn or other song, and she can play the notes!"

To prove Miss Pearl right, Mary smiled as her fingers flew from key to key playing softly and singing a song I'd never heard while Miss Pearl and I looked at maps and globes. The school also had a well-used copy of *Grimm's Fairy Tales*, an assortment of story books, books for older readers, a telescope, a stack of slates, chalk, and a basket of paints and brushes.

When Miss Pearl told me she used to take the children out of doors to study plants and look for insects and such to use in science studies, I finally found myself getting truly excited. That was like what Father and I did. My favorite days had been when we went outside to study everything from the tiniest plants to beetles, trees, leaves, birds, rocks, the stars, planets, and all the animals and anything else that crossed our path. Now Miss Pearl was saying I could do the same with the children. I felt a lightness. A possibility of what could be swirled in my mind as I looked around.

Mary held onto my elbow when Miss Pearl led us outside to walk through a birch grove. We walked through the school garden, too. "The little ones love planting seeds each spring. Then in the fall they pull carrots for their lunches. They already have chosen which pumpkin they'll bring home for Halloween." As I walked through rows of herbs, squash, and tall corn, I imagined the children pulling and eating fresh carrots and chives.

When we came to a stand of maple trees, I heard a rustling in the branches. I looked up to see my raven perched next to another raven. They were touching their beaks and making soft sounds. A breeze rustled their feathers. Then I felt a little nudge on my leg. There was Shadow with two other dogs. Their tongues hung out, and they panted like they'd been running and playing. I got a tingly feeling that the raven and Shadow knew something I was just beginning to realize. They were telling me *they'd* found home.

A ray of sunshine pierced the tree branches and lit the path we followed. There was no blazing comet overhead bringing me a mystical gift. It was the raven, Shadow, the school, and so much more that were showing me a real gift. My hands didn't prick. I reached into my pocket and pulled out my moonstone. It warmed in my hand. Gentle yellows, greens, and blues swirled and soothed me. I now knew where I should be and what I could do. I made my decision. I would stay. It would be lots of work, but I could do it.

I was even more sure when Mary said in a soft and hesitant voice, "If you decide to be the teacher, I could help teach music. I can even teach our students how to play the piano with all ten fingers." Then she added with a shy smile. "It would be much better than stuffing sausages. But mostly, I'd like singing with the children, and we'd have so much fun working together."

Yes, I thought to myself. That would be fun, and even if Noah couldn't heal her eyes, she could still use her musical talents for good.

We neared the river. It sparkled in the bright sun. "Come," I said to Mary. "Help me pull my canoe onto the shore."

The ravens preened each other's feathers.
Shadow and the other dogs curled under a birch tree.
We heard Ahni and her friends laughing as they played.
Gromske and Miss Ruth waved from a hill top.

Being born under the blazing comet was far from my mind as Mary and I settled my canoe onto a patch of clover. I wouldn't need it to search for home anymore. The canoe in which I was born had finally brought me where I belonged.

I am Luna
I am home.

Acknowledgements

I thank my earliest writing teachers who encouraged me even though they read some of my horrible, terrible, awful beginning attempts. Thank you Mara Hart, Milan Kovakovic, Bart Sutter, Maryann Weidt, Jane Resh Thomas, and others. I also am thankful for my writer's group for all their patience and willingness to read chapters over and over again. I am especially grateful for my husband without whose support I could not spend hours lost in my writing world. Also, I appreciate the wonderful staff at the Cloquet Public Library. They encourage me and all the other readers and writers in our community.

MYSTICAL GIFTS

While there is no evidence that a comet or any other natural phenomena can gift people born under their influence with a mystical gift, some ancient cultures did believe that comets, eclipses, falling stars, etc., were either good or bad omens.

Even though these gifts are not scientifically recognized, parapsychologists have explored them. Various studies show that some people do test to have a Mental Telepathy ability. Also, water dowsers are routinely (and successfully) used to determine where to drill a well.

CHARACTERS AND THEIR MYSTICAL GIFTS
Luna: Portals of the dead—Enters mystical realms to interact with spirits
Liida: Precognition—Sees the future
Antti: Telekinesis—Moves objects using the power of his mind
Lukas: Pyro—Makes fire with his fingertips
Aada: Telepathy—Transfers her thoughts and penetrates the thoughts of others
Maya: Levitation—Lifts objects and people off the ground
Noah: Healer—Mends broken bones
Greta: Reincarnation—Recalls her past lives
Aivo: Shape shifter—Transforms himself into the body of an animal
Sage: Clairvoyance—Sees events and people at a distance or past time
Rosa: Rain maker—Creates storms
Sylvester: Enchanter—Casts spells
Grace: Maker of love potions
Hattie: Palmist—Reads lines in one's hand to predict the future
Beatrice: Water dowser—Uses a rod or stick to locate underground water

AUTHOR'S NOTE

My fascination with Halley's Comet is the inspiration I used for *Born in a Red Canoe* and *Born of a Blazing Comet*. I first became interested when I read a biography of Mark Twain who was born in 1835, a year when Halley's Comet streaked overhead. Twain was fascinated that his birth coincided with the appearance of the comet and correctly predicted that he would die when the comet passed again in 1910.

About the Author

Katharine Johnson lives in Northern Minnesota with her husband and a flock of wild turkeys. The woodlands with all the critters that come to their yard provide inspiration and setting for most of her stories.

Her six published books have brought her on journeys of self-discovery. *The Mukluk Ball* is a fun picture book. *The Wind and the Drum*, a historical fiction novel, was selected as the 2018 One Book Northland. *Born in a Red Canoe* was a finalist for the 2023 Minnesota Book Award. *Sylvie's Silence* has been accepted as a nominee for the 2023 Northeast Minnesota Book Award.

She has also published several short stories, biographies, and poetry in anthologies. One children's story "Company's Here" was published in the *Ladybug* children's magazine. Her short story "Ada" won the Jonis Agee Fiction Award.

She is a member of SCBWI, Lake Superior Writers, and a local writers' group.

Much of her "shelter in place" time was spent reading scads of MG and YA books to deeply explore those exciting fields of literature.